MAISEY YATES

Lone Wolf Cowboy

HQN™

HQN™

ISBN-13: 978-1-335-47464-3

Recycling programs
for this product may
not exist in your area.

Lone Wolf Cowboy

www.HQNBooks.com

Printed in U.S.A.

To anyone who feels like they might be beyond hope, or beyond love. You are precious beyond price. And you are worthy of love.

Lone Wolf Cowboy

CHAPTER ONE

VANESSA LOGAN HAD been avoiding coming home again for a very long time.

And for most of that time, she had been convinced that no one was terribly sad about her absence. It had been seven years since she'd seen her family by the time she'd come back to town about two years earlier for her sister Olivia's wedding.

She'd been in a haze then—not a drug haze—which she imagined was what her family would have assumed, but just a kind of strange, surreal sensation, returning to a place that she hadn't been to in so long.

It was different this time.

Different now two years later as she drove past the welcome sign all done up in blue and cheery yellow, welcoming her to the town of Gold Valley.

Back to the county that bore her last name, where she had been born, raised and let everyone down who had ever loved her.

She was closing the loop. That was why she was back. Anyway, there was an opportunity here, and she figured she might as well take it. Olivia had a baby. Olivia had a family, and no matter what had happened between them in the past, Olivia was her twin. It seemed… It seemed like she should be closer to her.

Geographically, and emotionally. Though she knew it would all have to be done in stages.

She imagined her parents would want her near eventually. Maybe. She couldn't say for sure. She wouldn't particularly blame them, she supposed, if they couldn't get over it.

She had been difficult. She'd caused them worry. They had assumed the worst about her...and in many ways, they'd been right to. At least, at the time.

Her childhood had been ideal for a while. Before she'd wanted to be anything other than Olivia's twin, and Cole and Tamara Logan's daughter. Before she ever got curious about the forbidden things her parents had warned her so sternly about.

She ached for that sometimes. For those simple days. When a hug from her father had healed all wounds. When she'd gone for long lunches with her mom after shopping in town.

When she and Olivia had whispered secrets under the covers. Until Olivia had gotten scared of secrets, and Vanessa's had gotten too dark to share.

She might never get back to those times. It might all be too broken. But even if it was... Even if it was, she was still glad she was here.

She was back for her.

Gold Valley was the last refuge for her demons, and the final locked door in her life.

It was her origin story. And everyone needed to revisit an origin story.

She'd gone out on her own, failed, hit rock bottom and healed. But she had healed away, not at the site of her very first fall from grace.

And it was time.

It was just time.

She maneuvered her car through Main Street, marveling at the brick buildings, the faded advertisements painted on the sides, the lone neon sign above the Gold Valley Saloon—allowed only because it had been installed in the early sixties and was considered historic.

Any new neon would *not* be considered historic.

And the fact that Vanessa still knew those things—could still hear her father explaining them in that cool, authoritative voice of his that Vanessa could've listened to forever—made her smile.

Though it wasn't an entirely happy smile.

Home was complicated.

That was for sure.

Well, home would be a little less complicated now than it had been, maybe. She had her own place, and the keys were waiting for her. All of her possessions fit in the back of her car, and she was ready to start a new job in a couple of days.

She had things lined up. She was responsible now.

Had been for a number of years.

And she'd been too cowardly to get in touch with her family and let them know that she was doing better.

So maybe she wasn't totally responsible.

She tried not to dwell on that as the road carried her through the main part of town and back out again, out into a densely wooded stretch of highway, with long, direct gravel driveways.

One of those long gravel driveways would be hers.

Well, hers and a couple of other people's. There were typically several homes back up one of those roads.

Her car's navigation system buzzed and let her

know that she was in fact at her road. She turned left and started to look for numbers. Every few trees, there was a sign posted and Vanessa kept watch for the four-digit number that marked her new home.

She would have hated this when she was a teenager.

She'd hated where she lived already, and a road like this—that took her out farther away from the nearest large town, that was several miles out of Gold Valley, and over all this dirt and gravel—would have mortally wounded and offended her.

Thinking of that girl, with her bright, big ambition, her seeds of dissatisfaction and her deep certainty she knew better than everyone else around her...

It was almost painful.

She'd had no idea what she was going to walk herself into.

And she supposed that was another reason she'd had to come here.

It was the last place she'd been *that* Vanessa.

It was also where she'd changed. Completely and utterly.

She saw the number for her rental, nailed to a tree. She turned her car onto a much narrower gravel road than the one she'd just been on.

The house at the end of the drive was small, humble, with white siding that was peeling in places, a shingled roof and a covered porch with a few hanging flowerpots.

She wondered if Ellie Bell, her contact in Gold Valley, was responsible for the flowers.

She doubted it was the landlord's work, given the state of the paint.

Rustic was a generous description. Both for the landscape and the house itself.

She got out and looked around, the pine trees that towered overhead seeming to swallow her whole as she stood there, feeling increasingly smaller. As if her place in the universe had shrunk significantly.

She didn't mind the feeling. She grabbed her shoulder bag from the car and began to walk up the porch steps, one of the pieces of wood creaking beneath her feet.

It was such a lovely little place and would make a welcome change to the apartment she'd called home for the past few years. Quiet. Isolation.

Well, except for all the teenagers she would be working with.

That wouldn't be very quiet.

She was okay with that too.

Teenagers shouldn't have to be quiet. They should get to live as loudly as they could, in safe spaces where they wouldn't be punished for trying and failing.

Of course, they needed boundaries too. She did know that.

It was just boundaries had been suffocating for her, and sometimes it was tough to remember that others suffered from a lack of them.

She heard the sound of tires on gravel, and she turned just in time to see a mint-green SUV headed up the roadway.

She frowned.

There was a blonde woman in the car, looking harried. She parked behind Vanessa's car and got out.

"Hi," Vanessa said hesitantly.

"Vanessa?" the woman asked. She moved to the

back of the car and opened the door. A little blonde girl hopped out, her hair bouncing with each movement.

The tiny child gave Vanessa a momentary feeling of discomfort.

"I'm Ellie," she said, walking forward and extending her hand.

"Oh," Vanessa said. "It's nice to meet you."

"I'm Amelia!" The little girl spun in a circle as she announced her name.

"Hi, Amelia," Vanessa said, not sure what to do with her hands.

"I didn't make it up here earlier to put the key out for you," Ellie said. "I'm really sorry. I was hoping to beat you here, but I had drama with Amelia's sitter. It's just been a day. Plus, everything at the ranch is a little bit nutty right now."

"I'd guess so, with you just getting everything up and running."

The whole endeavor sounded great to Vanessa. An alternative school for kids who were either having trouble in school, or at home. Or in the system. Kids who were at their last stop, basically.

As a kid who'd been there, Vanessa wished there had been something like that for her. Of course… she doubted her parents would have ever been able to admit she needed help.

That was if she'd ever been able to admit to them that she did.

"It should be. Now that we're getting all the bugs worked out. And just in time to get started. We're going to have about twenty students, most of whom are from out of the area and will be living with foster families in town."

"That…that seems like a good size."

"Yes. Well, I was really impressed with your work. Not just your art, but your explanation of how you've used art for therapy."

"It's something that I… That I really believe in." It had saved her. Finding a passion. She wondered what her parents would think of it now.

They would have disapproved if she'd said she wanted to be an artist back when she was in high school. But maybe they'd think trading in pills for paintbrushes was an all right idea.

"Okay," Ellie said. "I don't want to clutter up your day. I'm sure that you want to get settled. But if you need anything, feel free to give me a call. And if you have an emergency, Jacob is just up the drive. Jacob Dalton, I mean."

Vanessa's heart twisted. "Jacob Dalton?"

She could see that name, clear in her mind, on a name badge. His hand strong, firm. His expression full of concern.

Stay with me…

She blinked. "I…"

"Do you know Jacob?" Ellie asked.

"No," she said. It was the honest truth. She didn't know Jacob. Not really. "I know his name. You know how things are in a small town."

"Definitely," Ellie said. "He's home unless he's out fighting fires. Though the serious part of the season is mostly winding to a close. I don't… I don't like it when he and Caleb are out on fires."

"Yeah, that sounds like an intense job," Vanessa said, struggling to keep her mind in the present, when half of it was still lost back in the past.

"Yeah," Ellie said. "And it's just…my husband… Amelia's father…" They both looked over at the little girl, who was turning circles just next to the porch. "He died. He died out on a fire. The helicopter he was in crashed."

That brought Vanessa right into the moment. What an awful thing to have to go through. She couldn't even imagine.

She might not know that kind of pain, but she knew what it was like to be an oddity. To be someone with a wound other people had a hard time understanding. And if Ellie wanted to open up, to share her pain… well, Vanessa was here to listen.

She knew what it was to be isolated that way.

"I'm sorry," Vanessa said.

She meant it. She'd lost a lot of people in her life. But not to death. By her own systematic alienation of them. And in some cases, by them cutting ties with her. But those losses had other chances available, no matter how unlikely.

A loss like Ellie's didn't have another chance.

"Me too," Ellie said. "He would've been a good dad."

And Vanessa probably would have been a terrible mother. But she was here. She lost her pregnancy. And this little girl was here without a good father. Because the world was strange, and it was nothing if not horrifically imbalanced.

"I really am sorry about that."

"I appreciate it. It's been a while. But that is the thing. Jacob and Caleb being out on fires… It always makes me think of Clint. Of course, so does Amelia's smile. But that's a happy thing."

"Does she like to paint?" Vanessa asked.

"Oh, she hasn't really done much of it. I mean, besides at preschool."

"I'd love to do some painting with her," Vanessa said. She wasn't quite sure why she offered, particularly given her initial reaction to the child. But if she could do art, and help Amelia express herself, then she felt like that was a bonus. Anyway, it gave her a place to focus some of the rattling nerves that were jittering around inside her.

Jacob Dalton.

Well, so much for her particular setup being *less complicated.*

Not that he would remember her. There was no reason for him to remember her. She would just be one of the many phone calls he'd had during his time as an EMT in Logan County.

"All right, Amelia," Ellie said. "Say goodbye to Ms. Logan."

"Bye, Ms. Logan," Amelia said, her smile cherubic and sweet. Ellie waved and headed back to the car. As Ellie got inside, Vanessa had to wonder what the other woman knew about her, and what she didn't.

Vanessa's fall from grace was something she imagined people in town discussed. Or maybe they didn't. Maybe her parents had done a good job of hiding the activities of their daughter for the past nine years.

Surely, the label of rebellious had been given to her before she'd left town. That, she actually knew for a fact.

She had been running with the wrong crowd. Being wild.

But if there had been any knowledge or subtext to

her interaction with Ellie, Vanessa hadn't sensed it. And she usually did. When people knew her background, they often spoke to her as if she was fragile. Perhaps mentally incapacitated. And if not that, then simply with a slight curl to their lip and a bit of disdain. Ellie had given her none of that, and Vanessa was grateful for it.

If she could just find enough people to surround herself with on a daily basis who knew her only as she was now, things would be great.

And if Jacob Dalton could just not remember her. That would be even better.

Or, maybe, she wouldn't end up having to deal with him at all.

It was optimistic, but she could hope.

That was the thing. No matter what, Vanessa Logan could always hope.

It was the only reason she was still breathing now.

So she would cling to it no matter what.

She took a deep breath and walked back to her car, fishing a large duffel bag out of the back. It had everything in it she would need for overnight. That way, if she didn't get around to unpacking the other couple of boxes she'd brought, she would be fine.

She was feeling pretty exhausted, and mostly she felt ready to make herself a glass of lemonade and sit.

That was the point of this new life. This new pace.

That was the point of coming home.

JACOB DALTON WAS tired down to his bones. It had been a long-ass time since he'd done ranch work like he'd done today. But his brother Gabe was actively attempting to recruit him into a full-time capacity at the ranch, and somehow his sales pitch included working Jacob until his knuckles were bloodied.

He sat down heavily at the table, a beer clutched tightly in his hand. "You're a sadist," he groaned, leaning back in his chair.

"Hey, I got you to come out and drink. So I must've done something right," Gabe said.

His brother was in a good mood. He was in a good mood a lot lately, thanks to his recent engagement to Jamie Dodge, a little tomboy, hell-raiser cowgirl that Jacob would never have thought his brother would take an interest in. But it turned out he'd taken more than an interest in her. He had fallen in love with her.

Nice for him, Jacob supposed.

"Yeah, well, I wasn't going to turn down free beer." Though he had beer up at his cabin, so it wasn't like he couldn't drink there. And anyway, he couldn't drink to excess, because he didn't have anyone to drive him home but himself. One beer and he was out. He could get back to the solitude of his cabin.

"The place is really looking good," his brother Caleb said, leaning back in his chair.

Only eleven months younger than Jacob, Caleb was almost like a twin. Though things had been different since their friend Clint died in a helicopter accident. He had been a part of their band of brothers, he had grown up eating dinner at their house, fought fires with them. He had been such a hugely important part of their life. And something about losing him, about losing that piece, had made everything different.

It didn't help that he felt responsible for Clint's death in a lot of ways. He and Caleb were the ones who had dragged their friend into the orientation for wildland firefighting. It was along the lines of what Jacob had done in between riding and the rodeo, back in the day. Since he had gotten work as an EMT right outside high school. And Caleb…Caleb had just been looking for a hit of something.

He was close to his brother, or rather, he always had been, but something had changed when they became adults, and Caleb was difficult to read. He was friendlier than Jacob, had a readier smile and made conversation with people pretty easily. But if you paid attention, you would notice that it was light conversation. Easy. Nothing behind it all.

"I do appreciate you picking up some work," Gabe said. "This has been a pretty huge project."

"No kidding," Jacob responded.

The throb in his shoulder agreed.

Caleb nodded. "I've been enjoying it."

Jacob suspected that his brother's enjoyment had to do with the amount of time it allowed him to spend with Ellie, but he wasn't going to say anything about that. For the simple fact that Caleb never said anything about it. He didn't need to, though. He took care of her. As if it were his job, and Jacob didn't think it had to do with guilt. And maybe it was just caring. Maybe Ellie was like a sister to him, and Caleb worried for her now that Clint was gone. But Jacob somehow doubted it.

"I honestly never would have thought you'd get involved in opening up… Well, it's a whole damn school," Jacob said. His brother wasn't a particularly caring or paternal type of person, at least not in Jacob's mind. And yet he'd thrown himself into this with a passion. He had a feeling it was connected to the way that Gabe felt about horses, and the power that the land and the animals had to transform someone's life.

But still seemed surprising to him in a lot of ways.

"It all started with McKenna," Gabe said, referencing the half sister they'd found out about a couple of years ago. "I got to thinking about how different her life would have been if she'd had more help. And then especially thinking about Dad's other sons. There's all kinds of boys in that position, and we can't go back in time and fix what's broken. But we can go forward and make a place for those kids now."

"How is the half brother hunt going, by the way?" Caleb asked.

"The same," Gabe responded. "I know about West, and that's it. I haven't got names or locations for the others. West's mother was completely uninterested in helping me with that."

Jacob essentially wanted nothing to do with this whole endeavor. As far as he was concerned, if the other children sired by Hank Dalton wanted to come forward, they would have done it sometime ago. He wasn't under the impression that their parentage was a secret. Not from them.

Jacob felt…well, deeply unsurprised that his father had more children other than just them. Other than just McKenna. Really, the appearance of McKenna had confirmed things he'd always suspected.

And if he'd been careless once, with all the sleeping around he had done, it stood to reason he might have been careless twice. It turned out, it was more like four times.

And so Gabe had made it a personal mission to

track down Hank Dalton's other sons to try to make things right.

Jacob felt like he already had a surplus of siblings, but that was just his opinion.

He wasn't going to make a deal out of it, or argue with Gabe. Mostly because, as far as he was concerned, he could just do what he always did. He could go off and do his own thing. It wasn't that difficult. Someday he might leave Gold Valley altogether. But as for now, his cabin up the side of the mountain served him well enough.

He finished his beer and stood up, groaning a little bit. "I'm going to go and fall into bed now," he said. "Especially if we have to do all that again tomorrow."

"You don't have to," Gabe said.

That just made Jacob want to flip them off. Because Gabe knew that Jacob felt obligated to get involved in this venture and help. He wished he didn't feel obligated. That was the problem.

The baseline issue with being a Dalton. Their father had always been unreliable. Sending home a check, and rarely rolling in himself until it was good and convenient for him.

The Dalton brothers had always picked up the slack for each other, banding together strong. And, however Jacob felt about life at the moment, his inclination was to support his brothers no matter what.

"I'll be there," he said.

"Appreciated."

He raised his beer bottle, and Caleb did the same. Then he nodded and began to walk out.

As soon as his foot hit the top step out the front door, he realized his brother was walking behind him.

"Stay and drink," he said to Caleb.

"I will," Caleb said.

But Caleb stood there and looked at him. And there was something about that look on his brother's face that reminded him of old times. Easy times. Hell, all their times had been easy for a while, and that had been by design.

Jacob had learned a long time ago that if you didn't talk about bad things, you didn't have to deal with them. And he'd thrown himself into that hard during all his growing-up years. He and Caleb had been hell in cowboy boots. And inseparable at that.

And now he could feel the distance between the two of them. And he didn't know what to do about it. All he knew how to do was avoid it.

He'd hidden his pain as a kid because no one had known what he'd been through. But with Clint… Well, everyone had known what had happened with Clint.

And more to the point, it had dragged the other side of his carefree lifestyle out from the dark and shown the ugly side.

Dark things didn't go away because you didn't talk about them. They just festered. And waited.

And really, they were still there, not dealt with, not discussed. He was trying to change. Trying to be reliable and there for his brothers when they needed him. To never again be the one who let the world fall to pieces because of his own selfish stupidity.

"How are things?" Jacob asked.

Caleb looked shocked. "Um…me?"

"Yes, you. We used to talk. We don't really anymore."

They'd been best friends, the three of them: Jacob, Caleb and Clint. Losing Clint had changed it all.

Caleb looked down, then back up. "Good."

"How's Ellie?" he asked, his voice gruff.

He felt guilty about Clint because of Ellie most of all. Because if he hadn't wanted to stay in bed that day, sleep in and wrap himself around the woman in his bed... If he'd gone on that fire like he was supposed to, then Clint wouldn't have been in that helicopter crash.

"You see Ellie almost every day," Caleb pointed out.

"Yeah, but *how is she*?"

Damn but he still didn't like talking about the hard things.

"Good," Caleb said. "I mean, it's been four years, man."

But they both knew that didn't mean much of anything. Because they both felt the loss of Clint still, and how much more must his wife feel it? Every day that her daughter kept on growing without a father.

"Yeah," he said.

"How are you?" Caleb asked.

"Getting on," he said. "Hey, I'm doing this thing, right?"

"The school?"

"Yeah. I...I show up now," he said, lifting a shoulder.

God knew he'd spent years not doing that. Being the one who blew off family barbecues because he was hungover. Leaving texts from women he'd slept with unanswered.

Because avoidance...avoidance had been his friend since he was ten years old. Ignore the problem and pretend it was never yours to deal with.

It might not make it go away. It sure as hell couldn't

bring anyone back from the dead. But it made it so he never had to deal with it at all.

"You didn't cause the helicopter crash," Caleb said.

Jacob shifted. "No. But it happened. And you tell me…if it was supposed to be you, do you think you could just let it go? Do you think you'd ever quit thinking about it? Wondering?"

Caleb shook his head. "No." The answer was gruff. Thick.

"Sometimes it helps me to spend some time alone." His life was so different now than it had been when Clint died. He hadn't spent a night alone, not in those days. He'd worked, partied and lived on his own terms. Now he needed that solitude sometimes to get his thoughts in order. Because he spent his days trying to figure out how to be better, and he found that took a hell of a lot of energy.

"I worry it makes you think about it all a little too much."

"Well, I spent a lot of years not thinking at all. I kind of hope this is an improvement."

"It's different," Caleb said. "That's for sure."

"Damn sure," Jacob said.

Caleb tipped his hat and walked back into the saloon, and Jacob began to walk toward his truck.

He got inside and closed the door behind him, thankful for the silence.

His conversation with Caleb replayed on a loop in his mind, and he tried to let it fade. But inevitably, he thought of the crash. Being at the crash site. Feeling frozen.

Flashing back to another accident. Another death.

Knowing that whatever happened with this one, he

had to come out of it changed. Because last time he'd used it as an excuse. Live like you might die, because he'd been aware you could at any moment from the time he was a kid. And push all the bad things down because talking about it didn't fix anything anyway.

And that…that selfish crap he'd taken forward with him had been the reason Clint was on that helicopter in Jacob's place.

The reason Clint was dead.

Because the crash had been so devastating there was no way to rush into the rescue. No way to fix it. Everyone on that helicopter was dead. And he'd known it the moment he'd watched it hit. He'd been there, and that was bad enough. He supposed he should just be grateful he hadn't had Caleb's job.

Actually being the one to tell Ellie.

He would never know how Caleb had found the strength to do that.

He turned onto the gravel drive that would take him up to his house, the sound of the rocks beneath the tires creating white noise that filled up his brain and made it easier for him to think. Or not think, as the case may be.

The sky was pink, casting a glow off the tops of the pines the road cut through. But off to the left he saw a cloud of billowing smoke that he knew meant one thing: fire.

Well. Hell. He could radio in, but it might be better to just see what it was. He was trained, after all. There was a house over there, but it hadn't been occupied for a long time. He hung a sharp left and saw a little house up ahead, with flames coming out of the chimney.

Great. Someone had lit a fire without making sure the flue was cleared. The house itself looked like it was filling with smoke, and Jacob parked, springing into action.

The front door opened, and a woman came out, smoke pouring out behind her.

"Is there a hose?" he asked. "And an extinguisher?"

She looked around, bewildered.

"Is there a hose?" he repeated.

"Yes," she said. "I mean, I think so."

"Dammit, woman," he said. "You don't know if your chimney is clear. You don't know if you have a hose."

"I just moved in four hours ago," she said.

"Well, then, your landlords have something to answer for."

"Can you keep my house from burning down, please?"

"Have you called anyone?" He grabbed the hose that was hooked up next to the porch and went straight into the house. The hose was for backup. He hoped he didn't need it.

"No," she said. "I was just hoping I could figure out how to put it out myself."

"Lucky for you," he said, "a fireman is already here."

He stuck the hose right next to the fireplace, and then walked over to the kitchen sink, and was relieved to find a fire extinguisher underneath. "Let's start with this," he said. He went over to the fireplace and looked up. The heat and sound from the fire burning up toward the top of the chimney was intense.

"It'll get worse for a second," he said, opening up the draft stop to give him better access. Then he pushed the nozzle to the extinguisher into the chimney and directed the stream upward. It was easy, and it was handled in only a couple of minutes. And when he was confident that there were no sparks left, he straightened. "Next time, make sure your chimney is clear if you haven't lit a fire in the fireplace before."

The woman was pretty. Glossy brown hair, a slender figure and lips that put a man in a sin-filled mood. And it had been a long time since Jacob had gotten involved in any good sin.

She also looked familiar. But he couldn't place why.

"I've never had a house with a fireplace. I didn't know."

"That's fine." He looked around. "Hopefully nothing is damaged. It's going to smell like smoke for a few days…"

"Probably." She looked up at him, and there was something that felt like an echo from the past in her distressed expression. She looked dazed but upset, and for the life of him he couldn't figure out why those brown eyes caught something inside him and held on tight.

Olivia Hollister. She looked like Olivia Hollister. But she *wasn't* Olivia Hollister. The two women shared features, but they would never be confused for each other. It was strange because she was identical to Olivia on a surface level, and yet so apparently different too.

Then she lowered her head, and when she looked back up at him, an image from the past matched itself up with her now.

Him giving CPR. Praying that the woman would wake up.

And then she'd opened her brown eyes, and he breathed a sigh of relief.

The past faded away, and it was at that moment he realized that she knew who he was too.

"You're Jacob Dalton," she said. "And here I thought I could avoid you for a little while longer."

CHAPTER TWO

SHE HAD KNOWN that this would be a part of it. A part of coming home. It was unavoidable. She was going to see people she knew. That was how small towns worked. It was one reason why she had avoided coming back for so long. She had already stuck her toe into the shallow end of this particular pool when she had returned home for her sister's wedding.

But then, she had only dealt with her family. She had met her new brother-in-law. And no one had asked her any questions. Which was good. Because she hadn't been prepared to answer them. Though she had a feeling that the lack of questioning had nothing to do with her sensibilities, and everything to do with the fact that her parents weren't sure they were ready for what she might say.

That was fine. She had worked out her sobriety on her own. Still, she supposed, working it out with other people was the next step. Working it out here. Not that she felt like her sobriety was in any danger, but she also knew she had to continue to treat it seriously. She did not know how her family would deal with the fact that she'd been sober a lot longer than just these past two years. They had just been so happy to find out that she was sober at the wedding that they hadn't dug deeply about timelines. Once they did they would probably have questions. Wonder why she hadn't come home sooner.

It would be a difficult conversation to have and she wasn't quite ready yet.

But she was here. So there was time.

It wasn't a quick visit at an event that had nothing to do with her. That had been part of her debate over whether or not she should come for Olivia's wedding two years earlier. She didn't want to take her sister's big day and make it about her.

But neither had she wanted to miss her twin's wedding.

Everything had worked out fine in the end. At least, as fine as it could have.

Her parents had been uncomfortable, but that they'd been at Olivia's wedding had likely shielded Vanessa. Of course, nothing seemed to shield her from Jacob Dalton's insightful gaze. Nothing seemed to be able to shield her from the reality of the fact that her past had come barging into her house to put out a fire.

If she were a little bit less stunned she might be able to come up with an appropriate metaphor for the situation.

"Do you want some lemonade?"

He looked at her, his lips working upward into a half smile.

He was so handsome. She had always thought so.

She had seen him around town, over the years, tall and rangy and possessing that Dalton charm that they were famous for. Or maybe just their father was famous for it. And everyone naturally applied it to his sons as well. After all, they were handsome, and they were those exceptional men who could never blend in, even if they tried. Paramedics, rodeo riders. All-American boys.

There was something different about him now. The years, she assumed.

She could see a few of them around his eyes, etched into the grooves around his mouth. But it was more than that. There were things written on his skin, visible in his eyes that she couldn't quite put her finger on.

"I'm Vanessa Logan," she said, realizing she hadn't introduced herself. She knew him, so she hadn't thought of it. His face didn't change at all when she said her name. "I made lemonade," she continued. "Not for you. For me. But now you're here, and you kept my house from burning to the ground, so it seems like maybe I should give you some."

"I appreciate it. But I'm probably just going to head on up the hill."

"You live up there?"

"About two miles up, yeah."

He gave her a strange look, as if her wanting to make conversation after he had just put a fire out in her chimney made her the weird one. She personally thought dashing off without saying three words was weird.

Then, in many ways, she was behind on interpersonal interaction. She'd spent a lot of years cultivating toxic relationships. Her first being with alcohol and getting blackout drunk because that had been such a great way to lose herself. And then there had been her ultimate. The one. Her personal love affair with opiates.

Once she had come out of that tunnel, she'd had to figure out who she actually was, what relationships she legitimately prized and valued. What *she* wanted. Because for a whole lot of years she'd wanted one thing.

To get high.

And after it had turned dark, to get high how she'd used to. To recapture the feeling from the beginning. To have fun with it, instead of just taking it to keep from suffering bone-cracking withdrawals.

But she'd stopped. And she'd dug herself out and gotten on with the business of being Vanessa.

And everything else had fallen underneath that priority. Because how could she function, how could she do anything when that need loomed large above her? When it overcame every other appetite. Every other desire. Thinking about it now made her feel almost panicky. She hated it so much. That reminder of how much she had been controlled. Of how much her life had not belonged to her. It made her feel weak and sad. Terrified. And she wasn't going to think about it anymore.

"Well, it's nice to know that I have very competent neighbors," she said, "you know, neighbors who can put out an emergency fire if need be."

"There is a whole fire department for that. And next time you should probably put in a call."

"Seems like it might be easier to just put in a personal call to you," she quipped.

The expression on his face wasn't really amused, and she couldn't quite understand why. He seemed irritated.

"I'm kidding," she said. "I'm not actually going to call you instead of the fire department if I have a fire. I just hadn't gotten around to it because I was kind of still in shock that I had managed to do that to myself.

My parents had a fireplace. But the apartments that I've lived in for the past few years have not. And you didn't need to know that, probably."

"No," he said.

She was desperate to know if he remembered her. In kind of a strange, morbid-fascination sort of way. She hoped that he didn't. Of course, she had gone and made it clear she knew who he was, but he hadn't really missed a beat over that.

As if he expected it.

But she imagined that the Daltons did.

And anyway, he hadn't asked who she was. She'd offered it up. But she was identical to her sister... Well, as identical as two people who'd not spent any time in each other's presence over the past decade could be. They had made different style choices. And Olivia had fuller curves. Though Vanessa hadn't used in quite some time, she remained a bit on the thin side.

"Thank you," she said. "I'm really glad my house didn't burn down."

"Yeah," he said. "Me too. I mean, this is kind of what I do, so that would be a bad look. Though usually I fight wildfires, not kitchen fires."

She had no idea why it sounded both dangerous and sexy. Well, she knew why it sounded sexy actually, it was just that it sounded sexy because it was dangerous that confused it.

She wondered at that small kick of adrenaline inside herself. If it was something related to that flawed part of herself that seemed to want and crave a little bit of self-destruction. Or if it was just one of those things. Because women were often attracted to dangerous men. Even women who didn't have an unhealthy relationship with controlled substances.

It was difficult to say.

She hadn't had a real relationship since high school. And she hadn't been with a man sober in…ever.

Something about the idea of being with a man, while standing directly in the presence of Jacob Dalton made her hands feel a little bit clammy. Made her heart thunder like a dull ache inside her.

"You don't want any lemonade," she confirmed.

"No," he said.

"Okay. Well, thanks again."

"Just doing my job," he said, nodding his head, and she had the feeling that if he'd been wearing a cowboy hat he would have tipped it.

But then, that would be gentlemanly. And while gentlemen might exist in the world at large, they never seemed to be involved in Vanessa's world.

And they certainly didn't turn intense blue gazes onto her and look at her as though they actually *saw* her.

"Maybe I'll see you around," she said.

His lips tipped upward. "Doubt it. Anyway, I hope not. You know, considering that if you did—"

"Myself or my house would be on fire?"

"Yeah," he said. "That."

And without another word, Jacob Dalton turned and walked out of her house, leaving Vanessa feeling strange and empty.

She wasn't sure how she felt about the fact that her home was already the sight of an exciting incident. She had been looking forward to a quiet life. A normal life.

She turned a circle in the living room, gazing at the wicker furniture, the floral cushions.

It looked like the sight of a normal life.

But suddenly, Vanessa felt very strange within it. Wrong.

As if her surroundings knew that she could never be normal. That she could never have normal.

She rolled her eyes at herself. To hell with that. She'd had way too much therapy to go sliding into this kind of self-pity without a little bit of self-awareness. She was freaking out because she had changed things. And she was making innocuous everyday instances into signs and wonders.

There was no such thing.

There was only life. And the choices you made within it. The choices you made in response to what was happening around you.

The choice was with her.

The choice had been with her for the past five years.

And she would make sure that she kept it that way.

She had chosen to come back home to Gold Valley. And a little chimney fire was not going to shake her resolve.

And neither was Jacob Dalton.

WHEN JACOB GOT back up to the cabin, he immediately got himself a cold beer. He hadn't been counting on running into Vanessa Logan.

Now or ever.

He still couldn't quite credit why he remembered her so clearly. Obviously he knew her from around town. But as an emergency call… He never could figure out why that night lingered in his head the way it did.

Her terror, mostly. Her terror and pain, something that had shaken him to his core.

That she'd been alone. That stuck with him. For all that his family was a bit of a fragmented disaster. Illegitimate children, affairs and burning trucks on the lawn... They were there for each other. They always had been.

He looked around his cabin, three rooms and total isolation, and nearly laughed at that thought. No one was here for him now. But that had more to do with him than it did anything else. He was the one who had changed. Not his family. And that was between him and God, he supposed. Or maybe him and his best friend's ghost. It didn't matter either way. Because there were no answers to be had.

His phone buzzed in his pocket, and he looked down at it, seeing his brother's name flash up on the screen.

He thought about not answering. But he knew Gabe would just keep calling until he did. Ever since he'd confided in him about wanting to start the school, he'd been slowly getting more and more involved in Jacob's isolated-by-design life. And since Jacob was trying to be better, he was making an effort to not just tell his brother to jump in a lake.

"Hey," he said.

"Hey yourself. You coming in tomorrow?"

Jacob paused and tamped down the irritation that coursed through his veins. "I said that I was. I don't go back on my word."

"Fair enough. It's a big day at the ranch, and I just wanted to make sure—"

"I'm not leaving you high and dry," he said. He was aware that his irritation had amped up to a degree that it probably didn't need to be. But he took it personally. His brother questioning whether or not he would follow through. He didn't leave things to chance. Not anymore. When he was supposed to be there, he showed up.

Because damn, not showing up...

He took a swig of his beer.

"It would be good for you to focus on something else."

"Something other than wildfires?"

The work that he did traveling around the country putting out fires during the dry season paid his bills for the whole rest of the year. The fact of the matter was... he didn't really need to work on the family ranch. But whether or not he let his brothers into his daily life or not, they were the constants that remained in his world. And they were... They were family. Blood despite whatever else was going on.

"I'll be there tomorrow, ready to do whatever you need me to do. I said it. I meant it."

"All right. Is there... Is there anything that I can do to be there for you?" Gabe said.

Jacob chuckled. "What's all this earnest crap? Is this because you're in love?"

"Maybe. I have to talk about my feelings. A whole lot more now that I'm with Jamie. Because if I don't, no one will."

That made Jacob laugh genuinely. He could see his brother's fiancée not being overly touchy-feely the way that he tended to think women were. Jamie was all grit. But she seemed to soften for Gabe. But only Gabe.

Jacob liked that about her.

Jacob had never seen much evidence that romantic love could be anything other than a toxic wasteland or broken heart waiting to happen. But Gabe and Jamie showed him that there might be a little something else it could be, and he enjoyed feeling unusually optimistic about something. Anything.

"I'll be there tomorrow," Jacob said. "And the next day. And the next. Because I said I would."

"I trust you," Gabe said.

"Good."

"And I'll see you tomorrow."

"Yeah," he said. "I guess you will."

When he hung up the phone he did his level best to keep on thinking of the ranch. To keep his mind on anything other than Vanessa and that night all those years ago.

Though if there was one thing he could say for that night, it was that he had managed to keep her safe.

It was more than he could say for his dead best friend.

Clint was just dead. And no matter what anyone said, Jacob was never going to be able to do anything other than blame himself.

CHAPTER THREE

THERE WOULD BE no students in her class today. Today, Vanessa was simply going to familiarize herself with her surroundings. But when she got to the driveway, and saw the grand archway that stretched over the top of it, her heart sank.

The Dalton Ranch.

How had she not connected all those dots when she'd talked to Ellie last night? The ranch and then the mention of Jacob living up the road. And of course Ellie would assume that Vanessa would know whose ranch it was.

She felt like an idiot.

It was like some big cosmic hand had grabbed hold of her and decided that all that disconnected, airy-fairy stuff she thought about facing her past was going to become very real, very concrete very quickly.

Well, she'd already seen Jacob.

None of the Daltons were more personal to her than that.

It was just that Jacob Dalton, whether he knew it or not, was the only one who actually knew what she had been through all those years ago. At least, he knew a piece of it.

Her family didn't know. She had never told her parents about the painful, terrifying miscarriage she'd suffered on their bathroom floor while they'd been out of town.

A miscarriage for a pregnancy she'd been steadfastly ignoring and denying in spite of the fact that she had been rapidly running out of ways to continue to live in denial. Some part of her had believed if she just didn't take the test, her nausea, weight gain and lack of periods could all be due to something else.

A pregnancy that had come from a sexual encounter she didn't even remember.

Her stomach turned.

Everything felt closer to the past here. Perhaps because it was the jumping-off point of her past. The place that made her.

For better or for worse.

And frankly, for most of her life it had been worse.

Not now, she told herself. *It's not worse now. You are different. And there's nothing—no ranch, no town—that's going to break you.*

Following the directions Ellie had texted her that morning, she eased her car along the narrow dirt roads that lead through the ranch, spidering out around various outbuildings. Many of which were new. The art room stood apart, nestled away from many of the other structures. It was made almost entirely of windows, allowing the maximum amount of natural light to filter in. She'd never had access to a place like this, either to paint herself or to conduct lessons.

She had worked either in her old, cramped apartment or in a rec center.

And it had been good. Anything that had allowed her to escape into art had been good for a very long time.

But this was something else. Something more than escape.

This was beauty. The kind of thing you allowed yourself when you could move past basic survival.

She got out of her car and made her way toward the tiny structure. There was no one around, but when she tested the door it opened easily. The door itself was a smooth glass panel, like the rest of the walls. There were counters, a sink and a blank section that she imagined was for the easels that were stacked up against the wall.

There was a pottery wheel. The supplies were all neat and organized, and looked as if an art store had been bought in its entirety and configured into the building.

She had given Ellie a supply list, but this went beyond that basic supply list by quite a bit, and immediately she itched to make something. To do something.

"Sorry," Ellie said, rushing into the room. "I meant to meet you here. It just took me a little bit longer than I anticipated getting Amelia settled in with the sitter."

"It's fine," Vanessa said, looking around the space in awe. "This is beautiful."

"I'm glad that you like it. I think Gabe has done an amazing job. This is a really meaningful project for him."

"I can tell," Vanessa said. "Something with this much attention to detail has to be a project that comes from the heart."

"The Daltons are good men," Ellie said. "I know they have some conflict with their dad, with both their parents, really. But they're a good family. And they support each other. It's nothing like I grew up with."

"My family is…great," Vanessa said softly.

Complicated. They were great to each other, and had sometimes been less great to her. Complicated. Good. That seemed to be the theme of her life lately. Or maybe it was the theme always and it was only now that she was able to deal with the imperfections as well as the good things, without throwing out the whole rose just because it had a thorn.

That had been her method for most of her life. Particularly when she'd been using. When she couldn't separate out the good from the bad, she would throw it all out. Because it was too hard to do complicated. It was too hard to feel. So she had aimed for nothing. Aimed for numb. And she had been a bit too good at that.

But there had been a time when she'd been connected to her sister like no other person on earth. They'd shared a womb. They'd understood each other.

And Vanessa had ruined that. She'd gotten angry at Olivia for being a tattletale, but she'd said so many horrible things to Olivia.

They'd been close once. They'd changed and grown apart. But she'd changed again. And maybe…maybe they could be close again.

The idea of feeling close to Olivia again…

The idea of having her family again, imperfections and all, was enough to make her heart feel swollen.

"I've met your sister," Ellie said. "She's lovely."

"She is. It would be hard to have a different opinion on Olivia. She's truly one of the best people." Of course, *lovely* wasn't always the word that people used to describe Olivia. Olivia was complicated too.

Their relationship was complicated.

They were twins. Sharing a birthday, sharing facial features…and nothing else, really.

But the bond was real. And, oh, when she'd come back for the wedding…

She hadn't seen her sister in years, and in that moment, all the anger, all the pain, it had faded away. They'd just embraced. Cried. Held each other.

It had been the same with her parents. In those blissful moments it had been a reunion and nothing more. None of the weighted things. None of the hurt or pain.

They'd had some lunches since then and the cracks—especially with her parents, and with Olivia's protectiveness of them—had begun to show.

It couldn't be that reunion moment forever. Not for her sake or theirs.

But it was that moment that made her crave the reconciliation.

She wasn't quite ready to tackle it, not just yet. She needed to get established, to get everything in order, and then she would initiate further contact with her parents. With Olivia, and her husband, Luke.

They knew that she was here. There was no way to hide her presence in Gold Valley, nor would she have ever tried to. But they were very sensitive—perhaps too sensitive—to Vanessa's need for space.

Sometimes she wondered if it was sensitivity or if they just didn't want her around.

Either way, the ball had been left in her court, and she was actually all right with that.

"Classes start tomorrow," Ellie said, her fingertips brushing over the countertop. "It will be good to be back to teaching. A little bit strange. And this is so unusual. I've taught individual classes at the high school level, but I'll be doing…well, everything but art, and that's new."

"Is teaching your passion? Sorry. That was probably a weird-sounding question. It's just that I think about that a lot now."

Vanessa was lately very interested in the subject of passions. She'd never had one. Not when she was younger. She had felt superior to the world around her, to her parents, to her sister.

Especially when she had started using. As if she had crossed an invisible barrier that she believed other people were just too afraid to get on the other side of.

She had been smug and entirely certain of her choices. She had been an idiot.

Any potential she'd had to acquire a passion of her own had been poured directly into her opiate addiction. It had started with pills. Pills that could be stolen from her friends' parents, pills she could buy. Pills she could talk a doctor into prescribing. But eventually, after she'd gone to California and exhausted clinics that would give her pills, and most of her money, she'd fallen into heroin.

Her passion had become getting high.

Getting clean and sober had been like being spit out right back where she had left off.

She hadn't built a life with anything she could keep. She had no friends that she could continue relationships with.

She'd had no real education, no job prospects.

She had burned every bridge anyone had ever tried to build for her.

She had been twenty-two and starting over. Utterly and completely.

She felt lucky, every day, that she had started over that early.

"It was," Ellie said. "I'm hoping that I'm going to get back there."

"Did you want to start work again?"

"I needed to," Ellie said. "I have to do something. For someone else. I mean, I have Amelia. And that's been... It's been good. I lost the love of my life, and I don't have any answers about why. None of it makes sense. And when he died, it was like my passion for everything just faded away. I waited for it to come back. I had the luxury of that since Clint's insurance money was more than enough to keep us comfortable. But I decided that I can't wait for it to come back anymore. I need to do something to jump-start it. If I don't, I might never feel it."

"Fake it till you make it?"

"Maybe." She laughed. "Though I can't tell anyone here I'm faking it or they'll worry too much. But somehow I feel like I can tell you."

"You definitely can," Vanessa said. "I'm the queen of fake it till you make it. I don't have a story of hitting rock bottom and deciding to do rehab. I got arrested for possession and I had the option of entering a treatment program before charges were brought against me. So...I took it."

Ellie's expression was neutral, and Vanessa smiled. "I'm an addict. I've been sober for five years. I'm not sure what shows up in my background checks because... you know, rehab helped me avoid having a criminal record. Hopefully you don't want to kick me out of your school now."

"No," Ellie said. "Of course not."

"I'm not embarrassed," Vanessa said. "I've had a

long time to come to terms with myself. But I know other people haven't."

"Well, I'm fine with you. Honestly, it's been a really long time since I've had another woman to talk to about anything. I have Tammy, but she's more of a mother figure. And Caleb is great. But he's a guy. It's nice to have you here."

Vanessa tried to suppress her smile. Because she didn't want to look too thrilled by that statement. But she was.

"Court-ordered rehab is how I found my passion, by the way. One night they made us paint. They made us paint a feeling. I thought it was so stupid. But I did it anyway. And at first, I thought I would just phone it in, but then suddenly it was like… It was like seeing myself on a canvas."

She remembered pouring out red, orange, yellow. Her rage, all over the canvas. She remembered feeling a sense of catharsis like she hadn't known she could feel. She'd been in some strange space where she had been able to experience a negative feeling to its full extent, and when she was finished, it had been out in front of her, out in front of the world, and she hadn't felt like she needed to use.

For her it had been a revelation. To feel so much over something so simple. Something that amounted to little more than finger paint.

After that, she'd had direction. She had pursued art school. Had pursued every opportunity she could possibly have to learn as much as she could. To get into the studio when she could. And the end result had been the opportunity to teach art. The opportunity to help others use it as therapy.

"I stumbled upon my passion late," Vanessa said. "At least, compared to a lot of other people. But I have it."

"That's all that matters. Not having it..."

"I'm sorry," Vanessa said.

"I know. Everyone is."

"That's kind of nice, though. In a way."

"Yes."

Silence lingered between them, and Vanessa let it. There was a definite difference between the kind of sorry you could be for someone who had lost a spouse to circumstances beyond anyone's control, and the kind of sorry people felt for a drug addict who had made all of her own choices. She had encountered every single reaction possible over the course of the years. Some people pitied her. Some people judged her.

Everyone had a story about drugs or alcohol, how it had affected them or those around them.

And oftentimes what had happened to the addict the person knew informed their own feelings about drug use. About the odds that Vanessa would stay clean. About whether or not they saw it as a disease or a moral failure, or a mix of the two.

But one thing Vanessa knew for sure. No matter the reaction, it often robbed her of the opportunity to be seen as a person separate from her addiction.

She wasn't ashamed of her past. Letting go of shame had been a key part in her finding sobriety. But sometimes she wished... Sometimes she wished she could find a way back to when she was just Vanessa.

Yeah, sometimes she wished that.

"I'll leave you to get set up," Ellie said.

"Thanks," Vanessa responded.

She appreciated Ellie, and the way that she looked at Vanessa without judgment. That she had hired her to work with these kids. In spite of the fact that she had a past herself. Hell, maybe she'd hired her *because* she had a past.

Vanessa was fine with that.

The one thing she couldn't do was pretend those years spent in hell and oblivion didn't exist. And she *wouldn't* do it either. Not for someone else's comfort.

That was what shame boiled down to, after all. Being afraid of what someone else's feelings were. If you, your past, your pain, were hard for them to deal with.

Vanessa did her best not to feel it anymore. There was too much crap in life as it was.

"I'll see you around," Ellie said, giving her a small wave before she headed back out the door. Vanessa took a deep breath and surveyed her surroundings.

She almost didn't need any of the things she had brought with her. But she was going to get them all set up anyway.

This was her new place. This was why she was here.

And maybe it was a little ironic to have a fresh start in a place where so much of the past existed. But she didn't really mind that either. This was her classroom. Her studio. Her life.

Control was hers. It was no different than it had been back in California.

Her own life, her own terms. And now she was doing it in Gold Valley.

She'd spent a long time avoiding the deep end. So, her new method was to fling herself right down in it. All things considered, she felt pretty optimistic about it. She'd made a decision long ago about optimism. Whether she believed something would be good or not, if she tried and failed it would hurt. So she might as well look at it positively. Optimism cost nothing. And it made the world around her much more pleasant.

She busily worked to get her things in place. Her paintbrushes. Her favorite supplies.

When she was done there were still hours left in the workday, and she decided that she wanted to get a look around the entire ranch.

Maybe she should send Ellie a text to see if she was up to giving a tour. But Vanessa had enjoyed the quiet, had enjoyed the hours spent alone, and she wanted to wander around in her own head for a while.

She walked out of the studio and into the pale early-autumn sunlight. It was still fairly warm out, the summer season seeming to grow longer and later every year.

But there were differences. The light that filtered through the trees had a more orange glow than the heat of summer typically did, and there was an underlying crispness in the air, different from the typical early-morning summer chill that arrived for a few hours at night and began to burn off starting at around 9 a.m.

Subtle changes and hints that the season was shifting.

The kind of thing she never would have noticed when she was younger. When each and every day spent in Gold Valley was just a long bore running into the next.

The difference in her own feelings was perhaps the

strangest experience about homecoming. She craved everything she had hated back then. A sense of simplicity. Of sameness. A pace that was slow enough that she could ponder the way the air felt, and how that signaled a change in season.

She wanted to buy a wreath for the front door. Something that existed to simply be pretty and allow her to enjoy a moment.

She had been running from quiet moments for a lot of her life.

Because it was in those quiet moments that bad feelings often took hold.

The ability to be quiet, to be alone, was something that she had only cultivated in sobriety. She had avoided it at first. Staying busy, learning new things and engaging in group sessions had been the best thing for her for a good while.

But the pace of LA had gotten to be too much, not to mention the cost was prohibitive. And if she wanted to be able to slow down, she was going to have to get the kind of life that didn't demand such an intense working schedule.

Plus, she hadn't wanted an apartment anymore. She wanted a house. Something else she hadn't cared about for all that long.

But in many ways it was like waking up. Like a cautious, tender plant just breaking through the soil and reaching for the sun.

She'd heard before that five years was a magic number in sobriety. That it was when your brain became yours again.

In her experience, it was true. She felt so different now. Like a new person entirely.

But that had come from hours of therapy. Of groups. Of finding ways to fill the black hole she'd imagined Vanessa Logan was with feelings, thoughts and aspirations instead of pills. Until—bit by bit—she'd become a person and not a void.

It had started with hating herself. Blaming herself.

For taking the pills. For drinking too much. For blacking out.

For everything that had happened after.

And oblivion, more often than not, had seemed like salvation.

But it was just drinking poison, thinking it was water.

She pushed those thoughts to the side and decided to focus on the warmth of the day. She hadn't spent as much time marinating on befores and afters in her other life.

But it was this place.

This place that made her get just a little bit more ponderous. And while, to an extent, she was happy to embrace that because it was a part of her healing process, she would also just like to have a day.

A normal day on a beautiful ranch where she was starting an amazing job she was more excited about than she had been anything for quite some time. She smiled. It felt good to be here. Felt good to have hope. Life just felt good. And she was enjoying the hell out of herself.

The entire spread of the ranch was beautiful, with large barns built in a modern style, with clean lines and windows and neatly manicured arenas all over the property.

There were wide swaths of manicured lawn in deep rich green with white fences bracketing the borders.

It was perfection, though Vanessa knew just how much this kind of perfection could hide pain.

But she wasn't going to think about that. It wasn't her pain either way.

Whatever politics the Dalton family had to navigate weren't her problem. She was just here to work. To teach art.

She felt almost giddy with the freedom of it. All of it.

She paused at one of the barns and saw that it was open. Curiosity got the better of her. She wandered through the door, her eyes taking a moment to adjust to the dim light inside. It was cool, even with the front door and back door open, it seemed to make a good job of letting breeze filter on through.

She heard movement in a stall and assumed it was a horse. So when a man appeared, she startled and leaped backward.

"Oh!" She put her hands up in a defensive position, like it would do anything to stop…well, anything.

The man whirled around, his cowboy hat pushed low over his face, his height and breadth almost overwhelming her.

But even so, she knew exactly who it was.

Of course, yet again the person she encountered was Jacob Dalton.

Because he was the guardian angel she'd never asked for, or something. Except, he felt a lot more inconvenient than she had imagined a guardian angel should.

"Vanessa," he said. "Is something else on fire?"

"Not that I'm aware of. I would have thought you have a radio for that kind of thing."

"I was just trying to figure out exactly why you were here."

"Well," she responded, "I'm the new art teacher."

CHAPTER FOUR

JACOB COULD ONLY stare at Vanessa Logan, the second time in the space of twenty-four hours. Which seemed strange considering that, until yesterday he hadn't seen her in about ten years.

"Of course you are," he said.

"Yeah," she said. "Though I'm not sure why you say it like that."

"Like what?"

She sighed heavily. "I'm not going to play games with you. You didn't really act one way or the other yesterday. But you remember me?"

It occurred to him then that of course she might doubt that he did. Or at least, that he might not have ever connected her with the sad, pathetic girl who he'd handled while in distress all that time ago. And he could say no. Could keep them both from having the conversation.

But then, there was no real point to that. She didn't seem embarrassed. In fact, she was staring at him with her brown eyes glittering.

She was a strong woman, was Vanessa Logan. He didn't have to know anything about what had happened to her in the ensuing years to know that.

All he had to do was remember that night, when she'd been scared and in pain, but not broken. Alone and holding herself together.

"I remember you," he said. "I remember the emergency call."

"I thought you might." She swallowed hard. "You didn't say anything yesterday."

"Well, I didn't really want to bring it up, in case you didn't want me to."

Which was crediting a hell of a lot more decency to him than he deserved. The fact of the matter was, he just hadn't wanted to bring it up because he didn't do heavy subject matter. Not if he could help it.

"That's nice of you. But ten years and a whole lot of therapy later, I can talk about it."

Therapy. Well, there was something he never wanted to talk about. "Right."

"I mean, in the sense that no one actually knows about that except for you and the other EMT that you were with."

"Right," he said again.

"There's just no point informing anyone new about it."

"It was a long time ago."

"Yes," she agreed. "A very long time ago. I mean, ancient history, really. Except that we obviously both remember."

"Yeah, I tend to remember things like that," he said.

He couldn't read her expression. "I guess I didn't think that you would."

"There's a reason I'm not an EMT anymore. I was good at my job, but I saw a lot of things that you can't just forget. And to an extent, you don't really want to. You get called to the worst moments in people's lives. And sometimes, to moments that are just going to make for a funny story later. I did help get a bead out of one of the Miller kids' noses. Scary for a few minutes, but once we were there everything was fine, and his mom knew that he would be. But I've also seen the kids who weren't going to be fine. And that's just the kind of thing that… It stays with you. There was a time limit on how long I can do that."

"So you moved into firefighting?"

He shrugged. "Yeah, saving people, but less directly most of the time."

"More dangerous for you personally."

"It was never about my own safety."

"Right," she said. She took a breath. "Well, I look forward to seeing how everything is going to run around here."

"Oh," he said. "Me too. My older brother, who has really no experience with children, has decided that this is a great way for him to give back to the community. And…I guess he thinks it's just easy."

Vanessa laughed. "I doubt he thinks it's going to be easy."

"Oh, I'm damn sure he does. Gabe Dalton is nothing but overconfidence and good intentions. Let me tell you."

"You don't put a lot of stock in good intentions?"

He didn't speak for a moment. He didn't know what there was to say about that. Except to bring it back around to when he had worked in emergency services. "Good intentions never stopped a tragedy, and they never saved a life. Actions and reactions are all that matter. And believe me when I tell you, I think my brother has a pretty good reaction time. Considering that he used to be a bull rider and all. But I don't think he knows what he's getting into."

She tilted her head to the side. "Do *you*?"

"No. But I don't intend on doing a lot of work with kids. Not specifically. In part because I don't have to. I won't be teaching or anything like that. Gabe's fiancée, Jamie, is going to be the riding instructor. I'm just going to help facilitate things."

"Well, it sounds good anyway."

"What about you?" he asked. He realized then that he really didn't know anything about her life. He had no idea that she was coming to be the teacher at the ranch. And yeah, he had gone to her house last night, but he hadn't looked in any of the other rooms. For all he knew she had a husband. Maybe by now she had children. "Do you have experience with…this kind of thing?"

She laughed. "Not a lot. But I've done a lot of art therapy. So I've worked with troubled kids in the past. I've also done a lot of free art classes at rec centers. And a lot of adult painting classes. I have experience working with a variety of people. But I never expect any one group of people to be the same."

"Why not?"

"Because people are all different. One particular personality can completely change the dynamic of an entire group. No matter how much experience I had I wouldn't venture to think that I could anticipate how a group was going to behave."

He frowned. "I'm not sure I agree with that. In my line of work I've seen a lot of human nature. And in my estimation there's just a few types of people. All the window dressing might be different, but the basic way that we behave is the same."

"The window dressing is what makes us interesting," she insisted.

"Yeah, and the blood in our veins is what makes us human. And that's essentially all the same."

She squinted. "I can't decide if your outlook on life is incredibly hopeful or if it's sort of sad."

He tilted his lips up into a smile. "Consider the source."

"I don't know the source. You were a part of a pretty dramatic moment in my life, but I don't actually know you."

"I'm not a hero," he said. "That's about all you need to know about me."

BECAUSE GABE CALLED that night's drinking session a meeting, Jacob really had no choice but to go. Not that he minded having a beer. Far from it. But he might have preferred to stay in and have one. Alone. But whatever, for the second night in a row he found himself sitting in the Gold Valley Saloon with Gabe, Caleb, Ellie and Jamie.

He was allowing them to talk because he didn't have much to say. Not really. As long as they were happy to let him sit in silence, he was happy enough to sit there. Or maybe happy was overestimating it.

"I want to thank you all for getting this far with me," Gabe said. "It means a hell of a lot."

Jamie grinned. "Well, you couldn't have done it without us. Let's be clear."

"It's true. I couldn't have done it without you. Any of you. You most of all."

Jamie seemed to take that as her due. And he supposed that was fair enough. Being with Jamie had changed Gabe. And if Jacob were given to thinking much about that stuff, he would say that it was for the better. But he didn't do all that navel-gazing stuff if he could help it. Thinking of navel-gazing, though, he did wonder why Vanessa hadn't come out, when the rest of their ragtag staff was here.

"Where's the art teacher?"

He didn't call her by her name because he didn't especially want to give them the idea he and Vanessa had a link that extended beyond the ranch school.

"She said she was busy."

Gabe went back to talking, as if the reasons that she might be busy weren't interesting to him at all, and Jacob found that they were of interest to him. Whether he wanted them to be or not. He wasn't in a space in his life where he could be interested in a woman.

Hell, even back in the day his interest hadn't had anything to do with what a woman did when she was at home by herself on a Sunday night. Unless that something involved every masculine fantasy, where the woman drew herself a bath and lit some candles and briskly sought her own pleasure, preferably while on the phone with him.

And now he wasn't even in the position where that did much for him.

Although the minute he let himself have that thought, his mind immediately superimposed Vanessa over it.

The visceral reaction he had to that was extreme and swift. His stomach tightened, recoiling. He pushed that thought to the side, forcing himself instead to think of her as she had been, in pain and alone, all those years ago.

Not because it was a happy way to picture her, but because it was safer. At least for him.

He wondered if she had manufactured an excuse because of him. Though the woman who he had talked to earlier at the ranch hadn't seemed like she would avoid difficult situations. She seemed like she charged right into them headlong.

"We have files on all the kids who are coming. And Ellie has done a lot of comprehensive reading on the subject. I decided that, for a while at least, one of the men needs to be in the classroom with Ellie or Vanessa. At least just until we get an idea of how all of this is going to work."

Jacob frowned. "Really?"

"Yes," Gabe confirmed.

"Like a classroom marshal?" Jacob pressed.

"It's not a bad idea," Caleb said.

But of course Caleb would think that. And Caleb would be first in line to work in Ellie's class because he was her personal protector at all times, and Jacob couldn't see why this would be any different.

"So we're just supposed to sit there and observe and make sure that none of the kids cause problems?"

"Some of them come from pretty difficult circumstances," Gabe said. "And obviously I don't think they are bad beyond redemption or I wouldn't have them out at the ranch. But I wouldn't say they're all just good kids with tough centers. Some of them have been in violent altercations. No sex offenders. But some that are definitely physical scrappers."

"I'll be fine," Jamie said.

Gabe shot her a look. "You're going to be with me."

Jamie looked particularly annoyed, like Gabe was

her overprotective dad. "I know how to handle myself. It's not like any of you can shoot a gun straighter than I can."

"You're not going to shoot anyone," Gabe said.

Jamie shrugged. "I'm not above a little bit of brandishing to prove a point."

"No one is brandishing," Gabe said.

"We might have to brandish," Caleb said. "I mean, if things get real."

"This is a *school*," Gabe said.

"You're the one who brought up the subject of protection," Caleb said. "I was just saying—"

"You're going to get all of our licenses taken away before we even get started."

"You're paranoid," Jamie said, patting him on the shoulder.

His future sister-in-law was another of those women who didn't back down from a challenge. Jacob appreciated that about her.

"I suppose that means I'm assigned to the art room," Jacob said. Because of course he was. Of course he was being put right in the path of Vanessa Logan.

He couldn't figure out why it bothered him.

"Yes," Gabe said. "Feel free to take up painting if you have the urge."

"Yeah, I can't say that I am exactly itching to explore my artistic side." As far as he knew, he didn't have an artistic side. He was completely fine with that.

He had a hard-drinking side. A selfish side. An adrenaline-junkie side. But art was not his thing.

"I'm going to head out," Jacob said, standing up. He had the urge to go and drink a lot more than he could here. He needed to be able to drive home.

"I'll walk you out," Gabe said, his brother's eyes watchful.

"That's mighty kind of you, Gabe," Jacob said. "Do you want to hold my books?"

"Stop being a dick."

Jacob waved goodbye to everyone else, and he headed toward the door, weaving through the crowd of people, the floor slightly sticky beneath his boots thanks to the revelers getting in their last weekend hurrah, being careless with their beers and syrupy mixed drinks.

Jacob pushed the door open—the handle of which was a little bit sticky itself—and stepped out onto the street, the night air flat and temperate. It was strange. Not warm like it was in the height of summer, and no crispness yet like there would be once fall took hold.

It was quiet out on the street, everyone safely tucked away in the bar, or in restaurants. It was dark, the glow from the streetlights bathing the uneven cement sidewalks in a golden glow and making each and every crack look deeper, wider.

His truck was parked two blocks away up against the curb, beneath a sign claiming a time limit that he knew wasn't going to be enforced at this hour.

"There a reason that you're walking me out like I need a babysitter?" Jacob turned to his brother and shoved his hands in his pockets.

"I just wanted to make sure if there was anything you needed to tell me."

"Oh. I take that back. You're acting like you're my dad."

"Don't be silly. Our dad never asked if there was something we needed to tell him. At least not so he could scold us or make sure we were okay. Mostly to see if he needed to give us a high five for doing something particularly questionable."

"Fair enough," Jacob said.

"I promise I'm not busting your chops or trying to make things harder on you by putting you on classroom duty. And I really did think that you would mostly just be doing outdoor stuff. But I got to thinking about it, and I was a little bit concerned because, hell, I don't know what these kids are going to do. They've never had structure in their lives. And I don't know anything about kids."

"And yet you decided that this would be a great idea for you in terms of what direction to take your life in."

"Yeah." Gabe said this as if it wasn't a little bit weird. "Don't you know what it's like to want to make amends for something? Hell. I know you do."

"I think you overestimate me," he said. "There's no making amends to a dead man, Gabe. I'm not fool enough to think that there is. Not even me."

"Then what are you doing?"

"People change," Jacob said. "I spent a lot of years being the asshole middle kid. I just wanted to skate along. I did the bare minimum."

"I'm not sure very many people would say that an EMT turned wildland firefighter is selfish."

"Yeah. Because they think everyone does jobs like that to help other people. Some of us just do it for the thrill. That's why I didn't keep working as an EMT. The kind of crap that you see doesn't make up for the thrill, all right? I think you have a warped view of me because you're my brother, and you want to believe that I'm a really good guy. But I'm not. The older I get, the more I realize that. But my younger days are what they are. I can't do anything about it, it is what it is. But thirty-five-year-old me is not twenty-five-year-old me."

"I know that. I've changed too. It's just that…"

"You think I'm punishing myself. I get it. I haven't done a whole lot to make you see it differently. I'm not. Whether that makes you think better or worse of me, I don't know. But it's just the truth. So don't worry about me. I may not be exactly what you expected me to be. But I'd like to think that I'm better. Hell, I'm helping your ass out, aren't I?"

"True enough," Gabe said.

"I think we both know that I probably wouldn't have done that not very long ago."

"Also true," he said gruffly.

They both knew it was because of Clint. He'd spent months isolating himself. Dealing with his grief alone. And then he'd started to change. He'd quit drinking as much. He'd started asking how he could help around the ranch. He didn't go out to bars, didn't hook up.

Too late, he was trying to be the man who would have gone on the call that day. Not the man who'd blown off his responsibilities for a good time.

"If you're worried about someone punishing themselves, look at Caleb," Jacob said.

"Caleb, huh? We usually sit around talking about what you're doing to yourself."

"I know. Because he's a dumbass. Look at him. He's with Ellie all the time, acting like a husband without getting any of the benefits. Come on. What would you call that if not punishment?"

"He cares about her. She's our friend."

"Yeah. But he acts like he has to be her personal bodyguard for the rest of her and Amelia's lives."

"Or for him that's just friendship. Maybe that's just being there for people. And were you saying you were trying to do that?"

"Yeah. I was. Still, if you're looking for someone broken, look somewhere else. I think you just don't get how I could be happy living up away from everyone else. Spending time by myself."

"I'm happy," Gabe said. "I want you to be happy."

"And that's great," Jacob said. "Really great. I'm glad that you're happy. I think happy might not be what I'm aiming for. I did happy. For a long time. People got hurt."

"I thought you said you weren't doing the blame game."

"I'm not. But I am speaking the truth." His words landed like a rock between them.

Gabe could say whatever he wanted. That there was no way he could have known. That there were any number of reasons a person could miss a shift. He could have been sick. Then would he feel guilty? He could be dead. Would that be better?

But the fact was, Jacob hadn't been sick. He'd wanted to have sex with his one-night stand again. Had wanted to sleep off his hangover in peace. He'd thought only of himself.

He'd told them to call Clint. To have him cover his ass.

He'd lost his life.

Those were the facts. And no matter how much he might wish them different, they couldn't be.

Clint had lost his life.

The least he could do was own the guilt.

"All right. Hey. Whatever."

"Yeah. Whatever. I'll be fine, Gabe."

"Okay. See you tomorrow. Dumbass."

And then Gabe turned and walked back into the bar, leaving Jacob standing alone on the street trying to find a feeling in his chest. To figure out if he was lying or telling the truth to his brother. The thing that bothered him the most was that he wasn't sure.

CHAPTER FIVE

VANESSA FELT LIKE it was her first day of school. Like she was in junior high again. Waiting to walk into a classroom full of people, feeling like nothing more than a square peg being shoved into a round hole. Of course, back in school it had not been classrooms full of strangers. No. She'd never been given the benefit of a classroom full of strangers. She was Olivia Logan's twin. Her family among the most influential in town.

She had known everyone and everyone had known her from the first. And there had always been something about that that she found disconcerting. Maybe it was because no one actually knew her. They looked at her, they saw her name and they overlaid an expectation that had never matched up with what she was. There had been so much credit given to her, at least by anyone outside her family. People would have had no idea.

She was the chronic underachiever. She was the one who was not expected to try. She was a little black hole that happened to be shaped like a girl. And nothing more.

At least, that was how it had always felt to her. But no one understood that. And she had never wanted to confess it. Because it was sad. And weird. And no one would believe that a girl who had money and a beautiful house in their small town could be anything but deliriously happy. That the girl who was part of a family who had such a tight-knit bond in the public sphere would feel isolated and alone. That a girl with an identical twin could possibly feel like a singular misfit who was like nothing and no one.

Never.

She wasn't that girl now. Not the girl people had believed she might be. And not the black hole that she'd been inside. She was something else entirely. Something belonging only to her. And, more to the point, she was the teacher. She had taught classes before. But it had been different. Really different. She had taught at rec centers. Had taught people who had chosen to be there.

These kids were like she had been just a few short years ago. Angry. Disenfranchised, in a place they didn't want to be.

They were going to think she couldn't understand that pain. That she was stupid. And she couldn't say that she blamed them. Nobody wanted to be forced into something. But it wasn't too late for them. It wasn't too late for them to make different choices. And that mattered to Vanessa. It mattered deeply. She had gone over a cliff and no one had been able to reach her. If she had the opportunity to take kids' hands, she was going to.

She parked her car as close to her classroom as possible and got out, taking a deep breath and trying to calm the beating of her heart.

She was an expert at what she was teaching. She had something to say. She had things to teach. She was going to offer the help she'd had, and she was privileged to be able to do it.

She took a deep breath and rolled her eyes at herself. "I'm good enough. I'm smart enough. Gosh darn it, people like me." Then she laughed because it was all a little bit—or rather, a lot—ridiculous.

"Some affirmations before you head into battle?"

She whirled around and saw who else but Jacob.

"Yeah. I didn't have time to do them in the mirror before I left the house. I only barely had time for mascara."

"Well, that's a shame. Though I don't really think you need mascara."

"Thanks. I'll be sure to change my routine established over the course of years because you told me I didn't need it."

"Sorry," Jacob said. "Habit. It's…bar banter."

She snorted. "Bar banter? Is that a fancy way of saying a pickup line?"

"I guess."

"You don't want to hook up with me," she said.

"No." Jacob looked somewhat mystified. Like he'd been hit on the head with a hammer. "But it turns out my conversation skills with women are maybe a little bit limited when I don't."

"Great. That instills a whole lot of confidence in you as a human. I didn't expect to see you."

"Well, the surprise is on the both of us. Though if you had gone to the meeting last night, we would have been surprised at the same time."

"Oh really?"

"Yes."

"I was busy."

"What were you doing?"

She frowned. "That's a little bit invasive." She

began to open up the back of her car and get out her art bag and the papers that she had prepared last night.

"I'm just curious."

"I was setting another fire," she said drily. "You caught me. I'm a very bad arsonist."

"Yeah, you are a very bad arsonist. Since you keep running into a firefighter."

"I like to live dangerously." She flashed him a wide smile. "I didn't feel like going out to a bar."

She turned away from him and began to walk toward the classroom.

"Does it bother you to go to a bar?"

"No," she said honestly. "I mean, I can go. I didn't feel like going to this particular bar in this particular town."

She would run into someone. There would be questions. And as much as there was a kind of perverse self-righteous joy in being able to answer those questions in a bar with a club soda in front of her, she wasn't really looking to do that here. Not yet.

"Bad memories?"

She crossed her arms. "You're very nosy for someone who claims to not want to sleep with me."

"Just making conversation."

"You're bad at it. And no. There aren't any bad memories in the Gold Valley Saloon. Not mine. I'm sure there are plenty of other bad memories that belong to other people soaked into the wood over there. I was barely eighteen when I left town. And believe me when I tell you, a fake ID doesn't work when everyone knows your family. Or when your identical face is wandering around being underage also." She looked at him. "But I don't feel like I should have to tell you about how difficult it is to try to get away with things in a small town. I doubt you were a model citizen back in your high school days."

"No," he said. "But we didn't have to hide anything. If we wanted to have a party my dad would buy the booze."

"Really?" She had seen parents like that on TV. The cool parents. But she hadn't known of any in Gold Valley. The Dalton brothers were old enough that she would never have partied with any of them.

And many of the people her age that she'd met in LA had been running from the same kinds of things that she'd been. If they had cool parents, they didn't remember them. Or they were dead from overdoses.

"Yes. But then, I don't think Hank Dalton was ever going to win father of the year. I mean, growing up with him was pretty fun." Jacob nodded, a strange expression on his face. "When he was around."

"Your dad is famous for riding in the rodeo, isn't he?"

"Yes," Jacob said. "Though so are a lot of rodeo riders. There are a lot of champions quite frankly. It takes a lot more than that to become a personality. Hank Dalton is a personality."

"Wasn't he in commercials for chewing tobacco?"

"You know, if you're asking that you know he was."

Vanessa snapped her mouth shut, bemused. Because he wasn't wrong. "True."

"Yes. He advertised chewing tobacco. And of all the vices that my dad has, I don't even think that's one of them."

"It's funny. Because my dad is kind of famous. But

in this town. Not really anywhere else. For completely different reasons."

"Yes. It's my understanding that Cole Logan is a model citizen. Of whatever town you might want to put him in."

Model citizen. Inflexible. A good heart, but a hard heart. One she'd always desperately hoped had held love for her. And maybe it had. But she'd tested the limits of it. Vanessa had a lot of thoughts about her dad. But she wasn't going to put any of them to words. Not now. Talking to Jacob about mascara and bad memories she didn't even have was one thing. Getting into issues with her parents was another.

"A true-blue cowboy in every sense of the word," Vanessa said. "If he had any interest in politics he definitely would have been mayor of the town."

"Well. The county is named for you, after all."

"Yes. Because our ancestors happened to show up here. I've always thought that was kind of funny. I mean, don't get me wrong. My parents, my grandparents, they did a lot for the community. But I have the feeling that all they would've had to do was exist and they would have been important. Because they have the same last name as a weird uneven circle on the map."

"That's how that kind of thing works, isn't it? Names create a legacy long before a person ever has a chance to get their say on what they might want their legacy to be. If you live in a place like this, you aren't born with a clean slate. You're born with your family ties wrapped around your hands, and you can either spend your whole life trying to wiggle your way out of them, or you can figure out a way that they can work for you."

"Can I help you carry anything in the classroom?"

She turned to the side and treated him to a cursory glance. "Are you a gentleman?"

"Oh no. At least I don't think so. My dad is about the furthest thing from a gentleman there is. But even he wouldn't let a woman heft things from the car to the classroom when he has two good hands and could easily offer to help."

"Well, that I will accept." She handed him all of her materials and then passed him, leading the way inside the classroom.

"It's my understanding that I'm going to be taking two to three kids at a time," she said. "And that they won't start until they've had a tour of the ranch."

"Yeah. That's how it was explained to me. I actually don't know much about any of it."

"You haven't asked?" she pressed.

"Not really. Look, I want to help my brother. But this whole thing with the kids isn't something I'm particularly invested in."

"Why is he?"

"Our dad. I told you already…our dad is a little bit of a mess. He's selfish. And it turns out we have some half siblings we are collecting more and more of as the years go on."

She blinked. He admitted to secret siblings like some people might mention they had a cold at Christmas last year. "And you don't want to find them?"

"I don't feel anything about it one way or the other, to be honest."

She could tell by the tone of his voice that wasn't strictly true. She took her supplies from him and set them on the counter, began setting up. "Okay. So you don't feel anything about it particularly. But you also have gone out of your way to not be invested?"

"I'm investing. I'm here. That's about as good as it gets, right?"

"Oh sure. You grudgingly and angrily helping him live out is his dream come true. I don't know Gabe that well, but I'm certain all he requires is angry servitude."

"Believe me. That is all my brother requires."

"I was being serious, actually."

"Oh, I have no doubt you were."

"I don't really understand what your half siblings have to do with this school."

"I think Gabe feels responsible in some ways. Basically he knew about my father's illegitimate children. And when our half sister showed up a year or so ago…"

"Oh. You're going to have to explain 'half sister' to me."

"Okay. McKenna showed up out of the blue a year or so ago."

She snorted. "That is not clarifying. That's repeating."

"Sorry. There's not a whole lot to clarify there. It just is what it is. We found out we had a half sister, which seemed pretty unique and crazy. And now we know we're lousy with half siblings." He paused. "You're setting them up on easels on the first day? I don't think you're quite prepared for just how feral this group of kids is."

She shot him a sideways look, wondering if he'd switched the subject away from personal things deliberately. "I thought you said you didn't know anything about kids."

"I don't. But as a relatively feral adult who used to

be a feral teenager, you set me up in front of one of those things…"

"And now that's my goal, Jacob Dalton. So congratulations to you. But I think you might be underestimating me. What is it you think? I'm the town princess, like my sister? Not true. I'm sure I have more in common with your half sister."

"Maybe. Anyway. My half sister was the catalyst for a lot of this. She grew up in foster care. I think Gabe sees this as a way to right some of our father's wrongs."

"Does Caleb feel that way?"

"As far as I can tell Caleb feels allegiance to one person and one person only."

"And that is?"

"Ellie."

"Oh right. You were… You were friends with her husband. She mentioned that you all fought wildfires together."

Jacob grew visibly uncomfortable. "We were good friends with Clint for most of our lives. And when he brought Ellie into the fold we accepted her right away. I don't know. I think Caleb has decided that he's doing something for Clint by making Ellie and Amelia and their happiness his mission on earth."

"And you?"

"Everything I've said to you about my dad—minus the secret kids—could have been said about me. I was the middle child. The wild one. Live while you're living because you never know when you might die."

"You were…worried about that even before Clint?" she asked.

"Yes," he said. "Not worried, just aware. But since Clint… Well, now I see it different."

"His death changed you, didn't it?" she pressed.

He looked at her, his reluctance to answer her clear. "I think if the death of your best friend doesn't change you, there's something wrong with you."

She lifted a shoulder. "There's something wrong with all of us."

"True. And after he died I realized there was something wrong with me. So I'm trying to fix it."

"So, for you that means fixing the ways you were like your dad?"

He looked at her, his blue eyes connecting with hers. And she felt it down deep. She was curious about him, and she didn't want to be. Curious about who he was before Clint. About who he was now.

About who he could be.

"Yeah," he said. "I'd like to fix that. I can't bring Clint back. But he's not here and I am, and it seems like I might…make the space I'm occupying here worth something."

Words got caught in her throat, all tangled together. "You know, for what it's worth, the space you occupy has always been worth something to me."

She expected to feel gratitude when she looked up at him, because that was what she'd meant by what she'd said. But it wasn't gratitude for his help when she'd had her miscarriage that she felt when she looked at him.

It wasn't about him being a savior.

It was about him being a man.

And she really didn't need that.

"Let's get these easels set up," she said, changing the subject on herself.

Because she didn't want to think about what the tension in her chest, the tension between them, could turn into. She had an art class to focus on.

And that would be enough for now.

CHAPTER SIX

JACOB HADN'T KNOWN what to expect with an art class like this. Hell, the closest he'd ever been to a paintbrush was when he'd helped paint one of the barns for the ranch. He didn't do…art. At all.

And it was clear to him that most of the kids coming into this place didn't either. The first two boys were sullen most of the time, and Vanessa had happily spent the hour intermittently talking or staring at them while they refused to do anything, their aggression seeming to feed off each other.

And Jacob knew even less of what to do with kids than he did with art.

He was basically no help. And he looked like exactly what he was. A potential bouncer if the situation called for it. Which he imagined didn't exactly ease the situation. If anything, it probably counteracted the general sense of therapy that was supposed to be happening here.

When the two of them left, they had a small break, and Vanessa looked around. "No need to clean out paintbrushes, I guess."

"What happens if they keep doing that?" he asked.

"Then they keep doing it. But they won't. Eventually, even if it's out of anger, one of them is going to pick up that brush. That was my experience with it. A few strokes of defiance. But then I found out I wanted to fight with a whole lot more than just the person in front of me. That I had a lot more to get out on that canvas than I thought."

"What if they don't?"

"They're going to get it out somewhere," she said. "And long term... I suppose art isn't for everyone. But it isn't going to hurt someone to do a painting. And if all they learn from this is that it isn't going to hurt them to comply when someone asks them to do something, even if it's outside their comfort zone, then they've learned something."

"I didn't think you had a whole lot of experience teaching kids."

"I don't. But I have a whole lot of experience being this kind of kid."

"It's hard to imagine."

It was. Vanessa was beautiful. Glossy brown hair, and a willowy frame. Her skin was clear and glowed with health. It was difficult to imagine it ever being any different. Difficult to imagine that she had ever been the drug addict she so freely claimed to be.

She more than claimed it. She'd worn it like a badge when she'd talked to him that first day at the ranch. Like a shield.

Not that he was in any place to go psychoanalyzing anyone.

She leaned back against the desk, her thin, cream-colored blouse molding itself over her breasts. He didn't really want to psychoanalyze anyone. But he didn't mind having a look at her.

It'd been a long damn time since a woman had stirred his interest.

Ever since Clint had died.

But then, that had made sense to him this whole time. His friend was dead. He couldn't go home to his wife, would never hold his baby. Why should Jacob continue to live life as if nothing had ever happened?

Vanessa tilted her head back, lowering her shoulders and stretching gracefully. And his mouth went dry.

He was positively struck dumb. Not just by the attraction that centered low in his gut, and down lower still, but at the fact that it existed at all.

And just how intensely it presented itself.

Why do you think that is? Because you want to cling to the time that you did something good? And she represents that somehow?

Hell, he hadn't even picked up a paintbrush and here he was getting overly thoughtful about blood rushing to his dick. There was no point in that. He was a man. She was a woman. She had a fine set of breasts, and he hadn't touched any in a while.

It was as simple and complicated as that. He was certain.

About the time he was thinking about how nice her rack was, and how long it had been since he had touched a naked woman, the next couple of students came in. Marco, Calvin and Aiden. He would forget those names as soon as they walked back out. But he imagined for the purposes of getting through the next hour he ought to remember.

Not that Vanessa seemed to require much of anything. Just as she'd done before, she calmly outlined the purpose of the class while Jacob leaned up against the counter in the back of the classroom.

She spoke with a no-nonsense tone, but it wasn't brisk or unkind. In fact, she somehow managed to seem both soft and laced through with steel all at the same time. She was something, this woman. And he could see that the rebellion against the assignment sat uncomfortably with the three boys, who had likely never met a rebellion they weren't entirely at peace with before.

But just like the first two, they didn't make a move to do as they were told.

"You can paint whatever you like," Vanessa said after sitting there for a good ten minutes and simply observing the inactivity of the three boys. Her hands were clasped in her lap, her expression serene.

"What is this dumb shit for?" Calvin asked.

He had a permanently angry expression, with light brown hair that stuck out at odd angles. He was skinny, the collar of the white T-shirt he was wearing stretched out, revealing protruding collarbones. His pale green eyes glittered with anger. He was a sharp contrast to Marco, who was at least six inches taller, with dark hair and a carefully blank expression. He seemed content to watch and maybe follow the lead of the other two. Or maybe just pick whichever path would work best for him.

Aiden had the smirk of a cocky bastard. And Jacob should know because he was one from the cradle. Aiden didn't possess the self-preservation inherent in that careful neutrality on Marco's face. Nor did he possess the earnestness required for the kind of anger that Calvin carried around on his scrawny shoulders. No, that boy was 100 percent pure smart-ass, and when he chose to speak—and Jacob knew he would—he was going to take the path of greatest irritation for all involved.

"You might like it," Vanessa said. "Have any of you ever taken art class before?"

The smirk on Aiden's face deepened. And Jacob could see the smart-ass remark coming before the kid's mouth opened. "I've been told what I do in the bedroom is something like art," he said.

"Didn't know your right hand was so chatty," Marco said, his expression still blank.

And Jacob found himself pleasantly surprised by that boy. Because it was a good burn, but not one that Jacob would have been able to level at a seventeen-year-old without causing some trouble. He imagined.

"It's not," Aiden said. "But your mom has a lot to say."

Jacob sighed heavily.

That earned him looks from the boys and from Vanessa. He shouldn't get involved. He didn't have a right to, not really. He was here to observe, not to… say things. But this just reminded him of…well, him.

He hadn't used anger. He'd been brash, he'd been inappropriate and loud and quick with a joke. He'd never taken much of anything seriously, and his willingness to play the fool had often given him the upper hand in social situations.

The control.

And as a bonus side effect, it kept it from being sincere. And nothing had scared him more than sincerity.

These kids needed a dose of it.

"Predictable," Jacob said.

Aiden frowned. "What?"

"That was boring. If you're going to bother to open

your mouth to shock the world you might want to make it a little something better than a joke that has been around since the early 90s."

"And you are?"

"The asshole that has been making jokes like that since before you were born."

"Are you a teacher?" Aiden asked.

Jacob snorted. "Hell no. And good for you too."

"Thank you," Vanessa said. "But I won't be requiring your intervention."

"You're welcome. But I'm not offering an intervention. I'm just responding to this kid's lame-ass commentary."

"If you're not a teacher, then what are you?" Calvin asked.

"I'm here to make sure you don't get out of line."

"Are you a cop?" Marco asked.

"Also no. I'm just here doing what I'm told."

"Well," Calvin said, "I'm not."

"Yeah. And look how far it's gotten you. Shipped off to school in Nowhere, Oregon. Congratulations. That whole rebellion thing is going great."

"Do you guys want to start painting so he'll shut up?" Vanessa asked.

"It's better than where I was," Calvin said.

"Then maybe you should lose the chip on your shoulder and pick up a paintbrush," Jacob said, ignoring Vanessa.

Vanessa was beginning to look testy, but she didn't interject again.

"Why? So we don't fail art class?"

So you didn't destroy your life. So people didn't get hurt. So people didn't die.

"Let me tell you something. From one screwup to another. There's going to be a hell of a lot of battles in your life. But there isn't one in here. Just a paintbrush and a damn can of paint. You can fight but for what? To prove you're a badass? To prove that you are tougher than a canvas? Or you can just do as you're told. Maybe you'll like it. Maybe you won't. But you won't have wasted your energy on a battle that doesn't actually matter to you. At this point, kid, I think you're so angry you would fight anything. But you better save it. Because life is gonna come try to kick your ass, more than it already has. I don't care what you've been through, and I don't care what you think I've been through. Believe me when I tell you, life is gonna keep kicking your ass. It's not going to decide that it's done just because you already had a bad time. So if I were you…I'd paint a damn picture in here. Fight the dragons when they show up."

"Thank you," Vanessa said, her voice soft. But he had a feeling he was going to earn himself a lecture later.

The glitter in her dark brown eyes told him that she had identified her own personal dragon. And that right now it was him.

The boys sat frozen, but after a few minutes, Calvin picked up a paintbrush. And then, so did Marco.

Aiden sat resolutely, his arms crossed, his dark brows locked together. But the other two painted. And then, with five minutes left, Aiden picked up a paintbrush and with just a few intense strokes wrote *fuck this* on a blank canvas.

Jacob was about to get in the kid's face, but Vanessa wandered around the back to look at the canvases, and her expression was completely different to what he had imagined it might be.

Calvin had done the canvas all in black. Except red at the center. Marco's was a mix of colors, all dark, blending together until they were muddy.

And then there were the simple words scrawled out by Aiden.

"I know you're trying to show me that you didn't participate," Vanessa said quietly. "But I hate to tell you this, even that says something about you. And that's okay. Whatever you feel. I'm not here to judge you, I'm not here to grade you. I'm here to help you figure out how to put what's in here on here," she said, touching the canvas again.

"You don't want to see what I feel," Calvin muttered from his position next to Aiden.

"It doesn't matter if I want to or not. Maybe it will make me uncomfortable. Maybe it will make the people around you uncomfortable. Art isn't supposed to be easy. This is a place where you don't have to worry about what anyone wants to see. Fighting me… There's no point. Just paint."

And with those words, the session ended, the three boys walking back out, where they were met by Ellie, who was ushering them to one of the larger classes of the day.

"I didn't mean to step on your toes," he said.

"I mean, I guess it worked," she responded.

"Still."

"I didn't think you wanted to do anything with the kids."

"I don't. But they're such little punk asses."

"No argument," she said, stifling an amused smile.

"Where did you get all that?" she asked, her voice softer now.

"Where did I get what?"

"Everything you said. About saving your battles. About fighting dragons."

"Everyone's fighting. When you're angry…that's what you do. You fight yourself. You fight the people around you. Kids like Aiden…they're fighting too. They do it with that shit-eating grin, but they fight. They do it by giving up. By not trying. And it's all going to blow up in their faces eventually. So you have to know. You have to know why you fight. You have to know what matters. Because if you don't, eventually nothing will matter. Or at least, you'll treat some very special things like they don't matter. And it will be too late to do anything. You won't realize it until it all goes to hell. I'm an expert in that."

"Well, look at you. You're much more self-actualized than you led me to believe."

"I'm not self-actualized. I'm not even entirely sure what that means. But I recognize a mirror when I see one. And that kid…"

"You know, it probably wouldn't hurt you to paint a giant *fuck this* on a canvas."

"What are you talking about?"

"I think you have some issues."

He frowned. "I don't have punk-ass kid issues. I had a friend who died. That really messed some things up."

"You think these kids are just rebelling against their parents? Some of them have suffered pretty serious abuse. Abandonment. Just because they're young doesn't make their issues less."

"I get that," he said. Except, he hadn't really given it any thought.

"You don't have to," she said. "But you might try taking some of your own advice."

"I'm not fighting against anything. I'm here. I'm helping. I'm done with being selfish. With being thoughtless about my actions and how they affect other people. I lived life like that for a long time and it cost my best friend. I'm different now."

"So you'll paint me a picture?"

"No," he said. "Because I'm not a troubled kid that got sent to a special school. And I don't need therapy. Your brand of it or otherwise."

"A pretty bold statement."

"Well, that's the kind of guy I am."

"Great. Since it's not your class, though, you can tone down the boldness there."

"Sure."

"You can just sit quietly until there are some dragons to slay."

Jacob had spent long hours on the fire lines. He had pulled all-night shifts driving ambulances. He had put in punishing twelve-hour workdays on the ranch. And he didn't think he had ever been so tired before in all of his life as he was after dealing with a bunch of kids all day.

They weren't even kids. It wasn't like he had been dealing with a passel of toddlers. No. He had been sitting in an art class with teenagers. That should have been easy. Nothing.

It was a strange kind of exhaustion. Not the aching muscles he was accustomed to having at the end of the day. It was a foreign, sand-behind-the-eyelids sensation accompanied by no small amount of brain fog.

He walked into the main schoolroom, where Gabe had asked the group of them to meet after the day was over.

Yet again, Vanessa was nowhere to be seen, but Gabe was seated on top of one of the desks, his feet propped up on a chair. Jamie was sitting down in a chair beside him, her arm draped over his thighs. Jamie looked about as exhausted as Jacob felt.

Ellie was seated on the floor next to Amelia, who was playing with two bedraggled-looking plastic ponies, one of which was wearing a tutu. Caleb was standing on the periphery of the group, his hands clenched into fists at his sides, as if he didn't know quite what to do with them.

Jacob assumed a similar position.

"Now that we are all here," Ellie said, giving him a smile, "how was the day?"

"Good," Gabe said.

"Exhausting," Jamie replied, draping yet more resolutely over Gabe's lap.

"You normally lead fifty-mile trail rides, girl," he said, shaking his leg. "Why are you so tired?"

"Youths," she said.

"It's not for the faint of heart," Ellie said.

"You don't look tired," Jamie responded.

"I have experience teaching. And for me…it was good to get back into it," she said softly, looking down at Amelia. "It was good to have something other than our little world to focus on."

"Where's Vanessa?" Jacob asked.

"She said she would email me a full report," Gabe

said. "I don't require anybody to be social as long as they get their job done."

"Wait a minute," Jacob said. "You didn't say that to me. Do I have to be social as long as I'm getting my job done?"

"You do, because you're my brother. And I want you here."

"I don't know why."

"Because the alternative is that you're going to be up at your cabin all the time."

Jacob couldn't really argue with that.

But he thought of the way his interest had been sparked looking at Vanessa's body earlier today, and he wondered if he just should have stayed up in the mountains.

"So all of the kids hate us," Caleb said. "I'm not the only one that noticed that, am I?"

"I felt like they liked me," Jamie said.

"I think they like your ass," Gabe said.

Jamie looked up at him and glared. "That is inappropriate."

"It wouldn't have been more appropriate for anyone else here to say it."

"He has a point," Jacob said.

"Are you saying they don't like *my* ass?" Ellie asked.

"You were in a classroom environment," Gabe said, having the decency to look slightly perturbed by the line of conversation. "Jamie was showing them the horses. And bending over and grabbing things."

"I think *you* were looking at her ass," Ellie said.

"I was," Gabe said. "She's my fiancée, and I'm allowed."

"Can I not be reduced to my ass, please? And that is not a sentence I thought I would ever have to say."

"Sorry," Gabe said, not looking at all sorry.

"My point is, these kids are kind of miserable," Caleb said.

"They're going to be miserable for a while," Ellie said. "And you know what, they might not even be miserable. But they don't know how to show that they aren't. Not without losing their shields. And those shields are very, very important to them."

"So basically, we signed on to do this job where a bunch of kids snarl at us twenty-four hours a day?" Jacob asked.

"Not twenty-four hours a day," Gabe said. "They're gone now."

"True," Jacob responded. "So tomorrow, same as today? Verbal abuse from snot-nosed teenagers and then collapse into a heap?"

"Yeah," Gabe said.

"Great. Then I'm out."

"Just a second before you go."

Jacob held back a groan. He wasn't going to let his brother know he was irritated with him. Because of maturity. Or something like that.

Gabe followed him outside, and Jacob waited. Because he had learned that if he came at Gabe swinging, snapping at him and asking him what the hell he wanted, then his brother would only feel all the more justified in prying.

He and Gabe had never been the close ones. Not really. That had been him and Caleb. Always. But the thing with Clint had done strange things to his relationship with Caleb. Hell, it had done strange things to his relationship with everyone if he were honest. But the biggest difference was Caleb.

"I heard from West," Gabe said.

"Really?" West Caldwell, their half brother who none of them had ever met.

Gabe had come clean with them all a few months back about the fact that their father had illegitimate children not even he'd known about.

They had a half sister, McKenna, who'd found them last Christmas, but the revelations of other children were more recent.

Their mother, Tammy, had known about them. Some twenty-five years ago she'd paid off women who'd attempted to extort money from her husband, and they'd left with their money, and without Hank or anyone else other than Gabe knowing about the kids.

Gabe felt compelled by guilt now to find the other kids and bring them into the fold. They'd managed to track down one of the women and, through her, had found her son West. But she'd been unwilling to share the names of the other mothers, so they were at a standstill.

"Yes," Gabe said.

"Why are you telling me? Separately from everyone else."

Gabe looked around, as if he hadn't considered that. "I told Jamie."

"McKenna? Caleb?"

"No. Because I have the feeling that all of this bothers you, and I can't really figure out why."

"It doesn't bother me. Not any more than anything else."

"I don't believe that."

"I can't help what you do or don't believe," he said, feeling frustrated. "I'm not going to live my life trying to make you feel comfortable."

"I didn't ask you to."

"You've been weirdly up on me about your plans. About all of this. About your plans for the ranch, telling me about all of it before you told anyone else, and about this. I'm not sure exactly when you thought I became a safe space, Gabe."

"Somebody has to be," Gabe said. "I mean, someone has to be for you."

This came close to sending Jacob straight over the edge into a rage. He was trying to reach him, or whatever. Trying to turn him into one of the troubled kids he was helping out on the ranch, and Jacob didn't know what the hell was going on in his brother's psyche to put him in this space, but he was definitely in it, and Jacob didn't have any desire to be part of it.

"I feel like you're doing some kind of metaphorical baptism or emotional stuff here," Jacob said. "And I'm not buying into being part of it."

"What do you mean by that?"

"You found love, great. I'm really glad for you. You decided to leave the rodeo and that you'd found a calling here. Great. I'm happy for you there too. But you changing has nothing to do with anyone else around you needing to change."

"That's not true," Gabe said. "We all have…stuff. And we can let it go."

"Do you hear yourself? You're a smug married man and you haven't even said your vows yet. You think that you know what everyone else should do? Gabe, that's bull. You don't know what I need to do, or what

Caleb needs to do. When anyone needs to do it. I know that you cared about Clint. But it's not the same."

"It's the same enough," Gabe said. "And it's not the only thing. We have to deal with the half siblings."

"Why? Why do we have to deal with them? Because you had an attack of conscience. I didn't."

"Why didn't you? Why doesn't it matter to you?"

"Because I don't want to deal with the brothers I have right now," Jacob said, knowing that he might regret that little outburst later. But he sure as hell didn't regret it right now. Because right now it was true.

"Listen to yourself. You sound like an arrogant dick. Deciding that everybody just needs to get with the program and get on the same page as you."

Gabe had the decency to look ashamed about that. "That's not what I'm trying to do."

"But it is what you're doing."

Gabe said nothing. He let everything settle between them into silence. "I didn't come and see you on the mountaintop all those months ago to tell you about my plan so I could shame you into action. I promise. I came to talk to you because I thought you might be the one person who would understand. We all live with guilt. To differing degrees. And as much as Caleb seems more…available, I feel like he actually isn't. I thought I could actually talk to you about it. I thought you might understand."

"I understand about guilt. But you're talking about the kind of guilt you can do something about, Gabe. There're people you can find and bring here and you can put salve on all those wounds that you have. Clint is dead."

"It's not because of you."

"It is."

"That bull about how you could've traded flights, and he wouldn't be dead."

"I declined going on that fire. I wasn't late and missed it. I was in bed with a woman. And I didn't want to get up. I got the call. I said no. Call Clint."

Gabe's face went pale. "You never told me that."

"Yeah," Jacob said. "I never told you that because it exposes what a dick I am. You think that I'm…the way that I am because I made up some story to tell myself about how if I had done things differently Clint would be alive? I didn't have to make up any story, Gabe. It's just true. And maybe in the end we can't figure out the cosmic exchange that might've happened. Maybe with our slight weight difference the helicopter wouldn't have crashed. Hell if I know. All I know is I sent my friend on that job."

"With good intentions. He had Ellie and she was having a baby. He needed the money…"

"You act like I thought any of that through. I never thought a damn thing through in all my life. All I've ever done is live for myself. All I've ever done is live to make myself happy. At least Hank never killed anyone."

He turned and started to walk away from his brother.

"You're not like Dad," Gabe said.

"No," Jacob said, stopping in his tracks. "You're right. I'm not like Dad. Because Dad is likable. And at the end of the day, he's turned out to be kind of a decent guy. I don't know what I am."

"You're trying."

"Trying doesn't matter when Ellie doesn't have a

husband. Amelia doesn't have a father. Dammit, Gabe, I can barely look at that little girl. If it weren't for me her dad would be here."

"Jacob…"

"I'm a piss-poor trade-off, Gabe. At least for them."

He walked away from his brother, feeling like he'd just had an epic tantrum, and he hated that more than the guilt.

Showing it. Bleeding it.

When everything settled down, and he was in the cab of his truck, halfway on the road back to his cabin, he realized that this was the first time he had ever told the story of that morning Clint had gotten sent out in the helicopter that had ultimately crashed.

He was surprised he didn't feel more about that either.

If anything, he felt slightly relieved. Because maybe now Gabe would quit trying to fix him.

Maybe now he would see that there were some things beyond fixing.

And Jacob might be doing his damnedest to be a physical help to Gabe, to Ellie. But it didn't mean he had to like it.

Maybe Gabe would just quit asking him to like it.

If he would just let him show up and do the work and leave, let him go off and be alone, they would both be better for it.

CHAPTER SEVEN

As Vanessa pulled her car up to Olivia's quaint little front porch, she began to wish she would have made an excuse and stayed behind for the staff meeting.

She had been back in town for long enough that it was strange she hadn't seen her sister, so when Olivia had texted her, Vanessa had asked if she wanted to get together.

She had an endless inner monologue running. An if-then flowchart of conversations she might have with Olivia. *If Olivia said...then Vanessa would say. If, then. And on and on.*

The two of them hadn't actually talked alone in... years.

Granted, Luke and Emma would be there. But Emma was a baby, and Luke was a man, so she didn't feel like they would do much of anything to diffuse the weight of the conversation. Emma probably more than Luke at the end of the day. Well, she'd made dinner plans, and she wasn't a coward.

Well, maybe she was a coward, but she wasn't going to let those feelings win.

She took great pride in that. When she could come up against a hard moment and make it her bitch.

Because she used to fold like a house of cards beneath hard feelings. Fold into a pile of blissful nothing. Chasing a haze to help wear the sharp edges of life away.

And now, she just let them cut her. Just let herself bleed.

In many ways, she was at peace with discomfort.

But that was in a generalized sense.

In this very personal sense that reopened old wounds rather than creating new ones, it felt different.

It was times like this she was reminded of why she had stayed away during the first few years of her sobriety.

Her new life, all the new growth, made her feel like a new creation. Like something with a past wiped clean and nothing but bright clear skies stretching out before her.

Here, she could feel the sins of the past wrapping themselves around her like old, dead roots, curling around her arms, making it feel difficult to breathe.

She did not want to use, though, and she supposed that was a very good realization.

In fact, the idea made her feel even sicker here than it had back in LA.

Like a memory of someone else. But one that was strong and more haunting than she would've liked. She steeled herself and walked up the front porch, and before she could knock, the door opened, the dainty little wreath hanging there shaking slightly as it did.

And there was a mirror image of herself. A slightly rounder face, longer hair, but very clearly a person with the same collection of features.

They were a very definite example of a person's looks not extending beyond the surface of skin.

Because they had never been the same, and the years had only widened the gulf between them.

Even in her recovery, Vanessa just wasn't the same. She couldn't explain how, not right then, or why she was so certain of it. But she was. And as she stood there facing her sister, she really wished that she hadn't come. But she had. So she had to buck up and deal with it.

"I'm glad you could make it," Olivia said, reaching out and folding Vanessa into her arms.

Maybe the warm show of feelings should have made Vanessa feel welcome. Should have made her reevaluate her emotions about being at Olivia's house.

It didn't. If anything it only further entrenched the feeling of wrongness that had settled over her from the moment she had pulled into the driveway.

"Me too," she said, forcing a smile and following her sister into the sitting room. It was an old-fashioned home. A Victorian-era farmhouse with spindly wood beams on the porch and matching detail inside. Lace curtains that fluttered over windows that offered a view out to the field, currently dotted with yellow flowers, a woven rug on the floor.

"This is different," Vanessa said, looking around.

She thought her sister would have preferred something a bit more like the house they'd grown up in. More classic, with additional modern conveniences.

She also realized that every time she and her family had seen each other since reconnecting, it had been on neutral ground. A café or restaurant.

But not her sister's house.

"Is it?" Olivia asked, looking around. "I thought it was rather classic."

"I didn't mean different in the grand scheme of things. I meant different for you."

"Oh. I guess so. It's like that dollhouse we used to have. Don't you think?"

Vanessa couldn't remember the dollhouse. And she didn't know what it said about her that said dollhouse, which had clearly been so formative for Olivia, didn't seem to exist in Vanessa's memory at all.

"Right," she said.

"Have a seat. Would you like something to drink? I mean, a soft drink."

The words hit like bullets, even though Olivia probably wasn't meaning to make her feel bad. She was probably making sure Vanessa knew she had something for her to drink. Which often, as a nondrinker, Vanessa found to be an issue. Some people didn't seem to understand the concept of drinking for hydration, and not for altered consciousness.

But even still, it made her feel…different. Separate.

"Sure," she said. "Iced tea?"

"I have some," Olivia said, smiling cheerfully and wafting from the room.

Her sister was wearing a feminine floral dress and white sandals, and it was lovely, not as prim as she remembered Olivia being. In fact, Olivia did seem much more relaxed than she had when they were younger.

Being with Luke had done good things for her. Vanessa knew that. She could see it.

Olivia returned a few moments later. "You can take a seat," she said, gesturing to a blue floral sofa, which was new but had an antique quality to it.

"Thank you," Vanessa said. "Are Luke and Emma here?"

"Yes. Luke was just getting Emma up from her nap, and I suspect she's wet."

Olivia said that with such casual flippancy. Vanessa couldn't imagine being that casual about something of that nature.

Wet babies.

Vanessa was not in a space to think about babies. She supposed if she hadn't had a miscarriage all those years ago she would have already been through this stage and offering sage wisdom.

But instead she'd lost a baby. Gained an addiction.

Lost herself.

Found herself again.

She was going to focus on the last part. That she was found. That she knew who she was.

"Right."

Olivia stood in the doorway of the seating area, her hands grasping her elbows, her smile looking a little bit strange. Vanessa busied herself sipping her tea.

"I hope you still like barbecued chicken," Olivia said. "The kind you just do in the oven. With barbecue sauce. I remember you liked that when Mom made it. So I made it. You don't have to take any green beans, though."

Olivia's overearnest offer surprised Vanessa. It had been her favorite. Except for the green beans. Her mom had always made barbecued chicken with green beans, and Olivia loved green beans. So she and Vanessa had always engaged in a stealthy vegetable transfer at some point when their parents were distracted.

Just a small amount of subterfuge. But it had always meant something to her because Olivia hated subterfuge.

"Good. Well, hopefully it will be good." Olivia twisted her hands. "I'm not as good at cooking as Mom is. I don't have as much experience. But I cook for Luke now. I mean, sometimes he cooks for me too. But he only knows how to cook on the grill, and he refuses to cook anything but beef or venison. So if I want something less…you know, I have to do it."

The simple words gave Vanessa a glimpse of her sister's world that made her ache to be part of it. "I'm sure it's good. You seem to have settled into…all of this pretty happily."

"*This* being the farmhouse?"

"Being a housewife," she clarified.

Olivia's lips turned down slightly at the corners.

She couldn't tell if she'd offended Olivia by that description. She hadn't meant to.

Everything seemed to be going well for a few minutes at a time and then… Thump. Rolling along, making conversation. Thump.

"You seem happy," Vanessa said, hoping to cover up any unpleasantness that was beginning to fester between them.

"I am," she said. "Very happy."

They were saved a moment later by Olivia's handsome husband, who came down the stairs clutching their daughter in his muscular arms.

Luke Hollister was stunningly attractive, there was no question about that. Tall and broad shouldered, with sandy-blond hair and a wicked glint in his eye. He was not the kind of man she would have thought her prim and proper twin would have ever ended up with.

But she glowed when Luke was in the room.

The two of them looked like they shared naughty

secrets that went way beyond smuggling green beans to the wrong plate.

He'd gotten her sister pregnant before marriage. Which in Olivialand was insane. The kind of…fire that had to exist between them to make her sister forget that her first true love was propriety was something Vanessa couldn't even imagine.

She had never been one to make the best choices, and she couldn't even imagine that.

Of course, she'd never made love to a man because she'd been so into it she'd lost control.

She was mildly envious that Olivia had.

And that she had that man for life.

Right, you're in a great space to have a man in your life.

No. Absolutely not.

Between her niece's antics—which mainly included blowing saliva bubbles and sitting in the middle of the rug slapping her chubby thighs—and Luke's easy conversational skills, they managed to avoid any thumps all through dinner.

There was coffee and cobbler after, and Vanessa forgot to be uncomfortable by the time she took a bite of that mix of warm berries, cinnamon and ice cream.

"I'll go take Emma out to check on the horses," Luke said. "I'll be back in a bit. Save some cobbler for me."

Vanessa wanted to beg him to stay, but she had a feeling that wasn't the best thing to do. So instead, she said nothing.

She smiled across the table at her sister, who looked up over her coffee cup and returned the smile.

It wasn't a very genuine smile. She could feel it on

her own face, and she could see it reflected right back at her when Olivia tried it.

"So, how long are you planning on being back for?" Olivia asked.

Vanessa frowned. "I was planning on staying," she said, looking down at her cobbler and taking a bite. "I mean, as far ahead as anyone plans for that kind of thing, I guess. I suppose it depends on whether or not I can continue to have a job. But right now I don't have any plans to move on anytime soon."

"Oh," Olivia said.

Thump.

"What? Did you not think I was going to stay?"

"I just wondered. I know you haven't really been in touch with Mom and Dad…"

"No one has been in touch with me," Vanessa said, feeling defensive.

"Everyone wants to give you your space," Olivia replied. "You just…" Olivia swallowed, and she could see her sister grappling with emotion. That irritated her.

"I just what?" Vanessa asked.

"You just came back with very little explanation."

"I took a job," Vanessa said, keeping her voice steady.

"Yes, you took a job here. You're here, but you're still *not here*. And I guess I don't really understand that."

"I can understand that you have feelings about that, Olivia," Vanessa said, calling on the placating voice that had been used on her many times during therapy, and wielding it against her sister like a sword. "And I'm glad that you feel comfortable expressing them to me. However, what I'm doing isn't directed at anyone in the family."

"No," Olivia said. "I didn't think it was. It never is."

Her words hit Vanessa square in the chest, twisted like a knife. She didn't want to hurt her family, but it was very important to her that she didn't hurt herself. And she didn't know how to do both just yet.

She retreated. Behind her veneer. Behind all her careful therapy language because she was hurt and she needed something to help protect her. "I understand that you have some anger. You're certainly allowed to have feelings. But I am here. And I did call you back and set up dinner. So as you can see, I'm not avoiding you completely. I think some of that anger is a bit unfair, don't you?"

"No," Olivia said. "I don't think so." Another way Olivia had changed, because one thing Olivia hadn't done when they were children was fight back. Ever. She'd always sat there, pale and sad, or she'd run away. But she never fought back. Apparently, she did now. "You're back here with no warning. And now that you're here, you expect everything to be on your terms. You reached out for dinner, and I made myself available."

"I'm sorry, I didn't realize that was a confrontational move on my part," Vanessa said. "I thought asking my sister to have dinner with me was polite enough."

"I'm just trying to figure out what it is you're doing."

"It may come as a surprise to you, but my decisions aren't actually shaped around you, Olivia."

Vanessa worked very hard not to lose her temper,

because anger was rarely productive. But then, she had also learned that stuffing her emotions down deep and then trying to smother them with mood-altering substances didn't really work either. Olivia sat in judgment of her. Still. And she had no earthly idea what it cost Vanessa to bring herself back home. To face everyone in spite of her shame. To carry all of the secrets and traumas that she had carried for years.

And she knew her family was hurt. She knew *she'd* hurt them. And she felt awful about it. Guilty deep down. But she couldn't go back. She couldn't fix it. She couldn't change it. And she couldn't erase her own pain either. Her own feelings of loneliness.

She'd left, it was true.

But she often felt like they'd left her first.

Maybe not physically, but emotionally.

And yes, there were things she hadn't told them. Things she didn't feel she could tell them.

She felt the need to protect herself still.

"I wanted to be near you," Vanessa said. "But not everything can be about you or Mom or Dad. My sobriety is for me. Coming back home is for me. You've all gotten along fine without me for years now, so acting wounded by the fact that I was adjacent to you for a couple of weeks and didn't give you the entirety of my plans is a little bit disingenuous."

"No one would have chosen to live without you. You left. You left, and half the time we didn't know whether or not you were alive or dead."

"And you *let me* leave," Vanessa said, standing up, knocking her chair backward and onto the floor. She felt enervated. A disaster, yet again, in the face of Olivia's cool fury. But then, she always was.

The fighting might be unfamiliar, but the dynamic was not. They had always been like this. And as Vanessa had unraveled, more and more, Olivia had taken all that thread and wound herself tighter. And in the face of her tightness, Vanessa could only be more of a mess. It had always been that way. Because she couldn't compete. Not remotely. So she didn't even try. Why bother. She couldn't compete with all that perfection. So she became a spiral.

She could feel it happening now.

"You're so angry at me," Vanessa said. "Because you think I just left. That I abandoned you. That I made you worry. You watched your mirror crack in front of you and you didn't do anything to reach out and stop it."

"You pushed me away," Olivia said, angry tears in her brown eyes.

Vanessa wasn't going to cry. And she wasn't going to allow Olivia to excuse herself either.

"You never asked me what was wrong. You never… You saw me sinking and you couldn't even reach down a hand. You just doubled down on being the perfect one. On being the easy one. The one Mom and Dad loved best. I think you all did perfectly fine without me. And maybe my mistake was thinking that we could find a way to integrate back into each other's lives. But I'm not sure if that's possible."

She took a deep breath and then turned away, trying to gather her emotions before she walked out the door.

"I swear, Vanessa, if you came back to hurt Mom and Dad again…"

"I can't believe you just said that to me."

"You have no idea what it did to them."

And Olivia had no idea that their father hadn't even been able to look her in the eyes by the time she'd left.

"You have no idea what life has done to me," Vanessa said, anger pouring over her now. "I know I did hurt you. I know I hurt Mom and Dad. But what I did…it wasn't for the purpose of hurting you. I did it to escape. And along the way I hurt myself too. Getting sober was saving myself. And as much as I've wanted to restore our relationship, it has been a lot more important for me to heal myself before I try to heal things with other people. I went through everything I did alone."

"No one wants to upset you," Olivia said. "Mom and Dad are walking on eggshells, and now you're here yelling at me because we didn't reach out, when everyone is trying to be nice. No one wants to send you into a relapse."

Relapse.

The word was like a slap to the face.

"I told you, I did the work. And this is why I stayed away for a long time after I got sober, because I thought some distance might let us build new patterns. Might let you see more than a junkie. But you don't. And no amount of time is going to fix that, is it?"

"I changed my life because of you," Olivia said, her voice tight. "I almost married the wrong man. I had to do everything right because you did everything wrong, and you left Mom and Dad to collapse. If it weren't for me they would have had nothing."

The words hung in the hair, stinging Vanessa's soul.

"I'm glad you were there for them," she said. "But I did have nothing. And maybe if Mom and Dad had done some actual parenting when they needed to, instead of worrying about appearances, they wouldn't have had to lean on their daughter like she was their last remaining crutch."

"That isn't..." Olivia closed her eyes. "We never knew where you were. We thought you were dead half the time, and we were imagining you in a ditch somewhere, but you've been sober? How long did you wait? How long... How long have you been sober?"

Her own weakness, thrown back at her so clearly and concisely, burned. Because she'd felt guilt for that. She had. But she'd also felt fear for her sobriety when it had been fragile and new. Afraid of how well she could handle her new self if she went back to an old place.

She'd chosen herself.

And she knew Olivia thought she'd done that when she'd left, but that wasn't true. She'd chosen oblivion. And she'd chosen drugs. And she'd chosen to hide away. But she hadn't chosen herself.

She hadn't chosen herself until she'd stopped using.

"Five years," Vanessa said, knowing with absolute certainty that, as far as Olivia was concerned, that was a dropped bomb. "Because I knew that if I came back before I was strong enough, I would fall back into all my old patterns. Because look at us. We're right back to where we always were. And I can't afford to go back to where I was, Olivia. I can't."

She got in her car and started driving back up toward her place, almost blind with fury and pain. Disappointment in Olivia, and in herself.

But she wasn't going to cry. No, she was not. She didn't owe Olivia her tears any more than she owed her contrition.

She had... She had done an amazing thing out of

the shady things that she had gotten involved in. And no one would ever give her any credit for it because they would just maintain that she never should have become an addict in the first place. Like she had chosen to become a damn dentist and decided she didn't like it. She had just chosen to be an addict. That was definitely what they thought. And probably she had chosen it to hurt them.

She was breathing hard, feeling utterly and completely beyond herself now. She hadn't realized she was so angry at her sister.

But their fight kept playing over and over in her head, and the more that Vanessa listened to herself rant, the more she realized how deeply she believed those things. It was true. They had let her walk away.

They had let her sink into the swamp. They had all just stood there and watched. Unsure of what to do. Afraid to get their hands dirty. Maybe, when it came to her parents, they were afraid to investigate and see what they'd done wrong. Or what might have happened to her to make her behave that way.

She hated that she'd hurt them.

She'd hated that they'd hurt her.

Poor Olivia… She had the feeling her sister didn't know what to do with anything in life that wasn't pretty or perfect. Maybe that wasn't fair, but she'd never seen evidence of the contrary. All the way down to that beautiful husband of hers. Her perfect baby.

The perfect baby that she'd had while she was married and not a teenager.

Perfect Olivia. With her perfect house.

Who had probably never woken up next to a man

and not remembered how she had gotten there or what had happened.

Who had very probably never lain on a bathroom floor crying while endless cramps rolled through her body as a pregnancy she hadn't even been sure she'd wanted cut itself short.

Hadn't lain there in a haze while a beautiful paramedic with mesmerizing blue eyes stared down at her, telling her that she was brave while she gave up all semblance of control and screamed and cried like she was dying.

She had come to the turnoff for her driveway, and turned left, barely noticing the truck that was coming in the opposite direction, trying to turn in at just the same time. Instead of hitting the brakes, she floored it, powering herself through and up the driveway ahead of the truck.

The truck driver laid on his horn. And even in the darkness, when she looked in her rearview mirror, she could tell. It was Jacob. She lifted her hand, raising her middle finger, hoping that his headlights shone into the window just enough for him to see. He honked again, revving his engine and coming up on her butt.

She shouted obscenities, letting them fill the car.

Because she was pissed off, and she didn't have time to deal with his manly road rage issues.

She couldn't even begin to care how stupid they looked, worked up into an absolute rage on a dirt driveway over nothing in particular.

She whipped into her driveway, and the asshole followed her. She pulled up to the house, killed the engine and got out, pushing her keys through her fingers, making a closed fist. Realistically, she knew that Jacob wasn't going to get in a fight with her. But old habits died hard. And anyway, she relished the idea of coming at him with her makeshift claws, if nothing else. She was spoiling for a fight. She wasn't done with the one she'd left behind at Olivia's, and if he wanted to give her fodder for it, she was all for it.

And it had nothing at all to do with the fact that she had just been thinking of him and his kindness. Of him seeing her in the most vulnerable moment she'd ever experienced. No. It had nothing at all to do with that. She kicked her way out of the car, just as he was getting out. "You know what," she said. "Screw you. Screw you and your giant truck. What are you doing? Honking at me?"

"What the hell are you doing? Turning in front of me. You drive that pansy-ass little car, I could have flattened you."

"You should've seen me coming. I had my turn signal on."

"So did I. I had the right-of-way."

"Ladies first."

"I'm sorry. I couldn't tell that you were a lady by the way you were driving. I just thought you were a bog-standard jackass."

"I'm not a standard jackass. I am an extravagant one," she said, holding her fist up, her keys shining through her fingers.

"Are you honest to God threatening me with your car keys?"

"Do I have to?"

"No."

"I will cut you," she said.

"Great. I will…not let you, but I'm not going to hurt you."

"I don't know that."

"You sure as hell should," he said. "I don't punch anyone shorter than six foot. Look at you," he said. "You were just lecturing me about feelings, and here you are, acting like a hissing, spitting cat."

"You're the one who followed me to my house."

"To see what the hell was happening. For all I knew, you were some psycho pulling into your driveway. All those little red Camry cars look alike. I wasn't sure it was you."

"Oh, you knew it was me."

"Fine," he said, advancing on her. "I knew it was you."

She growled. Then she stepped forward, dropping the keys and opening her hands, shoving him. He didn't budge. "Oh, did you? Were you checking to see if I was high? Because I hear I'm a real lost cause."

"No," he said, the word so firm and sure it did something strange to her.

Washed over like a soothing rain.

But she was still mad. And she refused to be placated.

"This is not how I am when I'm high, I think. I don't really know. Because I usually don't remember in the morning. But I'll remember this. I will remember that you are an immature asshole who had to come have a fight about a turn."

"I'll remember this too. I'll remember that you're a crazy person."

And then, she curled her hands into fists, grabbing hold of his T-shirt. And she had no idea what the hell was running through her head as she stood there looking up into those crazy blue eyes, the present moment mingling with memories of that night long ago when she had cried and bled in front of this man.

While he witnessed the deepest, darkest thing she'd ever gone through. Something no one else even knew about.

He was the only one who knew.

The only one who knew what had started everything. Olivia didn't understand. Her parents didn't understand. And they had never wanted to understand.

But he knew. He knew and he had already seen what a disaster she was.

There was no facade to protect. No new enlightened sense of who she was. No narrative about her as a lost cause out there roaming the world.

He'd already seen her break apart. For real. Not the Vanessa that existed when she was hiding. Hiding her problems from her family. Hiding her feelings behind a high.

Hiding. And more hiding.

No. He had seen her at her lowest when she hadn't been able to hide.

And somehow, he seemed to bring that out in her. Because she wasn't able to hide her anger either.

And she wasn't able to hide this. Whatever the wildness that was coursing through her veins was. No, she couldn't hide that either. And she wasn't sure she cared.

So she was just going to let the wildness carry her forward.

She couldn't remember the last time she had done that. The last time she'd allowed herself this pure kind of over-the-top emotion.

It had been pain. The pain she felt that night she lost the baby. That was the last time she had let it all go. In all the time since then when she had been on the verge of being overwhelmed by emotion she had crushed it completely. Hidden it beneath drugs. Hidden it beneath therapy-speak.

She had carefully kept herself in hand since she'd gotten sober. Kept herself under control.

What she hadn't allowed herself to do was *feel*.

She was feeling now. And she wasn't going to stop it.

She launched herself forward, and her lips connected with his.

And before she knew it, she was kissing Jacob Dalton with all the passion she hadn't known existed inside her.

CHAPTER EIGHT

JACOB DIDN'T KNOW what the hell was happening. All he knew was that he'd gone from getting yelled at to being kissed in the space of about thirty seconds.

He had been there for the yelling. Fully committed to being involved in the insanity of anger that had exploded between them.

And he was no less involved in this case. No less committed to it. It was lightning. It was fire.

And it was nothing like he'd experienced for the last four years.

Four years since he'd touched a woman, and now one was pressed against him, all soft gorgeous curves and pliant mouth. Slick, tempting tongue.

He parted his lips and consumed her. Near about swallowed her whole.

He gathered her up in his arms, so that she was up on her toes, as firmly pressed against his body as was humanly possible.

She trembled, grabbing his face and pulling him more tightly against her, deepening the kiss, wonderfully. Impossibly.

There had been a purity in that anger that had erupted between them just now. It had wiped away the ghosts of the past, specters that had loomed above his head for years now. Guilt. Because there had been no place for it. The anger was too damn big.

But as big as the anger had been, this explosion of need was enough to decimate everything. Everything but this.

He didn't know why. He didn't know why her, when every other woman hadn't managed to arouse any interest in him after all this time.

But what had started as vague interest yesterday, as he looked at the shape of her breasts through her blouse, had turned into something completely beyond itself today.

There was no question of stopping. At least, not in his mind. He maneuvered them so they could walk and kiss, so he could guide her up the porch steps while he ate his way down her neck, sliding his tongue over her collarbone, until they stumbled backward, her back against the door. He arched his hips forward, grinding against her body, and she arched against him, a harsh, hoarse cry on her lips as she panted and rubbed herself against him.

He met her gaze, and it was the strangest thing. It was like looking into the past, and looking into the future all at once. He could remember her, scared but so very brave that night she called for help.

He could see her now. Reckless and untamed. But there was something else. Something deep and wide that stretched out beyond the present moment, and for the life of him he didn't know what the hell that was. What it meant.

It was so momentous, he had to look away from it. It echoed inside him, and in places that he didn't want her to touch.

And just then, she moved her hand from his face, right down to the front of his jeans. Where he absolutely did want her to touch. She pressed her palm over his denim-covered arousal, finding the shape of him through the thick fabric.

"Oh my," she murmured as she tested the length of him.

"I hope that's a good 'oh my,'" he muttered, nibbling on her ear.

"I doubt you've ever had a complaint," she said, working at his belt.

They weren't naked. They weren't inside. They weren't horizontal. But he wasn't about to complain.

Wasn't about to ask about foreplay or anything else, not when the woman was undoing his pants, which he wanted more than just about anything else.

He wanted her naked. He wanted to see those breasts, to see her nipples go tight with need. He wanted to get her completely naked so he could look at all of her soft skin.

But his brain wasn't working very well, and immediate satisfaction was at hand, so he was happy to just follow that.

His breath hissed through his teeth as she lowered the zipper, reaching her hand inside his underwear and curling her fingers around him. His hips bucked forward, his body in a state of shock over the skin-on-skin contact after being without it for so long. She made a sound that was somewhere between a feral growl and the noise you might make if you got a good bite of ice cream.

And he felt it, it went down his spine like electricity,

making his cock jerk. His eyes met hers again, and she bit her lip, working her hand over his length.

There was a strange expression on her face, something like wonder, and it filled his vision, filled his brain. Filled his every last need.

Dimly, he realized this was a terrible idea. Because they had to work together.

Because neither of them knew each other well enough to know how the other might react to a one-night stand.

Because he hadn't been with anyone in long enough that it felt a little bit like a watershed moment, when in the past, encounters like this were perfunctory at best.

She leaned in, capturing his lower lip with her teeth and biting down.

Damn.

He was wrong.

Encounters like this had never been perfunctory. Because encounters like this didn't exist.

There was no use trying to compare her to hookups from the past because they hadn't been like this. He moved his own hands, pushing her skirt up past her hips and pressing his hand between her legs, finding her wet and ready for him.

He swept her panties to the side, and she moved her hand, letting him push his flesh against hers. Her head fell back, and she gasped.

"You want this?" he asked, his speech slurred as if he'd been drinking, as he moved against her.

"So much," she sobbed, shifting and parting her legs, wrapping one around the back of his calf and opening herself to him so he could test her readiness with the head of his cock.

He almost bit out a curse when her moisture bathed his aching body.

She was perfect. She was just so damn perfect. Then he moved his hands down, gripped hold of her thighs and lifted her as he thrust inside her, pressing her against the wall.

He swallowed her cry of pleasure as he thrust inside her, again and again, his need like a wildfire. It roared through his veins, wrapped itself around his bones, made it impossible for him to do anything but burn.

He felt good. Damn good. All through his body. And he couldn't remember the last time that was true. He pounded into her, and she met him for every thrust, her hips grinding against his, little gasps of pleasure on her lips, ripples of need deep inside her, squeezing down on his dick as he continued to chase his release, as he continued to try to find release for them both.

Somewhere in the fog of his brain, he remembered that he was a gentleman. And that meant the lady was gonna come first.

He moved his hand between their bodies, centering his thumb over her clit and pressing firmly, making a slow circle and then a faster one.

She gripped his shoulders, her fingernails digging into him, even to the fabric of his shirt. And she screamed in his ear as she came hard around him.

And thank God. Because he had reached the end. He let go completely, thrusting into her, hard and deep, and then going still as his release ripped through him.

He shuddered hard, gritting his teeth so tightly he

thought they might break, hell, he thought his whole body might break.

With the force of his release. With the force of the pleasure that woman had made him feel.

It took a few moments. Quite a few. But he began to become aware of where he was. And of the ghosts that still haunted him.

Two lost friends.

A little girl without a father.

A woman without a husband.

Countless failures besides.

And he just wished that he could go back to a few moments before, when everything had been perfect.

Because that had been a fantasy made real. And now that it was over, reality was the only thing that was left.

And it was pretty damn terrible.

VANESSA WAS STILL holding on to Jacob when her breathing returned to normal. He was still inside her.

Dammit.

She had no idea what she had been thinking. She hadn't been thinking. Not at all. She had just been feeling. Wanting.

And everything had been so big and bright and foreign, she hadn't known what to do with it. And she really hadn't known how to resist it.

Right. It didn't occur to you to resist it until it was finished.

The idea made her feel panicky and a little bit sick.

Because it was true. She hadn't even considered turning away from it. It had been too compelling. Too shiny and neat and gloriously tempting. And she had gone headfirst into it.

With a man she was going to have to see every day for the foreseeable future. Because she was an idiot. An absolute idiot.

Pleasure was still vibrating down her bones even as she cursed herself, even as he moved away from her, and she stayed pressed against the wall. She had a feeling she was going to have siding embossed along her skin.

Jacob was righting his clothes, and she made an effort to do the same, realizing that they were outside, with only the porch light shining on them.

"Good thing your neighbors don't live very close," he said.

"Yeah," she responded.

"I…"

"Do you want to come in for lemonade?" The question escaped her lips before she could fully process it.

Then she realized this was the second time the man had come to her home and she had offered him lemonade.

Though he had put out an entirely different kind of fire tonight.

Or maybe he had started it. She had no idea.

She felt like a foreigner in her own skin right now, so she really didn't have much of an idea of anything.

"I… Probably not."

"Yeah. That's fine."

"We have to work tomorrow morning."

"Right," she said. "We have to work."

"I'll see you."

"Yeah," she said. She didn't wait to watch him walk to his car. She just unlocked her front door with shaking fingers and went into the house, ignoring the sick thudding in her heart, the restless ache between her legs. She felt overwhelmed. Stunned. Completely overwhelmed by the entire thing.

And the images of what had happened played in her head, over and over again.

It was different. The sex had been so different.

It was so bright and loud and physical. There was nothing hazy about it.

She could remember it.

She swallowed hard, sinking onto the couch, tears building in her eyes.

She'd never been with a man while sober before.

Ever.

She'd never had to replay the uncomfortable moments, the time that had led up to the encounter. She had never been so aware of why different parts of her felt lit up.

Hell, parts of her had never felt lit up before.

Because whatever the sex she had before had been like—and she really couldn't remember—she knew it wasn't like that.

The way he touched her. The way he looked at her with such intent.

He decided to get her off, and he damn well had. She sucked in a shaking breath. Today had been... She couldn't believe it had been one day.

Painting class. A fight with her sister. Sex against a wall.

There were so many emotions inside her, and she didn't know quite how to process them.

She flopped backward, spreading her arms wide, one over the back of the couch, the other resting listlessly on the floor.

There was nothing to do but simply sit there with the feelings.

And maybe by tomorrow morning sometime, she would have an answer for them. Maybe by then she could figure it out.

She would have to. Because whether or not she did, she would have to see Jacob again. He would be in the back of her class, his arms crossed over his chest, his feet kicked out in front of him as he leaned against that counter.

His eyes would be on her, and she would have to try to not imagine the way they blazed with heat.

When he used his hands, she would have to try to not stare at them, try to do her best not to remember what it felt like when he put them between her legs and used them with superior effectiveness.

"Get a grip," she said to herself. "You've made way bigger mistakes than this."

It was true. This was just sex. And he was that kind of guy. It would be okay. It would be. Because it had to be.

She laughed. Because what else could she do. She supposed her one consolation was that at least now his memory of her screaming would be in pleasure rather than in pain.

And maybe that was it. Maybe she had been reclaiming something.

Reclaiming the narrative that she had with Jacob.

Maybe that was the theme of the day. Reclaiming narratives.

Anyway, thinking that was better than admitting to herself that maybe she had just lost all of her control.

CHAPTER NINE

VANESSA KNEW THAT the day was going to be interesting, to say the least, when she woke up the next morning, feeling raw and sensitive, then practically shouted at her own reflection in the mirror, "I will not feel shame for being a woman."

When she opened being overdramatic with her own self, she had a feeling that everything was going to be downhill from there.

But while it took some time to gather her thoughts, and her sanity, she held on to that same feeling as she got ready for work, got in her car and made her way toward the Dalton Ranch.

She wasn't going to feel shame about a sexual encounter.

For some very good reasons, she had decided to abstain from sexual relationships while she got herself together.

It had gone on a little longer than she had anticipated, but she had been in a very serious process of removing various crutches from her life.

Learning how to be alone. Learning how to be lonely. How to be upset. How to sit in her feelings.

She had done that. So it was fine that she was making changes.

All of this was about making changes. Coming back

to Gold Valley. It was about finding a way to reconcile with the past.

And yes, her attempt at doing that last night with Olivia had been terrible. But maybe her encounter with Jacob hadn't actually been a bad idea.

Reclamation.

She had decided that last night before she'd gone to sleep.

And she had spent the entire night turning all that over, hence her early-morning pep talk with her reflection.

She pulled her car up to the classroom and got out. She took a deep breath and walked toward the room, grateful that she had a little bit of time before she actually had students in her class.

She needed to get a grip on her brain.

No shame. No shame.

Shame was something imposed on her by other people. People who couldn't handle her.

People who needed shame to exist around difficult choices, so they wouldn't feel quite so bad about their own lives.

The more they could stigmatize certain people, the more they could make them other.

Suddenly, she wanted to claw her own brain out of her head. Her internal therapist was getting to be a little bit much.

Sometimes it was very helpful. She relied on it.

She used it to distance herself handily from confrontation—like when she had tried it out on Olivia yesterday.

But sometimes…sometimes it was just a whole

bunch of bullshit oatmeal. Bland and lumpy, and not anything she was in the mood to try to digest.

She growled at herself as she pushed the door open, then shrieked and jumped backward like a scalded cat when she caught sight of the large, looming figure in the back of the room.

"You seemed happier to see me last night."

Jacob was standing there against the wall, that hot, built body of his in a tight black T-shirt and very nicely fitted jeans. He was wearing his cowboy hat indoors, which seemed egregious in many ways.

And it took her a full few minutes to realize he didn't even mean when they had sex.

He meant when she had been yelling at him in the car.

Probably.

"You startled me," she said.

"Sorry. But I'm exactly where I said I was going to be. Exactly where I'm supposed to be."

"True," she said. "I just didn't expect you here so early."

"I thought it would be best if we had a chance to see each other."

Well, he wasn't going to pretend nothing happened. Okay. That was probably good.

Therapist Vanessa was completely sure that they needed to have an adult dialogue where they got everything out in the open and set parameters, like the ones that said that what had happened last night was never going to happen again. Because it wasn't. Ever again.

Why not?

She shut that thought down.

Everything was tangled up enough. She had needed

a release last night. She had been angry, and she had needed desperately to lash out, and then…well, what had happened had happened. There was no pretending it hadn't.

"So obviously we need to set some parameters for work," she said.

"Do we?" he asked.

"I assumed that was why you were here."

"We screwed. We won't do it here."

She swallowed hard, completely unsure as to why she felt like clutching at pearls she didn't even own because of his statement. She was not a prude. Not remotely. But there was something about the way he said it. Casual and intentionally crass, that got to her.

"We're not going to do it again," she said.

"Works for me," he responded.

That made her even madder. Which was silly because she was saying no more, and he was agreeing, and really, she should be happy with that.

"I'm not in a space where I can have a relationship."

He laughed. "Did I give you an indication that I was looking to settle down?"

"No," she said. "It's just…casual sex is not something that I… I'm not currently in a space where I can do a physical relationship with someone."

"That's fine."

"I haven't been with anyone in a long time," she said.

She was not going to tell him that she hadn't been with anyone since she'd gotten sober.

That she never had sex sober, not once in her life.

And that the differences were rioting through her

body like dissatisfied civilians, demanding attention. Demanding that she look at them.

She didn't want to. She wanted to ignore all of it. Pretend it hadn't happened and give thanks for the fact that it had been quick.

It wasn't because she was ashamed. She wasn't. But it was a whole lot of intensity that she just didn't have a place for. Not even remotely.

"Well, glad I could break the dry spell," he said.

There was something strange and guarded about him today. She wasn't sure she liked it. In fact, she knew she didn't.

The man was impossible when he wanted to be. And it seemed that he wanted to be often.

"Control is very important to me," she said. And of course she realized he hadn't asked, but oh well.

"Okay," he said.

"Control is very important to me," she reiterated. "I lost control last night. I'm not…ashamed. Because sexual desire is good and healthy."

"Yeah, I sure as hell feel healthy."

"But that doesn't mean it was a good idea. And it definitely means it's something that I should…think better of."

"What happened last night?"

"I could ask you the same thing. You weren't in any better of a mood than I was."

"Show me yours and I'll show you mine."

"We already did that," she said.

The corner of his mouth lifted up into a lopsided grin, and she decided she liked this Jacob much better than the one that had first been in the room when she'd appeared.

"Fair enough. But how about this? I'll give you a little, and you can give me a little."

"All right. I'm happy to do that."

"Okay," she said slowly. "My sister is a sanctimonious ass. And out of all the people in the entire world, she's probably the one most able to pick up a rock during a sermon on how 'he that is without sin can cast the first stone.' So, it's even a little bit earned."

"I see." But it was pretty clear that he didn't.

She sighed. "We haven't exactly been close the past few years."

"I feel like I kind of knew that."

"Yeah, I imagine word gets around." She looked past him, over the white fence, to where horses were meandering around the paddock, and beyond them, the mountains rose up high, looking like a refuge. An escape. A place to lose yourself.

"People think addicts are narcissists," she said. "But I just felt like a black hole. I didn't exist. I felt nothing. I was nothing. So why not just throw as much as you can into the pit and see what hits the bottom? See what…feels like something. You can reduce the whole world and all of your anxiety and all of your pain into a little ball, and shove it down deep. Just live in the moment. You don't think about anyone. It's true. But you don't really think about yourself either." She took a breath and looked at him, met his eyes. "I wanted to lose myself."

She could tell he didn't know what to say. She was glad he didn't try to say something anyway.

She continued, "I'm gathering that my family has a lot of their identity tied up in me leaving. In me being an addict. It's a huge part of who they are. A huge part of their…pain, I guess."

His forehead wrinkled, his brows drawing together slightly. "Families hurt each other," he said. "It's kind of what we do."

"Yeah. I did a whole lot of work on myself in the last few years. And I figured out a lot of things about myself. But I kind of… In my head I have all of these scenarios. The way that conversations with my mother will go, my father. My sister. A guy I dated in high school. But I think sometimes I forget they haven't had to think about themselves in the same way I've had to."

He looked confused.

"If you want to get sober, you have to admit that there's a problem with yourself first. Because you can't fix something if there's nothing wrong. So I had to admit there was something wrong. I look at Olivia, and I see a lot of her pain. And I get it. But I'm also not the cause of everything that happened here at home. A lot of what was going on in our house is part of my pain. I'm not sure that she's recognized that yet."

"And is that what you want?" he asked. "You want them to acknowledge they hurt you too?"

She took a sharp breath. "Yes. I mean…you can't fix things when you're hiding the broken pieces. How can you ever put it back together that way?"

"But your sister doesn't seem to want to do that?"

"No."

"All right," he said slowly. "You might win."

"Is this a competition?" she asked.

"It could be if you want."

"Hmm. What do I win?"

"The honor of having had the worst evening, and having the most justified anger."

She tapped her chin, as if she was weighing it. "Well, I'd like the win. But you should have a chance to state your case. You go."

"My brother is on a mission to bring all of our long-lost half siblings home. I don't really care about it. He's pushing me to care. I told him why I feel responsible for Clint's death."

Silence settled between them. "Do you feel responsible or *are* you responsible?"

His eyes connected with hers, and there was something strange in them. She had been worried, for a moment, that what she'd said would make him angry. But what she saw right now wasn't anger.

It was relief.

"I am responsible," he said. "I mean, in that way life and fate and all that intertwine, and you can't really know how things would have played out if something would've gone differently. But what I do know is…if I hadn't been so selfish… If I hadn't… He wouldn't have died. Because I was the one that was supposed to be in the helicopter, not him."

"Okay. *You* win."

"*I* get to win?"

"That's a lot. I don't know how you live with that."

"You're not going to reassure me that it wasn't my fault?" He looked around. "You're not going to tell me that if I had gone instead of him, I would be dead, and what's the point of that?"

"You know all that," Vanessa said. "What's the point of telling you?"

"I was with a woman," he said. "I was hungover,

and I didn't want to get out of bed, because I wanted
to have sex again." Silence stretched on between them.
"I haven't had sex since then. I mean, until last night."

"You're such a jerk," she said. "Talking about my
dry spell, when you had one of your own."

"That's the thing that makes me a jerk?"

"It's not like you knew," she said. "If even part of
you had known, you could've told everybody not to
go up in the helicopter. But you know that. You just
want to hang on to the guilt because it feels like action. And maybe because it's what made you change."

"Are you a psychiatrist?"

She laughed. "No. I just… I just had a lot of stuff
to work on. It wasn't fun."

"So you're fully healed and all that?"

"Well, think back to how I acted last night when my
sister got in my face and ask me that question again."

"Right," he said, tapping his knuckles on the top of
the counter. "I guess none of us are ever fully healed."

"Not on this side of things." She looked up at the
clock and saw there were about two minutes before
the kids came in. "So here's a question for you. Why
is it so important for you to believe it's your fault? Because that's a question I had to ask myself a lot. And
for me, the answer was that if it was my fault, then I
could treat myself as badly as I wanted to. Because
there was no point saving myself."

Something in his face went hollow and blank. "Because I…I can't save anyone. It always happens. I can't
save them."

Just then the first kid came into the room, followed
by the second. And their conversation was cut short.
But Vanessa intended to pick it up again at some point.

She looked over at him, as she got the kids settled into painting positions.

She wanted to know more about him. That man with muscular forearms and strong hands. Who had been a cowboy, a paramedic and a firefighter. And still thought he couldn't save anyone.

She didn't need or want to be curious about him. But she was. And just looking at him made her body hum with deep, remembered longing. Of the way it had been when he touched her.

Right. You're interested in him because you think he's hot. You're not going to be that stupid again.

And with that, she set her focus firmly on painting. Because she had to keep her mind off him somehow. Though, with him in the room, it was basically impossible.

Still, she had done the impossible in her life. This was just once more.

JACOB DIDN'T LIKE the honesty that Vanessa managed to mine out of him. It was something to do with the way she went right at him and everyone else. With her trauma right in the front, and everything out in the open. She spurred him in ways that other people didn't. She also interested him in a way that he couldn't recall another person ever managing to do. Maybe it was because in some ways, no matter how different they were, they were also alike.

He knew what it was like to walk around using swagger as a shield. To lead with anger, to try to shock people.

Vanessa had done something similar with him that first day at the school.

Of course, when Clint had died, his whole shtick had burned up along with everything else in that helicopter wreckage.

It had carried him through for a long damn time, though.

Through every familial relationship, in every relationship with a woman, every friendship. It had gotten him through every job he'd done and bailed on.

And in the end, even he had started to believe a lot of what he'd said and done. Because he had learned something very early on in his life. If you acted like nothing was wrong, you never had to talk about any of the things that were wrong. If you pretended something hadn't happened, and no one else knew about it, then it was almost like it hadn't.

Like it was a dream. But he had already caused one friend's death, and the behavior he launched himself into after had been protective, and it had gotten him a long way.

But then it had led to the death of another friend, and it made him start asking questions about himself.

Questions he probably should've asked a long time ago.

And now here he was, standing in a classroom full of teenage boys, being what?

He didn't know the answer.

The role model that Clint wouldn't be able to be for his own child?

Because he related to these kids, who were teenagers, which Gavin had never gotten a chance to be.

He didn't think about Gavin often. Almost never.

It was the weirdest thing. Because he never had to.

Because nobody knew that he'd been involved in it at all. Because he was a liar.

Because he had called for an ambulance, and then he had run away.

Because he had lied and told everyone he'd been by himself that whole day.

Because he had pretended for so long that he didn't have any idea what had happened, that it had become the truth, even inside himself.

Clint's death had brought things back up to the surface because there was no way it couldn't. Because it forced him to confront the fact that living like there were no bad days didn't keep them from coming back up. Because it didn't actually change reality, even though it felt like it might.

Because no matter how many people he saved as a paramedic, as a firefighter, it didn't erase the past.

I'm not a hero.

He wasn't a hero. He was just a guy trying to pay a spiritual debt that he never could pay back, hiding behind so many damn half-truths and lies, moments of brashly produced honesty, that he didn't even know what was real.

Except that one bit of truth.

What he wasn't. What he could never be.

This time, when it came down to it, the boys had all done something in class. Though Aiden had stuck with a stylized *fuck this* painted all over the canvas. Jacob had to wonder if being given permission to do that made it feel less satisfying. It would have for him. But that was just the kind of asshole he was.

He worked to get his brain focus back on to the

present. Because the past was a whole lot of messed-up stuff that he just didn't want to deal with.

But when he thought about the present, he thought about Vanessa. Naked and soft. Which was all fantasy, since he had never seen her naked.

He wished he had.

He'd felt her. Felt her come all around him up against the wall.

He didn't know how he managed to make it through the rest of the day without having an inappropriate boner, but somehow he persevered.

And when it was all over, he was ready to get out of there. Because he didn't feel like it was the best thing in the world for him to be in close proximity with Vanessa. Not while everything was quite so precarious. While everything was still close to the surface.

"Today went better," she said once the room was empty.

"Yeah," he agreed.

"Aiden still went with his aesthetic." She frowned. "I suppose he is painting his truth."

"That's probably what I would've painted when I was a teenage boy. Actually. I think I would have painted my own porn."

"That seems like a lot of work for a little bit of porn. Even back when you were a teenager surely it was more easily accessible than that."

He lifted a shoulder. "Maybe."

"You're welcome to paint something," she said, gesturing around. "Anytime."

He crossed his arms. "I haven't seen any of your paintings."

"I…I'm teaching," she said.

"So you don't have to actually do any painting, because you're the teacher?"

"I do paint," she said. "And I make pottery. I do a bit of decoupage."

He shook his head. "I don't even know what that is."

"It's when you—"

"I wasn't asking."

"Talking about your feelings is hard," Vanessa said. "Art makes it easier to get all that stuff out. I know not everyone is an artist, but the ability to express yourself in nonverbal ways—"

"Does it ever get old? Talking like a therapist."

"I…I'm not talking like a therapist. I'm explaining why something matters to me."

"I don't think that's what you're doing. I can practically see you throwing an arm out between us."

"It's better for us to be at arm's length, don't you think?" she asked.

"You're the one with an issue about whether or not something happens between us again, not me."

"You know, it's kind of bullshit for you to comment on me using distancing language. I might be using therapy-speak, but you use that kind of ridiculous alpha-male thing. *I'm not a hero. I can't save people.* Because you're just so bad, and yet here you are, showing up for your family, exhibiting guilt over your friend's death. Helping these boys out, even though you don't actually want to. All those are things that good people do, Jacob, and I don't know what to tell you, but I think you might be a good person."

"You don't know me."

"Oh, there it is again. Standard cliché *male* response.

Not a good guy. Not made for commitment. Let me guess, you're just a lone wolf."

"Did you notice that I live on top of a mountain? Or did you not?"

Vanessa flung her arms wide. "Great for you and your mountain. Sadly, though, I think you're just wounded like the rest of us, and a little bit of therapy wouldn't hurt you. In fact, it might help you. And it might make you see that whatever else has happened in your life—good, bad or bullshit—it doesn't necessarily mean you're a bad person. Being good or being bad isn't even about wanting to show up and do the right thing. Sometimes it's about not wanting to and doing it anyway," she said. "Do you think that I wanted to be sober every day of my sobriety? No. I didn't. But the important thing was whether or not I actually shot up. Not if I wanted to. It's what you do that matters. And sometimes your action has to go before your heart. In fact, I would say the best people, the strongest people do the right thing most especially when they don't want to."

"You know, I kind of see why your sister got mad at you," he said, anger twisting up his gut, making him want to say things that would get her to shut up. Or get her to kiss him. He wasn't really particular. But he didn't want to talk. Not really. Not anymore.

This was why he just avoided people to the best of his ability.

"You're acting like you have all the answers. Acting like you're so superior."

"I've actually done a lot of work on myself," she said. "Things that other people have never even thought of. Because I've had to."

"You talk down to people. You talk to people like you have nothing left in yourself to deal with. And it all comes off as a bunch of condescending crap." He shook his head.

She opened her mouth to argue with him and he cut her off. Because she'd had her say, and he wanted his. "You know what, that's great. Talk to these boys that way because they need it. Because you're older than them, and you can teach them something about life. But the problem with you, Vanessa, is that you walk around with the certain knowledge that you have everything figured out, not just the way that you fixed yourself, but the way everyone can fix themselves. You also walk around being angry because you feel like nobody understands why you became what you did. Why you became who you did. You have all these secrets, and you mix it in with honesty."

He had the realization while he started ranting at her, because it was so close to what he had just thought about himself. Enough brash honesty and people would be absolutely certain you were telling them the whole truth.

Where were you last night, Jacob?

Sneaked out. Got drunk.

Jacob, what were you and the Thomas girl up to last night?

A slow grin. *Exactly what you'd think.*

And then no one had thought to ask, *Jacob, why don't you like heights?*

Jacob, why do you have nightmares?

If you would just admit to things that other people would be embarrassed to ever talk about, they assumed that you were the kind of person who walked around with their guts spilled at all times. And they would never figure out that you were holding up something shiny to distract them from what was really going on.

Yeah, he knew that better than most people. And he could see Vanessa doing the same damn thing.

"It never occurred to you that you might not know someone else's whole story," he said. "It makes sense to you that your family could live with you, that your sister could live with you, and not know you, but you don't think that could be true of her. Everybody hides. And just because you know that, doesn't mean you see exactly what's going on with other people."

"I didn't say that I did," Vanessa said. "I never said any of that."

"But it's how you act."

"You know what, you have no room to speak to me about any of this. If I didn't act like I was good enough, no one would ever treat me like I was. And even still, they don't. But I have to walk around acting like I'm worth it. No one else is going to give that to you when you come from mistakes like I made. You know what people think. That someone with addiction issues is garbage. Lazy. That we don't care about things."

Her eyes glittered, her brows locked together. "I care so much. So very much. And I messed every-thing up. I messed everything up trying to have a few moments when I didn't care. Trying to have a few mo-ments when I didn't feel quite so awful about myself. I never thought that I would become an addict."

She pushed her hands through her hair and looked up at the ceiling. "I was rich. And everybody liked to party a little bit. I was rebellious, but not any more than any of my friends. But then… But then the miscarriage happened and I couldn't cope. I thought I could just use a little. Just escape for a while. Because girls like me didn't turn into addicts. I thought that I was immune to it. I thought it wouldn't hurt. Everyone else got away with it. A little bit here and there, why can't I? All of that stuff is for other people. Poor people. Uneducated people. It's not for you. Until it is. Until it is you, your child, your sister. You're not immune to it. Nobody is."

Her words rang with a kind of conviction he wasn't sure he'd ever felt before. "Some people make bad choices, and they can come back from it a lot cleaner than other people. And you know what? I'm still one of the lucky ones. Because some people make those same bad choices and they die. So I'm sorry if my sense of superiority offends you in some way. But it was my sense of inferiority, my lack of value that brought me down a path I never want to go back down. So I refuse to allow anyone—you, my sister, myself—make me feel small."

She was so angry at him, her dark eyes glittering. And he supposed if he were a better man he would feel guilty. But he also supposed that she was used to people treating her like she might be fragile. But he knew she was tough. He might feel bad for some of the things she had been through, but he also knew that she wasn't easily broken. Not after the kind of life she'd had.

"You accused me of being a cliché," he said. "I have a feeling we could stand here and cliché each other to death."

"You want me to take you seriously? You want me to listen to you? Take me seriously."

She picked up a paintbrush and held it out toward him. "Paint me something." She tilted her head to the side. "Unless you're afraid."

CHAPTER TEN

VANESSA HAD NO idea what was driving her right now. What was possessing her. She prided herself on being a very reasonable person, and somewhere in the last couple of days she had lost all of that.

Obviously, the act of thrusting a paintbrush in a man's face and demanding he paint to prove he wasn't a coward was not the act of a reasonable human.

So maybe she wasn't a balanced person. For all that she had always imagined she might be.

It was good to know that she had always been just a drive down the long highway home away from being an absolute crazy person.

But it wasn't just her. Or this place.

It was *him*.

Something about Jacob had her on edge. Something about her family had her on edge, in truth, but that was to be expected.

Jacob wasn't expected. Nothing about him was. Not her curiosity about him, not how compelling she found him. Not how infuriating she found him.

"Really?" He raised his brows. "You're daring me to paint."

"It's becoming a thing," she said, "so it just makes me wonder, if you're so adamantly opposed to doing it, there must be a reason. And given that you are a stereotypical alpha male, I would suggest it's fear. Which masquerades as anger. Because that's what testosterone does."

His expression went hard. "You want me to paint, Vanessa, is that it?"

"Yes," she said, "I want you to paint."

"And then you'll be happy?"

She could hear the challenge in his voice, but she refused to be intimidated by it.

"Yeah," she said, smiling so wide she thought her face might break. "Then I'll be happy. So, so very happy."

"Great," he said. "I'll oblige you, then."

He took the paintbrush out of her hand, but then he set it down on the counter. He walked over to an open container of paint and dipped his fingers in it. The blunt, calloused tips coated in bright orange. Then he approached her, his blue eyes full of the devil and a challenge that she knew she had to either run from now or face head-on and accept whatever consequences came along with it.

She decided to stand up against the consequences.

He reached out and pressed those fingertips against her cheek, dragging a line of paint from there down the side of her neck. "I'm not drawn to traditional canvas," he said. "I'm very avant-garde."

Rage hit her in the stomach. At least that was what she assumed all this heat had to be. Utter fury. And her nipples were tight in her bra, her entire body on fire, she couldn't decide if it was arousal or anger or some mixture of them. Couldn't decide if she wanted to punch him in the face, or grab him and kiss him.

"Oh, is that how you're going to do it?" she asked. "You're going to act like a child?"

Except he so clearly wasn't a child. The broad muscular six feet plus of cowboy standing in front of her could be nothing but man.

She dipped her own fingers in the blue paint just next to her, and then she put her hand on his face, on those rough whiskers, and left three streaks from his cheekbone down to his chin. His whiskers were prickly, and his skin was hot, and being in a petty, ridiculous fight with him should not be sexy.

"Care to guess what any of this means I might be feeling?" she asked.

"Petty," he said. "At least, that's my guess."

"Petty," she said. "And willing to give better than I got."

And then she reached into the blue paint one more time and got more, this time dragging her fingertips down the side of his neck.

Very quickly, she found herself being pulled up against his hard body, her breasts pressed right against his chest. He held her steady, as he reached for the blue himself and painted another swath of color over her face.

She wiggled, and he released his hold on her. Then she reached for the red, dipping her fingers in but letting the excess coat her palm before slapping it directly over his chest, onto his black T-shirt.

"Now, see," he said, "I was going to be nice, and I wasn't going to ruin your outfit. But now you're screwed."

He took some red and got it on his fingertips, flicking it over her blouse.

"This is a nice shirt," she said.

"Well, that's too damn bad."

She launched herself at him, reaching out and getting the orange paint and dumping it over his shoulders.

Dimly, she realized that they were being ridiculous, just like they had been last night. But she wasn't sure that she cared enough to stop it.

She had five years of some kind of controlled existence.

And before that, she'd been out of control in an oblique, tragic way. And the only way she'd ever been able to see color was with the help of a substance.

She saw color now. Brilliant, bright anger and no small amount of excitement.

She didn't know why being with Jacob seemed to push everything over the top.

Except...

Except there seemed to be something about the way she could let go when he was around.

A sense of safety.

Like she had felt that night she lost the baby.

He was tied to that, linked inextricably, whether either of them wanted him to be or not.

He might not feel like a hero, but—for an hour or so of her life—he had been one.

He had reached down when she had fallen.

He had been there when she needed it.

He had been there when her chimney caught fire too.

Okay, so maybe he didn't feel like a hero. And maybe Vanessa didn't feel like she deserved to have a hero.

But she had him now. A solid wall that she could throw herself against.

He wiped at the orange paint, getting his hand covered before he dragged it down the center of her chest, painting her entire top.

Her heart began to pound faster, a sick kind of slick friction building between her legs.

A steady beat of her pulse that echoed in her head, her neck, the center of her body.

And she was the one who escalated it. Again.

With a fresh coat of blue paint on her fingers, she pushed her hands beneath his shirt, pushed until the garment was up over his head, and she had left a trail of blue across his abs, across his chest.

He ripped the shirt off the rest of the way, but then she found her own shirt going the same way.

"If you have any attachment to that bra, I'd take it off if I were you."

She did. God help her, she did, and quickly. Goose bumps raised up over her skin, her heart racing.

"Now," he said. "You're a work of art all on your own. But it wouldn't hurt you to have a little color added," he said.

This time his movements were much more deliberate, his hands knowing as they went for the blue paint, as he pressed them against her stomach, tracing a line up through the center of her breasts.

Her nipples went impossibly tight. But he didn't touch her. Not there. No, he wouldn't give her the satisfaction.

Because he was *mean*.

He was mean, and what was happening between

them was inevitable. She didn't know why she felt that way, only that she did.

This man was everything that she feared about coming home. He was tethered to her trauma. Tethered to one of the most difficult events in her life. To her secrets. To all of the reasons that she'd left in the first place. And she couldn't seem to stay away from him. He was her deepest and darkest fear in that regard. A bad decision made flesh, after so many years of not making any bad decisions at all.

He's a normal bad decision.

Something about that realization washed over her like a wave. Relief. Utter and stark. This was the kind of bad decision that *normal girls* made.

And her life, from here on out, could not be about perfection. The desperate, yawning void inside her that she knew could never find perfect, had been the reason she had lost herself in the first place.

No, perfect wasn't her goal.

Not now, not ever. To live. To live and to feel, when it was hard, when it was messy, when it was real, that was the goal.

This was living. Here and now. Living and wonderful, and crazy and maddening.

And whatever lay on the other side of it, she wasn't going to worry.

Because this was what she needed.

She pushed the button on the wall that lowered the blinds and, after that, twisted the lock on the door.

Because she didn't want an audience for her insanity. That was certain.

"Is that how it is?"

"Just finish," she panted.

He didn't do what she expected. He didn't tear her skirt off. He didn't get naked immediately and climb on top of her and make it quick and hard like he had last night.

No. Instead, he went for the paint again. Then with one arm he lifted her up off the ground and set her on the counter in the center of the room. Starting at her collarbone, he traced her body. Traced a line down to the tip of her breasts, circling her nipple achingly slowly, leaving a trail of paint behind.

He was magic. His hands were magic.

She couldn't sort it out.

They didn't understand each other. They had just been shouting at each other about how little they were understood.

But he knew her body, and her body gloried in a touch from his.

And it was so bright and bold.

Last night, there had been no paint, but everywhere his hands had been left behind a trail of fire. She'd been sure that anyone who looked at her would be able to see the imprint of where his hands had been. And now it was true.

Desire right now was so much stronger than anything else.

He moved to red next, passionate strokes down her stomach, her back, her nipples. And then he took her skirt off, her panties, leaving her bare and sitting on the counter.

He forced her legs open, painted streaks of gold down her thighs, leaving handprints on her hips. And he hadn't even kissed her yet.

She was trembling, desire and fear fighting for equal place inside her.

And then finally—finally—he kissed her.

It was slow, and it was tender, and in strange opposition to everything else that had happened before, which had been all about passion, anger and other hard-edged things. His lips were gentle, his tongue exploring her mouth slowly, achingly. Paint-covered hands gripped her face, and she knew there was no way either of them could walk away from this encounter without being marked by it.

And she told herself she just meant the paint.

Because the paint was a much easier thing to handle than anything else.

She shifted slightly, and he knelt down in front of her. He consumed her. Stroked her slowly, the sounds he made so rough and perfect.

He was tasting her. Pleasuring her.

It hit her right then, the intimacy of sex. The way they were sharing the air, the way his body felt.

That his mouth was pressed against her.

The way she could hear his breathing. Match it in time with the pitch of his chest and connect it to the way his tongue played havoc between her legs. The way she could see, hear and feel how she affected him.

She looked down, right as he looked up, as he shifted. And in that moment she could see that hard, telltale ridge pushing against the front of his jeans.

He wanted her. And she could see it, up close and intimate, in the way his pupils dilated, the way his jaw tensed.

And he was a living canvas in front of her, all

streaked in paint and need, the colors haphazard and bright over his tanned skin and corded muscles.

There was a bit of orange in his chest hair, and she wondered if it would be difficult for him to scrub it out later.

And then she thought about helping him do it.

She licked her lips, thinking about how it would be to see him like that, water rolling over his body.

And then she realized the vague ridiculousness of having a sexual fantasy about a man while she was in the middle of having sex with him.

She didn't need to fantasize. Because he was right there.

Hot and hard and real.

She never even had a fantasy quite this good.

And the only real, clear memory she had of sex was with him.

This wasn't mottled or fuzzy. It wasn't vague.

And tomorrow morning she wouldn't wake up with a bad taste in her mouth and her head pounding and great blank gaps of wondering what had happened the night before. Sleeping next to a stranger, who was even more of a stranger than he might've been because she couldn't even remember the ways they'd gotten to know each other hours earlier.

This was like an entirely different thing. A different act.

She was doing it for different reasons.

She wanted him.

She wanted sexual satisfaction with him.

She didn't just want to be close to someone. She didn't just want a human comforter to keep the horrible, cold loneliness away.

She didn't just need a bed to stay in.

Thinking about that, about her past, made her chest get cold and frozen, and she didn't want that. Not now. Not while she was with him.

No, while she was with him, she wanted to be present.

In the moment.

She reached down, put her fingertips on his throat, right where his pulse was pounding hard, revealing his desire for her.

Then he lowered his head again and her fingers drifted up to his hair. And she watched her hands rest there, as he continued to tease her, pleasure her.

He nuzzled her inner thigh before beginning to consume her again, as he looked right at her while he continued to lap at her. She could feel him staring at her. Could feel the heat from those blue eyes right on her.

She couldn't look.

So she just looked at where her hands rested on him.

Because that was real. And it made her feel grounded.

Made it feel like she could breathe.

Forced her to quit living in the past and worrying about the future, and just feel the present moment.

Him.

Like an anchor in a whole uncertain ocean.

This moment was real.

And she wasn't *nothing*. She wasn't *empty*. She was filled.

With her need for him, with her desire for more.

They weren't gray. They were bright and brilliant, all their feelings painted across their skin, anger, stripped away and becoming need beneath that.

He rose to his feet then, and reached into his back

pocket, took out his wallet and set it on the counter next to her. And then he undid his belt, the button on his jeans, his zipper, and toed off his shoes as he pushed all the fabric away, leaving him naked in front of her.

He was beautiful. She moved her hand, pulling it back, allowing herself to look at his entire body. His broad shoulders and chest, tapering down to a narrow waist, abs that were streaked with paint, and then to his lean hips and muscular thighs, the part of his body that had no paint at all because it had been clothed during their war.

The evidence of his desire for her there was like magic.

This man, who wasn't a hero, wanted her, a woman who certainly wasn't one either.

But he wanted her.

He saw her.

He looked at her and didn't seem to wish that he could look away.

She didn't want to look away from him. Even though staring at him was a little bit like staring at the sun.

He made her burn. He made her ache.

He was such a beautiful man, with all of his scars. Oh, not on that perfect body of his, but they were in his soul. Something about those scars made her own light up bright and white-hot inside her. She recognized them.

She recognized him.

And he was right, she didn't know everyone's secrets. But she didn't have to know them to know that he had them.

"I hope the paint is nontoxic," he said, leaning down and capturing one nipple between his lips, sucking.

Pleasure pierced her like an arrow, and she arched forward. He stepped between her thighs, the hard ridge of his erection hot and tempting right there between her legs where she needed him most. He rocked his hips forward, curving his arm around her waist and pressing her tightly against him, riding her gently as he continued to suck her nipple.

She held on to his shoulders, pleasure building at the center of her legs and deeper.

Then he rolled his pelvis forward, the insistent pressure sending her over the edge.

Pleasure coursed through her, and she clung to him, shaking.

When he lifted his head, he was smiling.

"I know it was your orgasm and not mine," he said, his voice gruff. "But I'm pretty sure I felt that."

Heat washed over her, but she didn't have time to let it turn into embarrassment. He grabbed hold of his wallet, opened it and took out a condom.

He made quick work of it, tearing the plastic packet and discarding it, rolling the latex over the head of his arousal as he nudged at her slick entrance.

"Hold on a second." He wrapped his arm more tightly around her waist, lifting her up and back, laying her down on the counter and following her onto the marble surface.

He hovered over her, his gorgeous face less than an inch from hers, his broad chest brushing against her breasts. He kissed her then, every inch of his naked body pressing against hers, pressing her into the cold countertop, but she didn't mind.

She lifted her hips up, and he met her, sliding into her in one easy stroke, making her gasp as he stretched her.

He was so thick, so gloriously hard, she had a feeling he wasn't the sort of man she could get used to accommodating quickly.

And she didn't mind that either. She raked her fingernails down his back, down to his ass, holding on to him tightly as he thrust into her.

The way the counter braced her allowed her to feel the impact of each stroke, each brilliant burst of pleasure as he made contact with her most sensitive place.

She felt another release building inside her, even though it should be too soon. Even though it was absolutely too early.

But with him, it wasn't. Somehow.

He was magic for her body in ways that she couldn't explain.

In ways that she loved.

He moved his hands down to her hips, covering those handprints he had left behind, and he gripped her hard as he thrust home. He raised his forehead against her, those blue eyes blazing into hers as he filled her, over and over again.

She couldn't keep looking at him like this. She couldn't endure this. This deep, unending build of pressure inside her that seemed to have no end.

And then he thrust one last time, his breath leaving his body on a hard shudder, his body pulsing inside her. He closed his eyes, shaking, and that sharp burst of need she could feel coming from him burst inside her, her orgasm rolling over her endlessly, relief and regret all in one. Because she had wanted that to go on forever, as sure as she had been that it would destroy her.

But what a way to go.

At the hands of Jacob Dalton.

The rough, capable hands.

She was sweaty and covered in paint and buzzing with a kind of pleasure she had never realized her body was capable of feeling.

She had known her body could feel pain.

She had known it could feel trauma.

She had known it could feel sadness.

That it could feel like a blank void of absolutely nothing at all.

But she hadn't known it could feel like this.

It was like he had taken her body and gifted it back to her in a way she could never have guessed another human could.

Her eyes started to sting, and she blinked rapidly, moving away from him.

"You're covered in paint," he said, sitting up, his muscles rippling.

"I know," she said, looking around. "And my clothes are worse."

"Guess you better head straight home," he said.

"Probably," she responded.

She really didn't have any desire to try to explain this, not to anyone.

She gathered her clothes up and dressed quickly. She was dimly aware that he was doing the same. She wasn't sure what he did with the condom. Or the wrapper. But when she looked, both were gone, and he was dressed again.

He still had paint all over him. So did she.

She didn't know whether she found it disconcerting or comforting that it was impossible for the two of them to even pretend like nothing had happened. At the very least they looked like they had been involved in one of those weird marathons where people threw paint on you.

Except, on her hips, she knew that if anyone looked, they would find his handprints.

And there would be no way to pretend it was from anything other than exactly what it was from.

"Okay," she said. "I'll see you tomorrow."

"Hopefully you can get all the paint off," he commented.

"Yeah, you too."

"Hey, if I can't, I'm staying home. They don't need me here half as much as they need you."

"Don't you dare," she said. "You can't abandon me."

"You didn't even think you needed me."

"It is nice to have you here."

For the most part the boys had been good, but it was good to know that she had Jacob for backup if she needed anything.

"I'll have to make a record of that. Remind you several times a day that you said that. That it's nice having me here."

"I'll deny it," she said.

"Deny it all you want. I'll always know you said it."

"Look," she said, trying to find a way to take what had happened between them and make it light. To gloss over it. What she wanted to do was cry. Curl up into a fetal position and let herself howl. In happiness, and sadness. In just a motion. Because something in her felt fundamentally changed by having been joined to him. By the rawness of what had happened between the two of them. By the intensity of the pleasure that she had felt.

And she knew that she needed to figure out what exactly it was. What exactly it meant.

But that was something she needed to do alone, not with him.

Sex, for him, would mean something entirely different.

He hasn't had sex in years. You have no idea what it means to him.

You think you know everyone's secrets.

She gritted her teeth and shut that down.

"Obviously, being here is putting me through some things. Things I didn't anticipate. I appreciate... It's been very affirming..."

"Are you trying to thank me for the orgasms?"

"Yes."

"Affirming is not exactly the word I would use."

"Fine. Thank you for the amazing sex. Whatever else is going on in my life, that's not an unwelcome addition to it."

His lips quirked upward. "I feel the same."

"I really don't think we should keep doing it."

He shrugged. "You thought that an hour ago too. Look what happened."

"We should try not to?"

"Was that a question?"

"Maybe."

"Go home," he said. "Take a shower."

Part of her wanted to invite him to come along with her. But the part of her that was on a fragile, emotional precipice that was on the verge of cracking and breaking off into the sea very much needed to go be by itself.

"Right. Well, I guess I'll see you tomorrow."

"Yep."

"See you tomorrow." *And tomorrow there will be no sex.* She ignored the part of her that was deeply saddened by that internal statement.

She enjoyed having sex with him. She enjoyed it so much. But it wasn't good. It wasn't good for her. It couldn't be. Not in the long run. She felt so fragile.

That could be healthy.

As if words like *healthy* or *unhealthy* could possibly be applied to it. It was just life, she supposed.

Sometimes she felt like she was a good eight years younger than she was. Because she had lost so much time in a haze. Where she hadn't had real relationships of any kind, let alone healthy ones.

She'd never had sex sober.

And because of that this all felt very…new.

Yes. That was why. It wasn't just because of him.

It couldn't be.

She swallowed hard and got in her car, thankful that there was no one around.

And as soon as she was out on the open highway, she dissolved into tears.

CHAPTER ELEVEN

THE NEXT DAY it was time to get into the first of the ranch chores. They were having the boys help build a fence.

They were beginning with digging postholes. Three of the boys had three posthole diggers, and Jacob was supervising one section and one boy, while Gabe had the others.

They would be going in shifts throughout the day, the others seeing to their regular classes.

They would also be trading off checking in on those classes. So that meant he would probably only see Vanessa for a limited time today.

It was probably for the best. When he was around her his control seemed to go out the window completely.

Not that he had been known for his control when it came to women at any point in his life.

But the past few years, he'd been as celibate as a youth group leader with a promise ring.

Now? Well, now his body had been reminded of just how much he enjoyed sex.

Now he was preoccupied with it. Hell if he didn't feel a little bit guilty. Because there had been a reason he'd been denying himself in the first place. Because it had been part and parcel to trying to change.

Another parallel between himself and Vanessa, he supposed.

Maybe that was why they kept coming together like magnets. And then, the minute they flipped over, they repelled each other.

No, that wasn't true, not really. He enjoyed a fight with her in many ways. Because it gave him a chance to let loose and do something with all that anger inside him.

Maybe that was wrong. But if it was, he didn't particularly want to be right. Not right now.

It was a release. The sex and the fighting.

Maybe it was for her too.

"What the fuck am I supposed to do now?"

He was snapped back to reality by Aiden's surly question.

"What's wrong?"

"There's a rock in the hole."

"Dig it out with a shovel," Jacob said.

"This is probably against child labor laws," Aiden said.

He was arguing, but he was trying. And nothing spoke more to the changes he was making than that did. And Jacob... Well, he felt a sense of accomplishment.

He couldn't bring Clint back. But he'd wanted to make his place in the world matter a little more.

This made him feel like it just might.

"The government already knows you're here," Jacob said.

"Yeah, but I bet they don't know you're using us to build a fence for you for free."

"We could build this fence three times faster than you jokers. We don't need you."

"Then why are we here?" Aiden shouted.

"It's for you."

"Why? It's supposed to make us...better people? What do you think good people are anyway?"

"It has a hell of a lot of nothing to do with what I think a good person is. Why are *you* here anyway?"

"I got arrested," Aiden said. "None of the foster families can handle me anymore. I was basically headed for a group home. Though, all up, I think I'd choose prison first."

"Yeah, that's not about being a good person. It's about not having your ass in jail."

Aiden shook his head and looked away. "Whatever."

"Not *whatever*. There's a lot of mileage between being a good person and being a criminal." He needed him to understand that.

He needed him to want better for himself, because dammit, Jacob wanted better for him.

"Does it matter?"

Jacob shrugged. "I'm not a criminal."

"Are you a good person?"

The kid looked at him, a dark eyebrow raised, a challenge in his brown eyes.

"Not especially," Jacob said.

"All the posthole digging in the world didn't help you. Why do you think it might help me?"

"Look, kid," he said. "I don't know anything about anything. But I do know how to stay out of jail. So that puts me about a step ahead of you. And quite frankly, if I'm a step ahead of you, you should be concerned."

"Why do you care?"

Jacob frowned. "Did I say that I care?"

Except, when he said that, he found that he did. Because for some reason he identified with this kid and all that smart-ass rage. Because he knew that never covered anything good.

Probably something that happened to him when he was too young to understand the consequences. When he was too young to have had any say in the matter.

A kid who was a victim of his early circumstances. Not that Jacob felt like a victim.

"Why are you here, then?" Aiden asked.

"Okay, let's say that I do care. Just for the sake of argument. The thing is, there's no point running around trying to be the biggest badass. It doesn't prove anything. And running around like you are... Treating people like they're disposable comes back to bite you in the ass. Treating everything like it's a joke... It doesn't end well."

"Yeah?"

"My best friend is dead because of me."

Aiden's eyebrows raised. "You said you weren't a criminal."

"Carelessness kills more people than outright violence, I'm convinced of that. Look, I didn't kill him, but the fact of the matter is I didn't take anything seriously either. Not when I was your age, and not for a long time after. I didn't take much seriously until there were consequences that I couldn't ignore. I would rather you didn't wait until you were me. So honestly, that's my investment. Just that I know where your attitude leads. And if you can help it, I'd say stay away from it."

"Well, help me dig the rock out," Aiden said.

"Nope," Jacob said, handing him a shovel. "The rock is all you."

"It's huge."

"I'm sorry, Mr. Fuck This, you can't dig a rock out of a hole? What kind of inner-city badass are you?"

"Who said I was from the inner city?" Aiden grabbed the shovel and treated him to a baleful look. "You're stereotyping."

Jacob rocked back on his heels. "Maybe I read your file."

"Did you?"

Damn kid. "No."

"Then you're stereotyping."

"*Are* you from the inner city?"

"Of course I fucking am." Aiden scowled and went back to digging.

Jacob laughed and clapped the kid on the back.

"How are things going over here?"

He looked up and saw Gabe.

"Pretty good."

"Terrible," Aiden said, putting the shovel in the hole and trying feebly to get the rock out. He was a big kid. Strong looking too, but he clearly had never done any outdoor work in his life.

"Get the shovel underneath the rock," Gabe said.

"Put your boot on top of it," Jacob added.

"Not on top of the rock," Gabe said. "On top of the shovel."

After some more coaching, Aiden finally got the thing moving.

"You're a hard-ass," Gabe said.

"I thought that was what we were supposed to be doing. Instilling the value of a day's work into young, impressionable minds."

"Yeah, true. Can I talk to you for a second?"

"Are we going to have an interaction that doesn't conclude with you pulling me away from the group anytime soon?"

"When we quit having conversations that are best kept private?"

He didn't want to move away from Aiden, though, and it was hard to say why. Except that he needed the kid to understand. To understand that life and choices had weight.

And to be included. Not shuffled off to the side like something that didn't matter. Which he had a feeling had been too much of the kid's life already.

What would happen if someone treated him like he mattered? If someone pushed past the BS?

When he'd been a kid, no one had done that to him, and it hadn't ended well.

"If this is about what I told you the other night about Clint…Aiden knows about it."

Aiden looked up at them. "I do?"

"My dead friend," Jacob tossed back at him.

"Right," he said.

"You shouldn't feel responsible," Gabe said.

"Then you shouldn't feel responsible for our half siblings."

Aiden looked interested now.

"I knew about them," Gabe said. "I knew about them, and I didn't go looking for them when I should have."

"And I didn't go on the fire when I should have. I wasn't responsible. I didn't do the right thing, and because of that… So we can talk all you want about how it doesn't matter. About how it would just be a trade-off of him or me. But it's not going to make me feel any better than people telling you the half siblings aren't your fault does."

"There are half siblings?" Aiden asked.

"Our dad is a whole thing," Gabe said.

"I have half siblings," Aiden said. "I never get to see them, though."

"Yeah, we never see ours either," Gabe said.

"I'm not the one from the family, though."

It took a second for Jacob to realize what he meant. Aiden was the one who wasn't part of a family. He was the one shoved off to the side and kept out.

"Do you want to be part of the family?" Gabe asked.

"No. Anyway, I'm not allowed to because my stepdad thinks I'd be a bad influence on his precious kids."

So it was a little bit different, then.

"Guilty without a trial?" Jacob asked.

"Basically. So why try?"

The words hit perilously close to home because Jacob knew that feeling well. Because after Gavin had died he asked himself that constantly. Why try at all? He hadn't been able to save his friend. And so he had hidden what had happened, shoved it all down deep, never talked about it to anyone. Never let anyone know how badly it had hurt him.

That he could see his friend in his mind's eye, falling over the edge of the trail. Over and over again in his dreams.

And so he would push it down deeper. And deeper and deeper, so he didn't have to ever deal with it.

And he had always asked himself why it mattered.

Because Gavin was gone, and there was nothing to be gained by letting anyone know he had seen it. Because they would've wanted to talk to him and make sure that he was okay.

Because they would have been so worried about a little boy who had seen his friend fall to his death.

And Jacob hadn't wanted to talk about it. No, not at all. And what was the point?

It was a reason he'd become an EMT. Because he'd seen someone die already, so why not? He'd already had the trauma. He could protect the people who were injured. Maybe protect someone who hadn't seen that kind of thing before. Shoulder it in a small way.

He had been bad at that in his personal life. He hadn't known how to do it.

But he'd been able to do it for strangers. The one way he'd been able to matter.

It hadn't been enough. Because he hadn't engaged in his life, and that was where he'd let Clint down.

"Because somewhere down the road your behavior will impact someone else," Jacob said. "It will. I asked myself all the time why it mattered if I was an irresponsible dick. It didn't, until he died. Until I brushed off the responsibility, and now I have to live with the fact that my friend got on a helicopter that he shouldn't have been on because of me."

"Well," Aiden said, "I would just be glad that I wasn't dead. But maybe it comes back to that good-person thing."

"You'd feel guilty," Jacob said. "Every day. Believe me."

Aiden grunted and lifted the rock up out of the hole. "Done," he said.

"Good," Gabe said. "Next hole."

Gabe held Jacob back as Aiden moved down a few feet.

"That was good advice."

"I think he's a good kid," Jacob said. "Or I think he can be."

"You know, it's not too late for you either," Gabe said.

"Maybe not. Maybe the problem is I just don't care. But I'm not going to wander off into the woods, and I'm not going to get myself thrown in prison."

"What are you going to do?"

"This, I guess. Fires when I need to."

"And nothing else?"

"What else is there?"

"Marriage? Kids?"

"Hell no. I don't ever want to have that kind of responsibility. I've let enough people down. I'm hardly going to sign up to put any more lives in my hands."

"Whether or not you realize it, you do it every day with the fire. Honestly, that's something I've never understood about you, Jacob. You're very insistent that you're not a very great guy. But you left the rodeo to be a paramedic. And then you went and did firefighting…"

"This coming from you? You were so convinced that you are exactly like Dad, and you could never be married or anything like that, and are marrying Jamie."

"I'm not saying I didn't have my issues."

"Past tense?"

"Fine. I probably still have them. But I'm just saying that for somebody who's done so much to help other people, you're pretty convinced that there's nothing good in you."

"Good or bad, it doesn't matter. Intentions don't matter. Actions do. I failed in my actions, Gabe. And that means I can fail again. When you realize that—"

"You know, I don't think I've been very fair to you."

"Wow." Jacob looked around. "Should I be recording this? Am I on camera now?"

"It's just that I don't know how you feel. I mean, I think the realization that a random decision you make on a given day can have such an intense consequence is enough to mess with anyone's head."

"I think we all walk through life feeling like there's a safety net underneath us," Jacob said. "Whether we realize it or not. The first time you realize it's not there, it's a bitch."

"Yeah."

"I'm here. Somebody told me once that it doesn't matter whether or not you want to do a good thing, as long as you do it. That matters a lot more than wanting to do it."

"Who told you that?" Gabe said.

"Just someone… A therapist."

Aiden seemed to be listening to that part of the conversation. But as soon as Jacob looked over, the kid put his head back down and began to dig again.

"Well, I guess that's fair enough. But it sounds like a pretty miserable life if you don't want to do any of the things that you're doing."

He thought about Vanessa. About the way she had felt beneath his hands last night. The way she had looked, streaked with paint, all soft round curves and incredible beauty.

"I like some of the things I do."

"What?"

Jacob winked. "Nothing you need to know about."

Then he checked the time and saw that it was about the starting time for art class. "Aiden. Calvin. Marco. Art time."

"I already know what I'm painting," Aiden said.

As he led the boys over to class, all he could think about was just how much he had enjoyed painting. A hell of a lot more than he'd imagined he would.

And then he looked at Aiden, at the boy's shoulders, which looked square today, a little bit more certain.

He'd helped a lot of people in a physical way. Being an EMT, being a firefighter, he'd saved people, he'd saved buildings and trees, animals. But putting himself in physical danger didn't cost his emotions.

And then the strangest thing had happened.

Vanessa was the one person he'd ever helped who had come back into his life. And somehow now he wanted to...do more than just put a bandage on someone.

He wanted to help heal with it if he could. If his pain could help someone...

Well, then, he'd use it.

And it seemed like he might actually be making a difference.

SHE HAD MANAGED to not jump on Jacob again in the past week. Vanessa felt like that must be progress, even if she sort of missed how much fun it had been to jump on him. She was beginning to have a little bit of an internal argument with herself about whether or not there was a benefit to indulging in a little bit of casual sex with him.

They'd already done it twice, after all.

And the idea of having him in her bed… It made her smile. Rolling over in the morning, waking up and seeing him there. Naked. Gorgeous.

Maybe they couldn't have a conversation without getting a little bit too deep or fighting, but they seemed to be able to have sex okay. And that was something.

It was the weekend, so she had no real excuse to see him, but part of her wanted to make an excuse to go over there so she might run into him. Run into him when the classroom was empty, when no one was around…

She really was a little bit of a ridiculous hussy.

She wasn't sure she minded that.

The realization that she enjoyed sex so much was kind of a nice one. Once she had gotten past the feeling of horror that she had a lack of self-control, she enjoyed the normalcy of it. Most people seemed to like sex. She had blotted it out, put it in the category of nonessential needs so that she could focus on herself.

This was an expansion.

Maybe she needed to institute further expansion.

Of course, she could find another man.

But she wanted Jacob.

And that was another thing that came with her sobriety.

She didn't do what she didn't want to. She didn't suffer. Because that fake martyrdom nonsense didn't lead anywhere good. That didn't mean she didn't do things for other people. But she wasn't going to go out and have sex she didn't want, with a man she wasn't interested in, just to have it. She didn't eat cake with crappy supermarket frosting. She didn't wear uncomfortable shoes.

A refusal to have subpar sex went somewhere with those things.

If she was going to proposition Jacob, she supposed that she should get some condoms. She didn't carry them around because she didn't really need to. She'd been on regular birth control years ago, but she quit taking it when she had gotten sober.

She frowned.

She didn't carry condoms because she hadn't needed them. Jacob had had a condom in his wallet their second time together. Which was interesting because he'd been celibate for quite some time before, he told her that.

In the first time...

The first time he hadn't used a condom.

She'd known that. She had. It was just that she'd blocked it out. She hadn't really thought about it, mostly because she hadn't wanted to. She'd focused on the pleasure. On his body, the way it had fit hers. How she'd felt—wild and free and consumed. Present and hot, in the most beautiful of ways.

But she hadn't thought about condoms.

They hadn't had safe sex.

She knew she was clean. She'd gotten tested for everything years back, and since then hadn't had a partner. But that wasn't the only thing to worry about with sex.

It wasn't the only reason to use a condom.

She stood in the center of her house feeling like the floor had fallen away from her feet. She wasn't due to start her period until tomorrow.

She wasn't late or anything like that.

She should just wait it out.

But she didn't feel any cramping. And she didn't feel achy or even vaguely angry at the world. And that was the most common sign that she was about to start.

That was weird.

But didn't mean anything necessarily. She had a move, and things were strange. So that could obviously cause a delay in bleeding. Maybe. She wasn't a doctor.

She sat down on the couch. Then she stood up.

And then she went over to the fridge and opened it, taking down a glass and filling it up with some of the lemonade that was in the jug there.

She slammed the fridge back shut and took a drink.

The likelihood of her being pregnant was very low.

She was in her late twenties, which was not advanced in terms of age, but it wasn't exactly the most fertile either. And they had sex once. Standing. Against the wall.

It seemed like making them swim uphill like that would inhibit them.

The timing would have had to have been spectacular. Spectacularly bad.

She would just wait and see what happened. She would give it a couple of days. It wasn't an emergency. And there really was no reason to think that anything...

Anxiety made her stomach flip over.

This was all way too familiar. Familiar in a way that made her feel sick.

She could wait. She wasn't crazy. She wasn't crazy, and she wasn't pregnant.

But she could just be sure.

She didn't live very far from town. She could go get

a test, come back home and take it and ease her fears in the space of about twenty minutes.

It was either that or be panicked about it until sometime tomorrow.

No, she wasn't going to do that to herself. She wasn't going to panic.

She was making enough money at this job that however much a pregnancy test cost wasn't going to put her in the poorhouse.

Anyway, you couldn't put a price on peace of mind.

When she got to the grocery store, she saw that you could indeed put a price on peace of mind, and it seemed like kind of a high one, particularly for the ones that proclaimed they would give you a result two days before your missed period.

But that was the one she needed. Seeing as she was one day away.

She imagined it would be even more accurate in that case.

It was inconvenient to look so much like Olivia. Because if she didn't have somebody who was identical running around town, she wouldn't feel quite so conspicuous.

She would assume that everyone in town had forgotten about her more or less, and she wouldn't feel like anyone would be watching to see what she was buying.

But considering she had the face of one of the most beloved girls in town, it all felt very conspicuous.

Of course, Olivia was married, and she already had a baby, so if Olivia thought she might be pregnant again, it wouldn't even be that surprising.

She bought the test quickly, and the clerk didn't

comment on either the test or the fact that she was running around with Olivia Hollister's same face.

She was grateful for that. And relieved for a full minute, until she was back in her car and remembered exactly what she had in the little paper bag on the seat.

It was impossible to be Zen with such a package sitting there.

She had never bought a pregnancy test before.

She had been determined to ignore her symptoms the first time. Determined to pretend it wasn't happening. But she had known.

Her lips felt icy, her knuckles numb as she curved her fingers around the steering wheel.

She pulled over, her hands trembling.

And she didn't think she could do this alone.

Because it made her think of all those bad and horrible things.

Of waking up with a headache and a soreness between her legs that confused her.

Being afraid of what it might mean.

Having Jared get angry when she asked him about it. And then defensive, as he shouted at her about how she'd taken her clothes off, so of course it seemed like she wanted it.

And then the waiting. Waiting for blood. Waiting to bleed.

And it didn't come. It just kept not coming.

Until it did. Like a river.

With shaking hands she picked up her cell phone and dialed Ellie. She couldn't deal with Olivia. Not now. And Ellie was the closest thing she had to a friend in town.

"Ellie?" she asked, trying to disguise the fact that

she was on the verge of a panic attack. "Would you mind if I came over and used your bathroom?"

There was a slight pause. "Okay…"

"To take a test."

This time there was no pause. "Come right over," Ellie said.

She put Ellie's address in her phone's GPS and followed the directions to a little house in a neighborhood in town.

As soon as she pulled in the driveway, the front door opened. "Come in," Ellie said.

"Thank you."

Ellie appraised her closely. "I assume that you're not taking an algebra test into my bathroom?"

"No," she said, holding up the paper bag.

"Are you okay?" she asked.

"Do I look okay?"

"No. You look like you're going to throw up. And pass out. Though not necessarily in that order."

"Probably both."

"Vanessa—"

"It's probably nothing," Vanessa said, lifting the bag even higher. "I'm not even late. I just… I did something stupid. Really stupid."

"It's okay," Ellie said. "I understand stupid."

"I just have to see… I have to see how stupid I was."

"Go right ahead." She gestured down the hall to the bathroom, and Vanessa went inside.

She braced herself on the counter, her chest aching as she stared down at the pink box.

She blew out a breath, trying to ease the sensation in her chest, and tore it open, then wrestled with the thick white wrapping around the test itself.

A few moments later and she was sitting on the edge of the tub and staring. Staring at the window on the thing, watching as two pink lines materialized.

"Oh no," she said, covering her face and resting her elbows on her knees.

"Are you pregnant?" came Ellie's shouted question through the door.

Vanessa stood slowly, trying to catch her breath, and opened the door. "This means I'm pregnant, right?" She thrust the test outward.

"Yes," Ellie said. "Having taken many of these, I can tell you that is positive."

"You've taken many of these?"

"Yes. Every time I thought I was pregnant but hoped I wasn't. And also thought I was pregnant and hoped I was. It's not one of those things I like to wait around for an answer to."

"Me either. But now I kind of wish I had."

"It wouldn't have changed the answer," Ellie said softly.

"It might…resolve itself," Vanessa said, feeling numb as she walked out of the bathroom and into Ellie's living room.

"Yeah, but it might resolve itself into a…baby."

"I had a miscarriage. Once. A long time ago." She pinched the bridge of her nose. "I think I was almost four months pregnant. It was… It was painful. Kind of terrible."

"Do you know why? Did something happen?"

She looked at Ellie, so very grateful that her friend hadn't asked if it was her fault somehow. That she hadn't asked if it was because of drug use or anything like that.

For all Vanessa's sins, when she had suspected that she was pregnant, she hadn't done anything. It was of course coupled with her fear of blacking out again, considering what had clearly happened when she had done it the last time.

"I don't know," Vanessa said. "I didn't go to a doctor or anything. I was in denial. I was seventeen. And I really, really couldn't deal with it."

She wasn't sure she could deal with it now, ten years later. She certainly didn't feel any more emotionally equipped in this moment. Except she had told someone, or she had reached out to someone instead of going completely internal. So maybe that was a step? Toward something? She didn't know.

She didn't know anything. Not now.

"What are you going to do?" Ellie asked. Then she blinked. "I'm sorry. That's probably a terrible question to ask. You just found out."

"Have to... I..."

She had a whole new life now. She was a new person. She had learned to embrace difficult situations when they came. She had learned to be present for her choices. And she supposed that meant she needed to be active in the consequences of those choices.

Consequence.

That sounded like a really cold term to use for a baby.

A consequence.

She fought against the urge to put her hand on her stomach, because that was silly. She had only just found out there was something in there, and she had the urge to go grabbing on to herself like she was nine months pregnant.

There are consequences for your actions, Vanessa.

She could hear her father's voice, so very clearly.

Consequences.

She had been living in consequences for a very long time, at least as far as her parents were concerned.

Things that she had earned because of mistakes that she had made.

But she couldn't even really consider sex with Jacob a mistake.

She couldn't consider this…a mistake.

How could she?

She wasn't ready to go plan a baby shower or anything, but the fact of the matter was that she was a woman with a good job, she wasn't terribly young and she really didn't have designs on being in a relationship. In fact, this was probably her best bet at having a baby. And so, while there were certainly some things to sort through—namely the situation with Jacob—it wasn't a wholly unpleasant situation to find herself in.

"I guess… I guess I do a little bit of reading on child development."

"Okay," Ellie said. "I can… I mean, I have panic books."

"Panic books?"

"Books that I have bought in panics at various stages of either pregnancy or Amelia's development. I call them panic books. They're in my panic library." She gestured down the hall and Vanessa followed her into the living room, where there was in fact a bookshelf that covered the entire back wall.

"Panic library," she said. "There is the *What to Expect When You're Expecting* section, which is very effective at making you terrified of every twinge that you might experience during gestation. There is panic about the first year. General child development. I'm getting into panicking about the teen years now."

"Isn't Amelia four?"

"It is never too early for panic," Ellie said, her face utterly serious.

"You did it all alone," Vanessa said, looking at all the books. "Didn't you?"

Ellie looked away, then sucked in a sharp breath. "I can't even... I was so devastated when Clint died. And so terrified that something would happen to Amelia. She's the last piece of him that I have. At first I thought about her that way. I don't now. Amelia is herself. Wholly and completely, and it's wonderful. She's part me, and she's part him too, which is a gift. But..."

She cleared her throat and looked back at the shelf. "Those books were like my surrogate husband. Something to worry with. And I had to go through all of the what-ifs. Because somehow... I thought if I didn't I might be caught unawares again. I didn't worry about him. Not really. He was just so confident. He thought he was bulletproof, and he seemed like he might be to me. There was not a single part of me that thought when he went out on that fire I wouldn't see him again. You can't think that way when your husband is in a dangerous job anyway. If you do, it'll drive you crazy. It was just so...shocking. The whole bottom fell out of my world. On the top. On the sides. If I hadn't had Caleb... If I hadn't had the whole Dalton family, I would have collapsed. But panic books and family. They're family to me, even if they're not family by blood."

Well, that was complicated. Considering that Jacob Dalton was actually the father of her baby.

There wasn't going to be any...*not* telling him.

"I'm ready to do it alone," Vanessa said, feeling a sense of certainty. Jacob was a solitary man, and she would absolutely give him a choice. But her choice was already made.

She wanted to confess all to Ellie and ask for her opinion on how Jacob might react, but the fact of the matter was, Ellie already knew about the baby before Jacob did. She couldn't really add more to that by also telling her that he was the father before he knew.

Well, that would be a new experience. The thought was not a particularly happy one. Considering that the father of her first... Her first pregnancy...

Well, she wouldn't have wanted him involved anyway. And also considering the way things had ended it just wasn't a particularly fun thought.

You could just leave. You could leave again, run away. Nobody would be surprised.

Your family would just think you had a relapse. Jacob probably would too.

She could live up to everyone's expectations and swan off freely to start over again.

No one would have to know where she was. And she could raise her child on her terms.

Not with the stifling, unwinnable atmosphere of the Logan family hovering overhead. Not with her name attached to her like a millstone.

Totally new. Totally clean.

No.

That was what Vanessa would have done ten years ago. It was what she would have done five years ago.

Run and hide.

Bury the problem. Pretend that it wasn't happening. Pretend that it hadn't happened.

Fly under the radar because she could never fly above it.

She wasn't going to do that. Not now. Not this time.

"I have some conversations I have to have," she said.

"Is…is it someone here?"

Vanessa sighed. "I really probably should talk to him first."

"Right," Ellie said. "Understandably."

"I need to talk to him first."

"Yeah. Totally."

"Can I have one of your panic books?" Her voice sounded small in her head.

"Sure. Gestational panic?"

"Nothing about how to tell a guy he's going to be a father, is there?"

"Sadly, no. But then, that wasn't my particular hurdle."

"Yeah. I'm sorry. It probably seems silly for me to be worried about that, all things considered."

"No. I was actually terrified to tell Clint that I was going to have a baby, and we'd been trying. But I knew that it would change everything. Babies do. Though in my case…I've always been so grateful that with Amelia I had another person to love. Because I lost… I lost someone that I loved. And if I hadn't had someone else…I don't know how I could have gone on."

"I suppose you just would have," Vanessa said. "That is what we do. We go on."

And she knew that she had never lost someone, not

in the way that Ellie had, but she still knew that to be true. That you soldiered on as best you could. That you made a life, even when it was grim.

That was the thing. Her addiction years were completely lost years. In some ways they were, but in others… She had jobs. Lots of different ones. Sometimes she hadn't had them. Sometimes she'd had places to live, and other times not. She had big groups of friends. Loud and noisy and distracting.

She'd been happy sometimes. Sometimes happier than she'd been in the past five years. And sometimes, if she was completely honest in her memories, she felt like she had a greater sense of freedom then.

But that was only true when everything was perfect. When she was high and out with friends.

When she wasn't so acutely aware of the fact that she had a leash and a collar made of substances that her body craved in order to have those feelings.

That was the trouble with the past. It was tempting to make it all bad or all good. The truth was often much more complicated. But complicated wasn't comfortable. And nobody liked to try to wade through complicated feelings. Brilliant bright labels were much easier.

She often resented the lack of them. But that was another thing she'd learned. That painting with broad brushstrokes could be dangerous.

Comparison could be too. Trying to make what was happening now a direct parallel to what had happened ten years ago.

She couldn't. It was different. She was different.

The entire circumstances were different. And she didn't need to wonder how she would've handled it the first time, because it wasn't the first time, and she wasn't seventeen. She was strong now. Braver than she had been.

And most important, she had gone out and gotten a pregnancy test the moment she suspected, rather than waiting. That was symbolic of something. Her ability to face up to reality. Or whatever.

"Are you going to be okay?" Ellie asked.

"Yes," she answered definitively.

Because she would be. Whatever happened with Jacob. She just would be.

CHAPTER TWELVE

As far as Jacob was concerned it had been a perfect Friday so far. He'd gotten up early and hiked up to the top of the ridge behind his cabin, standing and looking down on everything below. From his vantage point on the rocky mountaintop, he could see the sloped, pine-covered mountains fade into a bright patchwork of fields and vineyards. Barns and houses rising up out of the landscape, horses' and cows' miniature black silhouettes against the green.

Sometimes, when he stood up there, he was consumed with thoughts of falling. Falling from the sky in a helicopter. Falling from the edge of a cliff like the one he stood on.

And inevitably when he saw himself fall, he saw a boy falling too.

Like his dreams. Like his memory.

He couldn't explain why he felt compelled to climb to the top of mountains, given they always gave him thoughts like that. But he had them quite a bit. And he found something good in standing there defying the feeling anyway.

The bad memories were there whether he stood on the mountain or not.

When he got back to the cabin he was sweaty and he stripped his shirt off as soon as he got out from beneath the cover of the trees and into the clearing in front of his house. He stopped when he saw a figure standing there, looking out over the view in front of his place. It was Vanessa.

She had her hands clasped in front of her, her dark hair blowing in the breeze.

She turned to face him and his stomach went tight.

Hell, if she was here for round three, he was ready.

In fact, that would make a good Friday a *very* good Friday. Physical exertion outdoors and indoors. He would take it.

"Hey," he said.

As opening lines went, it probably wasn't his finest. But she had come to him. So he assumed pickup lines weren't really required.

"Hi. I probably should have called. I think I have your number somewhere. But I just thought I would come and see if you were home. I guess you are."

"I guess," he said. "I was climbing." He took a few steps toward her and she took a step back.

He lunged forward, his arm outstretched, panic overtaking him. "Careful," he said, grabbing hold of her arm and pulling her back toward him.

"I'm not… I'm not close to the edge," she said.

He supposed she wasn't.

But…he had just seen her falling again. He could always see people falling.

"Sorry," he said, gritting his teeth. "First responder habits die hard."

"I bet," she said. "I bet you have definitely seen some things."

"Things I wish I hadn't," he confirmed.

"Okay, well. This is off to a great start."

"I'm in," he said.

She blinked at him. "I'm sorry, what?"

"I'm in," he said. "I'm already half-undressed anyway."

The corners of her mouth pulled down. "Did you think I was here to proposition you?"

"Yes," he said. "About the only thing we've done together alone is have sex. So I figured that was probably a trend that was going to keep going."

"Wow. No. That is not what I'm here about."

"Then what?"

She took a deep breath and looked off to the side, her hair ruffling slightly in the breeze.

She was beautiful. And it struck him hard like a punch to the chest. He didn't really know why. He'd seen beautiful women before. He'd seen a lot of beautiful women. But there was something about her. Standing there the way that she was. There was just something about her.

It wasn't the first time he'd felt it either. Like he was staring into his future every time he looked into her eyes.

"I'm pregnant," she said.

The word hit him like a slap to the face, and before he could react at all, she continued, "I would like to keep the baby. And there is no obligation on you. But I knew that there was no way I could walk around being pregnant and not acknowledge the reality of the situation."

"Excuse me?"

That was not the best response, and he knew it. But he didn't know what the best response was. He was still reeling from the first thing she'd said. He hadn't had any time to process the rest.

"I might not… I might have another miscarriage," she said. "Who knows. You know that I… You know that happened."

"I'm sorry. I need to back up about five steps. You're pregnant."

"Yes."

"Dammit."

"Yeah."

"I really thought that you got past this kind of thing in high school."

"Well, I did it then too. But I'm not sure why you would think that. Considering you can make a baby as long as you've got sperm."

"I just… I'm always…"

"We didn't use a condom. And I think I very deliberately didn't think about that. Because it was—"

"I always do," he said.

"But you didn't."

Yeah, and he'd known it, because he had to go buy condoms after their first time. And he put one in his wallet. But he very deliberately erased any concern that she might be pregnant. He had figured she was on the pill or something. Because she hadn't said anything.

Yeah, right. You didn't figure anything. You didn't think about it because, just like her, you didn't want to.

"I don't need anything from you," she said. "I made my decision, you're going to have to make yours. But I don't need you to do anything."

"I—I know that traditionally people get married in this situation…"

"I don't want to marry you," she said. "I profoundly don't want to marry you."

"My parents... If you knew... Marriage is..."

"I had that traditional family," Vanessa said. "You know, the one that's supposed to protect you from everything? Mom and Dad married, stable, owning their own house and everything. My mom stayed home with us. I had all the things that were supposed to make me successful and keep me out of trouble. My parents had a fifty percent success rate with that. I was doing absolutely everything you would be afraid your child was doing. And no amount of old-fashioned American family values could do anything about that. I don't need a nuclear family to create a safe space for my child."

"You're using therapist-speak again."

"Well. I'm just saying. And it sounds to me that you had married parents too."

"Yeah, but I don't know that you can call us a model for the great American family."

"Fine. But my point is, I think we can acknowledge that marriage isn't going to solve anything."

"Okay."

"Now, I'm not opposed to us trying to co-parent."

"Co-parent."

"Yes."

"That's...the stupidest thing I've ever heard. How are we co-parenting? We would just be parenting. It's always people doing it together unless somebody chooses not to, or the guy is a dickhead."

"So you think a guy who doesn't take his paternal rights is a dickhead."

Yes. He damn well did. He was not going to be like

his father. Not in that way. He had spent a damn lot of years doing a good Hank Dalton impression. Swaggering around and not taking a damn thing seriously.

And Jacob might not have designs on being a husband, and he may not have chosen to be a father, but the thing was…he was going to be one.

His own dad had a string of illegitimate children all over the country. And it was something Gabe was working hard to clean up now.

He thought of McKenna, his half sister, who had come to them just a couple of years ago. Who had been given such a hard run of life thanks to their father's lack of involvement.

And even though Hank hadn't known about those children, the fact remained that his irresponsibility was a serious issue.

"There's no reason on earth I shouldn't be a father to a kid that I'm actually the father of," Jacob said.

"Great," Vanessa said. "So we'll…we'll come up with an agreement."

"Okay."

"Why don't I… Why don't I wait a couple of weeks and make some doctor's appointments?"

The idea of waiting a couple of weeks for anything right now seemed like torture. It was only the rest of his life.

"You know, I need to make sure everything looks good. I never went to the doctor last time. So I don't actually know… I don't know what happened. I don't know if something was wrong with the baby or with me. Or if it was just one of those things."

"You seem remarkably calm."

"I've had a couple of hours to process it. But I didn't

wait long to come to you. The first time I was pregnant I was too young to be a mother. And…the circumstances were not great."

"I imagine," he said.

"I mean…really not great. The guy… He's not a good guy."

"Does he still live around here?"

"As far as I know."

He wondered if that had to do with her avoidance of the Gold Valley Saloon. Because most people in their age group hung out there on a given weeknight.

"Who is it?"

He'd wondered then. Because even though he had been intent on evaluating her situation at the time of the miscarriage he'd asked if she'd wanted him to call someone. And she had been emphatic that no one could know.

Terrified even.

He could remember that clearly. Her holding his hand and looking up at him, terrified, telling him her family couldn't know. That no one could know.

That included the father.

"I don't really want to talk about it right now. Honestly, for obvious reasons I have to think a little bit about my past right now. You know, for medical reasons. But I don't want… I don't want this to be the same thing. It isn't. I'm different. And I'm in a place where this actually isn't bad news for me." She met his gaze. "If it's bad news for you, you don't have to be involved. I know you feel like you have to be, and that it says something about your masculinity if you don't. But that's not how I want it to be."

"You just told me the other day that being good

isn't always about wanting to do right. It's not wanting to and doing it anyway. Or did that only apply to you?" he asked.

"No, it applied to me choosing to stay sober. But a person shouldn't be made to feel like you resent them. Like you had to choose them."

He shook his head. "Well, I suppose you and I have different definitions of why people should do things."

"No. I just don't want my child to feel unwanted."

"Whatever my feelings are right now, and I'm not entirely sure what they are myself, it doesn't change what I should or shouldn't do. Right is right whether or not you want to do it."

"Jacob—"

"No. I spent my whole damn life doing what was easy. Avoiding things. Doing what felt good. You know what? It's bullshit. Being happy is bullshit. It doesn't mean anything. Being irresponsible like that is just putting the responsibility on someone else. It doesn't go away, it just shifts. I learned that lesson the hard way, and I will damn well not learn it with you. I will not learn it on a child. I won't be the struggle that kid has to have in life. And if I don't feel thrilled about it, that doesn't change what I should do."

"You know what," Vanessa said. "Fine. I can't make the decision for you. I told myself that I wouldn't. It's just that I didn't expect to try to talk you out of taking parental responsibility."

"You thought that I would leave you alone to do it?"

He expected her to say something about men, about the fact that men tended to do that. Or maybe about him personally. Instead, her face went slightly waxen. "Everyone always has. Every major event in my life

I've handled alone. So yeah, I didn't just assume that this would be different."

"Every major traumatic event in my life I've done my damnedest to handle alone," Jacob said. "My thought always was that if you didn't talk about it maybe you wouldn't have to deal with it."

She huffed out a laugh. "I tried that. It didn't go very well." She took a breath. "Okay. Now…sometimes I'm not really sure. If everyone left me to handle my pain by myself or if…I hid it too well."

"You're not that good of a liar, Vanessa," he said. "I'm not sure how you could have hidden things that well."

"How do you know?"

"Just a feeling that I have." He didn't know how he knew. She hid things, but he could see when she was hiding something. He couldn't imagine anyone…not seeing it.

You'd have to be looking the other way.

Her family had clearly been focused on anything but her. And that pissed him off, even all these years after her trauma.

He was just a dumbass guy. He didn't know much of anything about the finer points of emotion or the finer points of women, and even he recognized all that.

A baby.

He didn't think any of it had fully sunk in yet.

He had agreed to being a father. Because he was going to be one. And from his point of view, that meant there was no debate on how he'd handle it.

But…he didn't think he was going to be able to grasp the enormity of it for a while.

Right now, it didn't look like anything. Her stomach

looked flat, her body still slender. Because of course it wasn't like he was going to be able to see it now. He knew nothing at all about babies or any kind of development. But he knew enough to know the thing was the size of a BB right now. That it was barely much of anything.

The absurdity of it all hit him, standing there with the edge of a cliff behind both of them. That either their lives would change, or they wouldn't. That everything they knew about themselves, about their futures, would either be altered irrevocably, or everything would go back to normal.

And it all depended on the fragility of what they'd created between them.

On how everything progressed over the next weeks. Or didn't.

How did people choose to do this? He couldn't even fathom it.

It all felt way too big to wrap his mind around.

He looked behind himself then, at the cabin. Dilapidated and run-down. When he bought it initially, of course his plan had been to build a new place on the property. Because he loved this spot.

He suddenly imagined a child toddling close to the edge of that cliff and he nearly doubled over.

Would he be able to make this spot safe?

Fences.

He would need a lot of fences. And he would have to teach his child everything he knew about safety out in the wilderness. Everything he knew about safety in the world.

Because that trail he and Gavin had been on as boys

hadn't been anywhere near their houses, it had just been a bad situation with a couple of stupid kids who hadn't known what can happen out there.

Everything in the world was dangerous. It was *so damn dangerous*. And he…he had never managed to protect people when it mattered.

He would just have to. He had to protect Vanessa. He had to protect the baby.

That meant making a safe space for both of them. And it would not be on the edge of this cliff face, no matter how much he liked the view.

Thankfully, the property sat on several acres, and he imagined he could get a pad dug out back farther. On a safer spot.

He would need something completely different than what he'd been thinking.

Yeah, you said you didn't want to marry her, and you're planning on making a house.

Well, his kid would need a house. It had nothing to do with Vanessa. Although, Vanessa felt like his.

She had already, and this only made it more so.

Co-parenting. She had talked about co-parenting.

Well, he wanted something more than that. And he wanted it to be complete. Right now, they lived close to each other, with nothing but a stretch of dirt road between them. But maybe there was something better.

"What are you doing?" she asked.

"What?" He looked back at her.

"You're staring at your house."

"Thinking."

Her eyes narrowed. "If you're making plans, it's too soon."

"It's not too soon. I have to figure out where I'm going to put a baby."

"What makes you think you're putting a baby anywhere? I'm the one *having* the baby."

"It's not going to stay a baby. It's going to grow up. And if you think I'm going to have him toddling around up here…"

"Him? It could be a girl."

For some reason that scared him even more. "Whatever. The point is, I have to figure out my living situation. Because this doesn't work."

She looked behind them. "Okay. Agreed."

"I bought this place because of the view," he said, looking behind her.

There was a whole lot of "but now" buried in that sentence. He'd bought it for the view…but now it wouldn't work. Now it was different.

Now everything had changed.

"But it makes you nervous," she said.

Yeah, he had certainly betrayed some of his feelings about places like this to her a few moments ago when he grabbed her arm like she was going to somehow stumble and fall twenty feet behind her.

"Yeah," he said. "It does. I figured I would buy a house that sat right on the edge of something that bothered me a little bit."

She cleared her throat. "I'm not sure I know what to say to that."

"Does that scare you?" It scared him a little bit.

"I don't know. We're all different kinds of messed up, Jacob. I guess it's not really my place to comment on your particular brand of it."

They stood facing each other for a moment, and the

largeness of it all seemed to expand between them. "We really can't be sleeping together anymore," she said.

He nodded slowly. He didn't have to ask why. Because they didn't need any kind of volatility in their relationship. They didn't need to have a relationship that had anything to do with each other.

He was not going to be in a Hank and Tammy Dalton situation, which was all fighting and drama, and didn't do anything for the kids.

And he imagined she had all of her reasoning too.

But the fundamental one was they couldn't guarantee that a relationship between them would be anything other than toxic.

They had to have a relationship based on that kid.

Anything else…anything else probably wouldn't last.

He had been the man who lived in the moment. Who did what he had to to make himself comfortable. He wouldn't do that. Not anymore.

All of this, this was about the kid.

And it was the strangest thing, suddenly he wasn't irritated or even afraid. Suddenly, he felt like he might just have something worth focusing on other than himself.

Clint couldn't be here with his baby girl. Amelia could never have her father.

But his child could. He might as well dig his own grave and march right into it if he didn't take hold of this with both hands because it would be the damn sorriest use of his time on earth.

If he didn't take responsibility for his kid when his friend never could.

It was so clear to him. It burned in his chest like fire.

And after four years of sitting in a whole lot of guilt and grief, he felt a weight on his chest shift for the first time.

CHAPTER THIRTEEN

OVER THE NEXT four weeks Vanessa's relationship with Jacob developed into a cautious pattern.

They would see each other—only at the ranch—and he would inquire politely about how she felt.

When she made a doctor's appointment, she gave him the date.

They otherwise didn't speak much about their potential future. And really, what was the point? Things would either progress or they wouldn't.

And Vanessa felt like everything was a little bit in a holding pattern until they got confirmation that everything was all right. She hadn't even told Ellie yet that Jacob was the father, and she knew her friend was dying for her to name names.

Her relationship with Ellie was different than any she'd had in a long time. She was a solid, steady presence, but she didn't demand Vanessa behave in a way that made her comfortable. When all her friends had been into drugs, so much of the lifestyle had been about the behavior of the person around you supporting your own.

It all felt normal because they all did it.

Which in hindsight of course said a lot.

But Ellie was content to let Vanessa sort things out

the way it worked best for her. This friendship was such an unexpected and interesting gift.

She hadn't come here for friendship. But she'd found it.

Still, Vanessa was in no hurry to confess that Jacob was the father of her baby, and she really didn't know why.

Control, maybe?

No.

Maybe if she didn't have that history of losing a pregnancy at an advanced stage, she wouldn't feel quite so cautious. But she did.

And if she was cautious with Jacob, then she was completely noncommunicative with Olivia and the rest of her family. And she knew that would have to end too. Especially when they figured out if the pregnancy was viable.

It was likely she would still want to wait awhile to tell anyone.

Today, she had an appointment.

And she had thought long and hard about whether or not she was going to have that appointment in Gold Valley, or if she would go farther afield to Copper Ridge or maybe to Tolowa to ensure a little bit of anonymity.

But the doctor she'd chosen was a gynecologist as well as an obstetrician, so she figured it was fair enough that she might be there for a regular old exam.

She also wasn't going to hide.

But when she pulled up to the parking lot and saw Jacob's oversize truck spilling out of one of the narrow spaces—clearly not designed for men and their man vehicles—she thought differently about it.

If there was anyone they knew present in the building, and it was entirely likely between the two of them, it was not going to look like an innocuous visit.

It was connecting the two of them in that way, if nothing else.

So what? What does it matter?

She didn't know. It was just that she was so entrenched in the idea of hiding herself when she was here.

It didn't matter. None of it did. If she had to explain the situation to someone, it would be fine. They would be explaining the situation over the next nine months…hell, the next eighteen years.

If everything went well, then there would be no hiding any of this ever.

Still, she hadn't realized he was going to come to the appointment.

She had given him all the information, but had just assumed he would wait for her to call him when she was finished.

But no. Her cowboy had come down from the mountain because he clearly needed to be there.

And he was there before her. Which just…

She sighed and got out of the car, then walked into the office.

She checked in, giving her name to a smiling woman sitting behind the marble counter, and then walked into the waiting area, which was made to look like a living room. Plush and welcoming and warm. There were two women sitting with chairs between them reading magazines, and thankfully, Vanessa didn't know either of them.

And there was Jacob. Sitting on a love seat with

his boots kicked out in front of him. He was not reading a magazine.

"You came," she said.

"You thought that I wouldn't?"

"I figured you might wait and see what the results were."

"No," he said. "I figured I would come and see what the results were."

"You don't have to."

"Sit down," he said.

"I don't have to do what you tell me," she said, but she took a seat beside him. "You really don't have to be here."

"This is how it is," he said. "I'm showing up."

She looked at him out of the corner of her eye. "You're going to be overbearing about this, aren't you?"

"Hell yes," he said.

"You have a thing about showing up," she said.

"Yeah, we both have some issues. And I imagine they're going to clash a little bit."

"Welcome to the next eighteen years of our lives?"

The question seemed to hit them both with equal force and settled between them like an overfed barn owl. She took a breath, ready to say something, and he was about to do the same when the door opened. "Vanessa?"

The girl standing at the door, dressed in scrubs, now, she looked vaguely familiar.

Probably from school. That was unfortunate.

"Right here," Vanessa said, standing up.

If the other woman knew who she was, she didn't give any indicator. Her smile was carefully bland, comfortably so. And Vanessa decided she didn't want to do any deep investigation on a potential connection here.

"Height and weight," the woman said.

Vanessa toed her shoes off and stepped onto the scale, keeping her eyes fixed on Jacob, who wisely didn't look at the scale at all.

"If we can get a urine sample first," the woman said, stopping outside the bathroom door.

"Sure," Vanessa said.

She looked at Jacob, who took a meaningful step back.

Vanessa sighed. This was going to be nothing but a long string of personal situations that she would rather not have Jacob witness.

But you slept with him.

Yes, she had slept with him. That was different. They'd had great sex. The kind of sex where they probably had both looked great too. It had been intimate, but it had been glorious.

There was nothing glorious about having to pee into a cup.

Then she vanished inside the bathroom and took care of that particular necessary evil before coming back out.

After that, they were led into a small room where Vanessa had her blood pressure taken and had to answer a few questions.

Including the date of her last period and last sexual intercourse.

She looked over at Jacob. "What day was that?"

He looked startled. "The twentieth."

She looked back at the nurse. "I figured he would know."

If a man was going to remember a date, she imagined it would be the date when he'd had an orgasm with another person.

If the woman thought it was strange it had been more than a month since Vanessa and her apparent partner had had sex, she didn't say anything.

She just took the information down. And again, Vanessa was grateful.

"If you can go ahead and get undressed and put this on, the doctor will be in shortly."

Then she left, leaving Jacob and Vanessa sitting there.

He stood up and turned his back.

She thought about telling him that gesture was a little bit ridiculous at this point, but decided against it. He was keeping boundaries in place, and for that she should be grateful.

For that she was grateful.

She undressed slowly, keeping her eyes on his broad shoulders, and couldn't help but admire the way that tight black T-shirt of his tapered to his muscles, the way it highlighted his narrow waist. Lean hips. And his Wrangler butt.

She was very much into that.

She had never really considered herself a fan of cowboys.

But she was a big fan of this one.

He made her understand the fantasy. Wild and rough, raw, somewhat untamed. But...

At the end of the day the man who would show up for a doctor's appointment.

Her heart clenched slightly. She put her clothes carefully on one of the chairs, put the gown on and sat up on the table, the paper crinkling underneath her butt. She wiggled, trying to smooth it all out.

"Are you done?" he asked.

"Yes," she said.

He turned to face her. "Nice," he said. "Hospital-gown gray is definitely your color."

"I like the socks," she said, holding her feet up and displaying the white cotton footwear she hadn't taken off. "I think it really adds something to it."

"Definitely." He reached out and took hold of her toe, squeezing gently before releasing, as if he'd remembered belatedly he probably shouldn't touch her without permission.

She would love to be mad at him for it. But really, she had liked it.

The connection that made her feel like he was there. Like she wasn't alone in this.

Her throat got tight.

She knew how to power through things alone. She wasn't sure she knew how to do it with another person.

A part of her really, really wanted to.

Another part of her, though, wanted to throw him out of the room and handle it all herself because having this big broad-shouldered variable in her life made things feel all a bit precarious.

The door opened and the doctor came in. "Hi," she said. "I'm Dr. Grant."

"Nice to meet you," Vanessa said.

Jacob held his hand out gravely, and the doctor shook it.

"Everything going well?" Dr. Grant asked. "No cramping or anything like that?"

"No," Vanessa said, shaking her head. "But I wanted to come and check viability. I had a miscarriage ten years ago. But I had never been to a doctor. So I'm not totally sure if the problem is me or..."

"Of course," the doctor said. "We can check for a heartbeat today."

With a sheet over Vanessa's lap, she had her lie back and lift the bottom of the gown before she put gel over her stomach.

"We'll try this way first," the doctor said.

"*This* way? What other way is there?" Vanessa asked.

"Transvaginal," the doctor said.

Jacob frowned. "That doesn't sound pleasant."

"A great many things about this process aren't pleasant," the doctor said, smiling. "But modern medicine is helpful, even when it isn't comfortable."

Vanessa sighed and looked up at the ceiling, hoping that nothing would end up needing to be done *transvaginally*. Although, on her list of concerns, that was pretty low.

The doctor placed a wand at her stomach, and a watery sound filled the room. But there was nothing that sounded like a heartbeat.

She continued to move the wand over different parts of her stomach, and suddenly the sound waves shifted, contracted and expanded. And again and again in a rhythmic fashion.

"There it is," she said.

"Oh," Vanessa said.

She was overtaken by emotion. By a feeling of being completely and utterly overwhelmed.

Because here it was. Evidence that what had happened was real. That the baby was real.

It was… It was alive. And inside her. And growing. And it bonded her to the man sitting across from her, who looked no less in shock as he continued to listen to the sound of his child's beating heart.

"Good," Vanessa said.

Which seemed a weak, insipid response to such an event.

"Yes," the doctor said. "Good."

The rest of the appointment went by in something of a blur, and before Vanessa knew it, she and Jacob were back out in front of the clinic, an appointment card clutched in Vanessa's hand for another month out.

"Something could still go wrong," she pointed out, staring down at the date on the card.

"Sure," he said, stuffing his hands in his pockets.

Something about that casual response and gesture let her know that he really didn't think anything would go wrong.

"I wish I knew… I wish I knew more about the first time. So that I would feel a little bit more secure." She looked up at him. "I don't even know what I'm supposed to feel right now."

"I say we move forward assuming everything will go like these things usually do."

"We can keep it a secret for another couple of months," she said.

He shook his head. "That doesn't work for me. That doesn't give me enough time to figure things out."

She scowled. "I didn't know that I was asking your permission."

"I didn't think you were. But I'm giving you my opinion."

"It's not your uterus."

"But this is something that affects my life too. Give me a really good reason not to tell."

"We could still lose it," she pointed out.

"I would end up telling my brothers about it if we did."

She sighed. "I don't know if I would tell my family."

"Telling my family isn't telling yours."

"Maybe. But rumors in this town."

"You think we're not going to start rumors coming and going from the doctor's office?"

"Fine. I guess I have some baggage. I still feel a little bit like I'm seventeen whenever I walk through town. Like I have something to hide. But we are adults. We're having a baby. That's fine. That's not utterly horrifying and terrifying onto my soul."

"So, you're doing great," he said drily.

"Yeah. Fantastic. How are you?"

"Ready to do what we have to."

"Great. So…we do what we have to."

"For me that means telling some people."

"Okay. For me that means going back to my place and eating pie."

"Do you want me to bring you pie?"

A funny little sensation hit her in the chest. "No. I can get my own pie."

"Suit yourself. I'll check in with you tomorrow."

"Okay," she said.

She stuck her hand out because she didn't know what

else to do. So there, standing in front of the ob-gyn clinic, she did about the most absurd thing in the world and shook the hand of her baby's father.

It was like an electric shock, even now. And that jolt seemed to freeze them both in place. She wanted to lean in. But she couldn't. They couldn't.

This was bigger than the two of them.

It was the three of them now.

When he released his hold on her, his expression shifted, the corner of his mouth lifting upward into kind of a rueful smile, and then he tipped his hat and walked back toward his truck.

And Vanessa was left to wonder why her chest felt like there was a rock in it.

CHAPTER FOURTEEN

THEY HAD EVEN managed to get Caleb to come out to the bar. Which meant that Ellie must be settled at home with Amelia, because God knew it was usually difficult to tear his brother away from his personal project.

Jacob had to wonder how long Caleb could possibly sustain an entire life built around supporting their friend's widow.

Mostly, he had to wonder what the hell Caleb's end goal was.

Because Caleb had to be in love with her. There was basically no other reason a man would give everything of himself to a woman like that. Maybe it was all guilt, but Jacob had a hard time believing it.

And Caleb…

Well, he was starting to wonder if Caleb was just punishing himself.

But Caleb's situation was not Jacob's concern tonight, and he was left to wonder why in the hell he felt so compelled to talk to his brothers about his situation.

Mostly because this wasn't something he could pretend wasn't happening.

He heard that heartbeat today in the doctor's office. And he didn't want to give Vanessa any kind of freakout, because she wasn't exactly in the best place either.

And he needed the plan. Dammit. He was going to have to build a house.

After he left the office he put in a call to Graybar Construction, talking to them about his property, and when he would need the house built by, how he would need it positioned. They said there was no way that Faith, their world-famous architect, could design a house for him in that space of time with her workload. And he said he hadn't given a damn about how famous the person who designed his house was as long as it could get built.

So they'd told him they could give him one of their standard plans and tweak from there.

It gave him details to control, and that made him happy enough.

Somehow, he had to get on top of this. Somehow, he had to make it…okay.

"I'm buying beer," Jacob said, clapping both his brothers on their backs and turning to walk toward the bar. Laz was there pouring drinks, and Jacob asked him for whatever he had on tap.

"Dark or light?"

"Amber," he returned.

Laz shook his head but produced three glasses of a local amber ale, which Jacob brought back to the table.

"I wanted an IPA," Gabe said.

"No. I judge you for that and we're not having it at the table."

"I don't think that's your choice," Gabe said.

"Sure it is. I just paid. Also, I have something to talk to you both about."

"Me too," Gabe said. "I offered West a job."

"I'm sorry, you what?"

"I offered West a job. At the ranch. And he took it."

"He took a job at the ranch. Here."

"He won't be coming until around Christmastime. But yeah," Gabe said.

"What about... What about the rest of them?"

"Still working to track them down. I've found West, but the other two...no leads at all. I don't even have names. I don't know where to begin."

"West's mom didn't give you names?"

"No. She barely wanted to share West's information with me." He shifted in his seat. "Anyway, what did you want to say?"

Why did he suddenly feel like a guilty kid?

An accidental pregnancy would actually be way easier to confess to his dad, who wouldn't have a stone he could throw. Telling Gabe and Caleb was another thing.

"I... Well, it turns out that I..." Somehow, it was damn hard to say the words. He wasn't going to lead with Vanessa being pregnant, because he wasn't going to lead with Vanessa's name. But the words that he was having difficulty forcing out were: *he was going to be a father*.

"You're training to be a ventriloquist?" Caleb asked in a rare display of humor.

"I'm going to be a father," Jacob said.

Gabe quite literally spit his beer out on the table. "What the hell?"

"No way," Caleb said.

"Yeah."

"With...who? A wolf that wandered up to your cabin?"

"Screw you," Jacob said. "No."

"It's just that as far as I know, you haven't been around any women in a while."

"I clearly have been."

"Wow. So…when?"

"Last week of August," he grunted, having way too easy of a time picturing how it had been on that hot summer night. Hard and heavy against the wall.

Again on the counter.

Though that hadn't been when she'd conceived.

But it was memorable.

"What?" Caleb asked. "Is she an elephant?"

It took him a while to realize they had been asking about due dates. Not conception.

He gritted his teeth. "Sometime in June."

"Oh. *Oh*," Gabe said. "Last week of August. After school started?"

Jacob hedged. "I don't know."

"She from around here? What the hell are you going to do? Are you going to marry her?" Caleb asked.

"*No*, I'm not going to marry her."

"Do not make me have a shotgun wedding," Gabe said. "I swear to God, if you knocked up someone's daughter from around here, and you're not going to marry her—"

"She doesn't want to get married," Jacob said. "And we're not teenagers. We're going to be perfectly able to work things out. It's not like we were in a relationship. We just know each other. And it's fine."

"Who is it?"

Jacob sighed. "Vanessa Logan."

That earned him nothing but stony silence. Until Gabe spoke.

"Really? You knocked up the art teacher?" Gabe asked, his voice laced with disgust.

"Hey," Jacob said. "She was completely involved in the knocking up. But it doesn't matter. She has a job, she'll be close. The kid will be close."

"You actually want a kid?" Caleb asked.

"I don't know. But I'm not dead. I'm not going to be. This is my responsibility. I intend to take it. I'm not like him. I'm not like I was."

They said nothing for a while. The sounds of the saloon closed in around them and they all lifted their beer glasses and took a long drink, setting them down with three distinct clicks on the scarred wood table.

"Well," Caleb said finally. "What do you need?"

The shift was so abrupt that Jacob wasn't quite sure what to make of it.

"What do I *need*?"

"From us."

Gabe nodded. "Yeah, I'm hardly going to exhaust a bunch of resources looking for other siblings while I let one that's right here twist in the wind. What do you need from us?"

"I don't know. I sure as hell didn't think I'd be the first one of us to have a kid."

"Well, neither did I, considering I'm actually en-gaged," Gabe said. "Of course, it's going to take Jamie forever to be ready for that."

Jacob winced. "Because of her mom?"

Jamie's mother had died shortly after she was born. Complications from childbirth had resulted in the death, and he had to wonder if that had made Jamie a bit nervous about having kids of her own.

He wouldn't blame her.

The whole thing was a minefield of horror.

"No," Gabe said. "She just isn't ready. I wouldn't mind. But I'm ten years older than she is. So I have to be a little bit reasonable."

"Fair enough."

"She's doing rodeo stuff sometimes. She's not done with that. When she can take a year off, then we'll talk about it."

"Don't look at me," Caleb said.

"You still seem more like father material than I do," Jacob said. "Hell, you've basically taken care of Amelia since she was born."

Caleb's expression shuttered. "She's not mine," he said.

"I know," Jacob said. "But you do know what to do with her."

"Yeah. Look, it's not that hard. Kids are…great."

"Yeah. They're just great. Except, for some reason, considering our current situation, I'm having visions of mine growing into a little hooligan who hates me and everyone else and has to go to a ranch to dig postholes."

"Well, you know how you keep that from happening," Gabe said.

"I know how to keep pregnancy from happening. You wear a condom. I failed at that."

Gabe winced. "I don't want to know. But I just mean…be there for the kids. If you see one pattern in these kids, it's that they didn't have anyone that was on their team. They didn't have anyone that was there for them."

Except he thought about what Vanessa had said. About the fact that she had all the things that were supposed to make a kid successful. That she had all the things that were supposed to make life easy. Guarantee success.

"Well, I thank you for the confidence. I'm not sure that I have it. Not yet."

"We can do that for you."

"I also have to build a house," Jacob said. "Any volunteers to pick up a hammer?"

"Can you hire someone? Or can I give you some of my money?"

"I can hire someone," Jacob said. "I've basically banked all my money that I've made going around fighting fires. I haven't spent anything in the past couple of years."

"Well, that's good. Because I was not about to be building things for you."

"That's great. You ask what I need, and then you put a hard limit on what you'll do."

"Of course. I'm your brother, not a parent. This is not unconditional."

Unconditional.

He supposed that was what parenting was supposed to be.

He'd just never...leaned on his parents. Not at all. His antics had earned him attention, and that had been enough. Anything he'd actually needed, he handled all that himself. His dad was more than willing to pat him on the back and say boys would be boys. His mother rolled her eyes but didn't intervene.

He'd learned that not staying still, not talking allowed for an easy relationship. Gentle ties that didn't require any depth. And that was the story of his whole life.

That had worked well enough for a long damn time.

And he realized his son could very well do the same thing. Or his daughter. Could live a whole life of pain and shove it down and never tell him.

He didn't want that. Not for any child of his. He wanted more.

He wasn't sure he knew how to get it, since he didn't know how to give it.

"You look terrified," Caleb said.

"Every few minutes it starts to feel really real. And I start imagining things like teenage years. I don't even know how I ended up being the one sitting here being worried about this."

"Chill out. It's a fetus still," Gabe said, clapping him on the back. "It can't give you any trouble yet."

"Yeah, but that's just not true. I have to get ready for the arrival."

"Well, first," Caleb said, standing, "you can get drunk."

And Caleb went back over to the bar and saw to ordering enough rounds to make sure he did just that.

VANESSA HAD DECIDED the first person she would talk to was Ellie.

Jacob had already talked to his brothers Friday night, and she had let it set over the weekend, figuring she would just talk to Ellie on Monday. So during break she wandered over to Ellie's classroom and found her sitting there eating a sandwich.

"You're just in time," she said. "Caleb just brought me lunch."

She wasn't exactly sure how close Caleb and Ellie

were. Though it seemed to her that they essentially lived in each other's pockets. And for the first time she realized that Caleb might have already said something.

And maybe Ellie was just waiting, not wanting to intrude.

"I don't know if Caleb talked to you already," she said.

"What? I mean…I've talked to Caleb, but not about you."

"Oh. Okay. Well…it's just that I know that Jacob talked to him."

"Jacob talked to…"

"Jacob is the father of my baby," she blurted.

The silence shrank down into a flatliner, a slight buzz rising up in her ears, like confirmation she'd officially killed the conversation.

"No," Ellie said finally. "No. *Really?* I mean, I figured that maybe I didn't know the father, considering you hadn't told me. But I was trying to be good and wait. And I really did not expect that it was a man who is basically *family to me.*"

"We just went to the doctor on Friday and made sure everything was all right. And he told his brothers a few days ago. I had to make sure they knew first." She winced. "Are you mad at me for not telling?"

"No," Ellie said quickly. "I'm not. I—I can't even imagine the added stress of dealing with not being in a relationship with the guy you're having a baby with."

Of course, poor Ellie had experienced the heartbreak of losing the man she loved before their baby came into the world. There were different hardships.

Vanessa, for one, was happy to bear this one. The other seemed too crushing.

"Did you know him?" Ellie asked. "I mean, before you left town."

"Not really. He's older than me. By a few years. But I knew who he was. And…when I had my miscarriage when I was seventeen, he was the paramedic who responded to my call. I called because it hurt so bad, and I was bleeding so much, I was afraid that something really serious was happening to me. I mean, I guess something was. But you know, I was afraid I was dying. Like, really dying. I called, and he helped me. I refused treatment. I didn't want to be taken to the hospital. I didn't want my parents to ever find out. I think he's the one who made sure the bill was sent in my name. So I was able to take it down to the office and deal with everything myself."

"Vanessa…that's awful. I can't believe you went through that alone."

"I mean, we all go through things. And that's the thing." She pressed a hand to her chest. "He was so kind to me. He made me feel not so alone. And it's a horrible memory, but I can't have it without seeing him there." She sighed. "Apparently I can't be alone in the same room as him without tearing his clothes off."

Ellie looked down at her sandwich as if roast beef could potentially offer clarity. "That is…a lot."

"Yes."

"You never told your family about the miscarriage?"

"No."

"Did you have anyone? Anyone at all?"

She shook her head. "I didn't want my friends to know, because I didn't want to talk about…any of it. Not about the conception, which I was too drunk to remember. Not about the… So I just went inside myself.

But myself wasn't a very safe space. It was sharp and sad, and I wanted something to dull it. And I thought, well, I had fun at parties. And I couldn't even remember having sex with my boyfriend thanks to pills and alcohol. And I wanted to forget. I stole some pain medication from my dad and it made me feel good when nothing else had." She swallowed hard. "I thought I could handle it on my own. I thought I was handling it. But I wasn't."

Ellie reached out and put her hand on Vanessa's. "You were so young."

"Yes. And I—I made some mistakes, but I've also forgiven myself for a lot of them. I was hurt and I didn't know what to do. I was ashamed of being pregnant in the first place." She took a deep breath. "That's why I try not to do shame now. Shame is what kept me quiet. And maybe if I'd… Maybe if I'd talked to someone… I mean, who knows."

Ellie offered her a small smile. "I know a lot about what-ifs. But the biggest thing I know for sure about them is they don't change anything, they just drive you nuts. You can't wonder what might have happened if something had gone differently. Because it didn't.

"I wish I'd known you," Ellie said.

"Me too," Vanessa said.

"I'm glad Jacob was the one who was there for you."

She nodded slowly. "Yes. I am too. But it's… The past and the present are just kind of a weird twisted knot of fate that I can't really sort out. He was there for the miscarriage. He's responsible for this pregnancy."

Ellie set the sandwich down and adjusted it self-consciously on the plate. "Are you in a relationship?"

"No," she said. "No. We're not. We can't be. Because what if it went wrong and ruined it? We don't actually know each other. That's the problem. There's this big chunk of shared history, and because of that, like, an unearned sense of intimacy. It's all just really messed up."

"Yeah, that is…a tangle."

"He wants to help me raise the baby. And I appreciate that so much. I also don't really know how to deal with another person." She let out a breath. "I'm not sure I know how to deal with anything very well."

"None of us know what we're doing," Ellie said, taking a bite of her sandwich. "I don't. I look at Amelia sometimes and I…I still can't believe I'm her mother. Some days I'm so bone tired I swear I'm a ninety-year-old woman. Other days I look around and think…how am I a mom? And a teacher? And a widow? How am I all these things when I still feel like a high school girl who hasn't figured any of life out at all."

Vanessa sat down on a stool and sighed. "That is… oddly comforting."

"To know I still don't know how to parent in spite of my wall of panic books?"

"Yes. Though I know all the things I don't want to be. I guess I can start there."

"Sure. But you know these things are little more… dynamic in practice than in theory."

"Yes," Vanessa said, feeling resolute. "I can figure this out."

Ellie chewed and nodded, but said nothing. And Vanessa had the distinct impression she was being placated.

Vanessa appreciated Ellie's input. And she appreciated that the other woman was trying to make her feel better. But in reality, a seed of certainty had planted itself in her stomach, and now that it was there, she was going to cling to it with everything she had. She could do this. And yes, Jacob was going to help her raise the baby, but they would live separately. They would have separate lives.

The baby would be the only bridge, and Vanessa would be able to control her world and in all the ways that she felt necessary. Jacob was a good man. She didn't know him that well, but the way that he took accountability for the death of Clint told her plenty. He was a man who understood responsibility.

And yeah, she had been a little bit stern with him about the issue of their child feeling like he was nothing more than a grim burden. But the fact of the matter was, there would never be anything wrong with the man standing like an anchor. Being that firm and sure backup. And another thing she knew about Jacob was that if their child ever made a mistake, he would never think less of them for it.

Her father had been that sure and certain man, but he had no bend. No forgiveness in him. And that had been half of what made it so difficult when she'd made mistakes.

And maybe she'd been testing him. Testing the bonds of his love.

But she'd found the end of it. So ultimately, it was difficult to regret testing.

Except the consequences had been so heavy in the end.

But she had a feeling that her arrangement with Jacob would be perfect in many ways. Her child would have endless support without parents who were concerned about appearances. Parents who had already taken an unconventional path and forged ahead in spite of any disapproval. The only expectation they would place on their child was that he be happy.

She felt like that put them ahead of most other parents, really. It wasn't going to be about them, or their expectations for what their child would become. It was all about their child's growth and happiness.

"You look…serene," Ellie said. She didn't sound like she believed Vanessa was serene.

"I *feel* it," Vanessa said. "I feel like this might be the best thing that could've happened." And she meant it.

"Well, that's good. Since it's happening."

"I mean, we're not bitter exes or anything like that. That should make it simple anyway."

"And what about when you meet someone else? And you want to get married?"

"I don't know that I will," Vanessa said. "I'll be focusing on my work and on raising my child. There will be plenty of time for a relationship later. I've gone a long time without being in one."

"Which ended well," Ellie said, looking meaningfully at Vanessa's stomach.

Vanessa's lips twitched. "That was different. And who knows, maybe I will discreetly have those kinds of relationships. But I'm really not in the market for a romantic relationship."

"Right. So what about when Jacob gets married, and he has a wife? And that wife is your child's stepmother?"

The thought made Vanessa feel brittle. "Then we'll cross that bridge when we come to it," she said, smiling widely. In her current state, she feared it might crack her face. "But honestly, the more people our child has in its life to support him, the better."

"Yes. People who don't actually have kids yet. They're always so confident in how that will work out."

"I understand that life is messy," Vanessa said, irritation riling her up. "I know that nothing is guaranteed. But I also already know that, and I'm not going to make things difficult for my child by expecting things to go exactly the way I have them planned."

"You are literally already planning things in advance."

"I'm planning on rolling with the punches," Vanessa corrected.

"Yeah, you're leaving out feelings, though."

"I'm *not*. I'm thinking a lot about support and love and warmth."

"And nothing about possessiveness, about worry and anxiety. All those things…they end up having a big part in what kind of parent you are. I'm not trying to be discouraging. I actually think it's good to accept that you can't plan everything. Because otherwise… well, otherwise when you find it's not going according to your plans you're going to think you did something wrong. When in reality it's just…you can never fully control what's going to happen in your relationship with another person. And that's what a child is. Another person."

"Well," Vanessa said, feeling resolved. "What I do know is that I'm not going to handle things the way my family did."

"It's not a bad place to start," Ellie agreed.

"Well, I better let you get back to your sandwich."

"I really can't believe that Jacob is the father of your baby." She wrinkled her nose. "He's kind of like a brother to me. But…I do feel like I have to know."

"Know what?"

The look on Ellie's face could only be described as "curiously appalled." "How good is he?"

"Really?" Vanessa asked.

"I'm a celibate woman," Ellie said. "Single parenting. Plus…other things."

Well, that answered Vanessa's question about Caleb anyway.

"Why do you need to know?" Vanessa pressed.

"Because I am perverse in that way. And it is a thing you sometimes wonder about men who you've known for a long time."

Vanessa could honestly say she'd never wondered about random men. But far be it from her to spoil Ellie's fantasy. "Well," she started. "We had a fight that ended in sex against the wall, and I didn't even think about a condom. I think that is a pretty decent answer to that question."

Ellie got a faraway look on her face. "Well, that sounds…nice."

"Nice isn't the word I would use."

She was not about to admit to the finger painting. Or to the fact that they'd had sex in a classroom. Not when Ellie was the one who had hired her. It all seemed just a little bit wrong.

"I've just kind of had to forget about sex," she said somewhat morosely.

"You don't…*have* to have," Vanessa said.

"Even if I could find the time, I don't know how to find the man," she said. "And anyway, right now it feels… I just haven't figured it out yet. I don't think I've moved on enough."

"Oh. I can understand that."

"It's just sex has always been linked to emotion for me. And that emotion is still tied up in someone that's gone. I don't want a romantic…thing. Not now. I could be with someone else, but I'm afraid of it becoming some weird sexual surrogacy thing and I really don't want that."

"Well, that's also fair enough."

"But it doesn't mean I can't wistfully ponder what it might be like to have a guy lose a little control and take me against a wall—"

"And get you pregnant," Vanessa said.

Ellie pulled a face. "No. My fantasy is dead. Another very good reason not to get involved with someone sexually at the moment. I love my daughter. I do not want to single parent more than one child."

"You're really selling the parenting thing."

"I don't have to sell it to you." Ellie lifted a brow. "You already bought the starter kit."

"Yes, yes, indeed. In fairness, they sell it to you as—"

"Sex against a wall." She nodded sagely.

"Yes. And then it grows into something else completely."

"You know if you ever need anything…"

"I'm sure I'll be reading your panic library soon."

"That's what it's there for."

Vanessa walked out of Ellie's classroom feeling very cheered. She could do this. And she would.

They would do it. Together.

But separately.

Yes, as far as she was concerned, it was basically an ideal situation.

CHAPTER FIFTEEN

It was…interesting to be at the ranch now that everyone knew. Well, the kids didn't know. And as long as Jacob didn't have to deal with that, he wasn't going to.

Today, they were painting outdoors because the warm fall weather was bound to wane into very *cold* fall weather without much notice, and Vanessa thought they might benefit from experimenting with how natural light changed the way the colors looked.

Of course, painting profanity looked much the same no matter what light you were in, so it was all the same to Aiden.

But not to Jacob.

Vanessa's light brown hair was loose and fluttering in the early-autumn breeze. She was also wearing a long dress that swirled around her slender legs, and Jacob couldn't quite help but picture how those legs had felt wrapped around him.

He shifted uncomfortably, taking in a deep breath as he watched her talk about color and light, her gestures broad and her face filled with enthusiasm.

"Is she your girl or something?"

Jacob looked down at Aiden. "What?"

"You look at her like she is," Aiden said.

"I'm just looking," Jacob said.

Aiden shrugged. "Not that I blame you."

Jacob crossed his arms and looked down at the kid. "Did I ask?"

"I was just saying."

"Well, she's not," Jacob said. Though the response felt disingenuous, considering that Vanessa felt like his in just about every way.

"Is there something you'd like to share with the class?"

Jacob looked up at Vanessa, who was looking at him. "No."

"We were talking about color and light," Aiden said, his tone serious.

Calvin didn't look up from his canvas, and Marco snickered.

Calvin had started to get into painting, his work becoming more and more intricate. Still not representative in a visual sense of what was around them, but it was definitely something inside him. Though today, there were lighter colors, mixed with abstract shapes of the outdoors. And Jacob was forced to really recognize the fact that this work that Vanessa believed in so strongly really did matter. And that it really was doing something to change these kids.

Even Aiden, who was a stubborn ass, was responding to his life here on the ranch.

Vanessa lifted a brow. "Somehow I don't believe that."

Vanessa stretched and fanned herself lightly, even though it wasn't that warm. "I'm hot," she said.

"Yeah," Aiden agreed.

That earned him snickers from both boys.

Jacob elbowed him. "Watch it."

Aiden looked up at him, his expression clearly telegraphing, *You said she wasn't your girl.*

"When I was a kid," Vanessa said, "we used to go to an ice cream place on the coast. Tillamook. And we would get marionberry pie ice cream. It was so good." She smiled. "I want some of that now."

"If you're not going to give us all ice cream, it doesn't seem fair to talk about it," Marco said.

"Just thinking. Sometimes I don't think I have good family memories," she said. "But I do. It's just easy to erase all of the good stuff when you want to be angry."

Calvin looked up at her. "I only have bad ones."

There was an uncomfortable silence that settled over the group. Vanessa walked over to him and put her hand on his thin shoulder. "But that doesn't mean it's all you can have. From today on, you can make your own memories. Your own choices. You might not ever be able to fix the situation you came from, but you can make your life whatever you want it to be. Make your own good memories."

"What do you know?" Marco asked. "You're an art teacher."

"I'm an addict," Vanessa said.

All three boys looked at her, their expressions shocked. "What?" Calvin asked.

"I'm a drug addict. So trust me, I've seen a lot of things. I've done a lot of things. I've had a lot of bad things happen to me. And when I was your age… the things that hurt me, they weren't my fault. But I made a lot of bad choices because of my pain, and that was my fault."

"You seriously did drugs?" Calvin asked.

"Very seriously," Vanessa said. "A lot of them. And I missed my rent, got evicted—more than once—lost friends. Terrified and alienated my family. Slept on the streets, on couches, with men I didn't know. But I got out of that. I got sober. Someone had to make me. And they handed me a paintbrush in rehab, and here I am. So when I say you can change your lives, when I say you can find good things, I say it because I've done it. Because I've had bad things happen to me. And I've done bad things. But they're not who I am."

The kids said nothing to that. Calvin bent his head and he just continued to work on his painting, but Jacob had a feeling those simple words had impacted him deeply.

That was the woman who was going to be the mother of his child, and a strong, visceral sense of possessiveness overtook him.

Something inside him, something primal and dark, that he'd never known existed, wanted to stake a claim on her. Make her the mother of all his babies.

All his babies? He wasn't even sure that he was on board with having one.

But there was a biological shift happening inside him that he didn't think he could control or explain.

They finished their paintings outside, and when they began to walk back toward the classroom, Aiden elbowed him, the way that Jacob had elbowed him earlier. "If I were you, I'd get her some of that ice cream."

"What?" Jacob asked.

"She said she was craving that ice cream." Aiden

looked at him conspiratorially. "You should get her some."

"Are you giving me...relationship advice?"

"Man, I don't know anything about relationships. But I know a lot about Netflix and chill."

"I'm not going to...Netflix and chill with Vanessa."

"Yeah, right."

"I'm *not*."

"Because you already have," Aiden said.

"I..." Jacob decided right then that he kind of hated kids.

But there was apparently nothing he could do about that at this current point in his life. He was surrounded by them. Teenage ones. And he was going to have an infant one soon enough.

"You have," Aiden said. "And if you want to *keep* doing it...ice cream."

The stupid thing was, the kid was right. He needed to get Vanessa some of that ice cream.

Because no, he wasn't going to...Netflix and chill, or whatever he'd said. But he was trying to build a partnership with her. Build some trust. And bringing her ice cream wasn't a bad place to start.

Actually, he needed to talk to her about the house. About the fact that he was starting to think the best thing for them to do would be to live together.

Yeah, okay, she didn't want to get married. But, at least for the first few years of the kid's life, while they were both single, it made sense for them to share a house. They were already down the road from each other. Why not share a space completely?

Instead of having two cribs, diaper-changing stations, whatever the hell else babies had. Why not just combine and have one?

Yeah. That was the kind of conversation you started with ice cream.

And Jacob felt determined.

"I'm going to make sure you get an A in this class," he whispered to Aiden.

"This is starting to feel creepy," Aiden said.

"You started it," Jacob said.

"Yeah, man, but I'm a troubled *youth*. I'm inappropriate."

"Something tells me that you're a lot less trouble than you get credit for."

Aiden shrugged. "I'm smart. Doesn't mean I'm not troubled."

"Good point."

"You know what she said about memories," Aiden said.

"Yeah."

"My memories of here won't be so bad."

Something felt warm at the center of Jacob's chest, but he didn't say anything in response to the kid. Instead, they just walked back to the classroom together.

And for the first time in a while, Jacob didn't feel quite so lost.

BY THE TIME Vanessa got home, she was exhausted. She was sweaty, and she was exhausted. And hungry.

She thought back to her memory of the creamery and her stomach growled. She should have stopped and gotten ice cream on the way home.

And *pie*. Pie would be so good with the ice cream.

Or if she could have found marionberry pie ice cream, just like her memory…

She stopped for a moment, suddenly a little bit wistful.

Good memories of her family, of her life at home, reminded her why she'd come back here originally. Reminded her that there was more than this stilted, painful relationship they had now.

So often she remembered her mother wringing her hands and worrying. Her father being upset. Disapproving.

And the worst part was…

She'd proved them right, hadn't she?

They'd been afraid that she would get herself in trouble, and she had.

They'd been afraid that the worst would happen and she would become a teenage mother, and she would have, if not for a malfunction in biology.

They'd been afraid she would take drugs. She had.

They had been afraid she would put her life in danger, end up in poverty, sleep with strangers.

She had done all those things.

She'd moved away and moved in with a bunch of friends, and that had been okay for a while. They'd all worked and paid portions of rent. But people left, and eventually it was Vanessa and one other friend, and two girls more interested in clubbing and getting high than working their part-time jobs and paying rent.

Eventually they'd gotten evicted. And Vanessa had not liked living without a roof over her head at all.

A boyfriend had solved that pretty quickly. But their

relationship had ended very badly when she'd ended up selling his Xbox for a bump.

She'd been back out on her ass. Bar hookups had gotten her a warm bed and sometimes drugs. A couple of times one guy lasted a few months, and she'd been pretty stable in terms of places to stay, but even guys who were into drugs didn't enjoy being around a serious addict. She couldn't keep a job.

When she'd gotten arrested she'd been living in a pretty well-known drug spot, in another group housing situation. One of her roommates had overdosed, and Vanessa had called an ambulance.

The other woman had survived the OD, thankfully. But Vanessa had wound up getting arrested for possession.

She'd been a mess. And her arrest had been the best thing that had ever happened to her.

Before that, she'd been her family's worst nightmare. Everything they'd said she would be.

Sometimes she even wondered if she was entitled to her anger.

She hated complicated. She hated remembering that her parents were good as well as frustrating.

That they'd bought her and Olivia ice cream and taken her to the ocean, that they'd bought her nice clothes and that her mother had taken her to lunch, just her, every year on her and Olivia's birthday. And she had taken Olivia out too, but separately. That she had always made an effort to let the girls be individuals.

But then, she always remembered her mother crying and saying maybe she shouldn't have.

Because maybe if she had dressed them alike,

maybe if she had treated them as a unit, Vanessa would've been more like Olivia.

Or maybe Olivia would have been more like me, she'd fired back.

No. Because Olivia is stronger than that.

Vanessa's throat got tight. She blinked rapidly and then put her hand on her stomach.

What would her family think about this?

It doesn't matter.

It doesn't matter.

There was a firm knock on her door, and she jumped. Then she walked over and looked out the side window and saw Jacob standing there holding a paper bag. She frowned and pulled the door open. "What are you doing here?"

"I brought you ice cream."

He held the bag up, and Vanessa's stomach went hollow.

He had brought her ice cream. Because she had been talking about ice cream today in the art class.

She really didn't know what to say to that. Didn't know what to do. So she was standing there in the doorway completely frozen, probably staring at him like he had grown a second head.

"Are you okay?"

"Yeah," she said, stepping aside. "I...I just didn't expect... Thank you."

He made his way inside and set the bag on the counter, pulling out a familiar pale ice cream tub.

"Marionberry pie," he said.

"You *really* went and found Tillamook ice cream?"

"I did. Though, to make sure no credit is given to me when it's not due...it's not hard to find here."

"I guess not. I'm the one that was away. Not the ice cream."

"Bowls?"

"You don't have to do that," she said.

"I want to." He made a move to open the cabinet and then stopped, his eyes resting on a painting she'd hung on a blank space in the kitchen wall.

One of hers.

It was one she'd done shortly after getting sober, of a girl standing next to a mountain, sun shining down on her face.

"Is this yours?" he asked.

She didn't know why it made her feel uncomfortable. When the boys painted she always painted with them, so he'd seen her work before, even if it had been in a classroom setting.

This was different from painting along with the boys. This was personal, and she knew that.

"Yes."

"Is she you?" he asked.

"Kind of." She shifted in her seat. "I did it right after I finished rehab. At the point when the decision to be sober was mine, and not the court's."

"Tell me about that," he said, his voice getting rough. "We've talked about your addiction but what about... What about what you've done since? What about making the choice to stop? And the art. I know it meant something to you but..."

Her heart stilled, then thundered forward.

No one had ever asked her about this. People were much more fascinated with addiction than with sobriety.

"My first paintings were rough. Just colors and shapes," she said.

"Do you still have them?"

She blinked. "Yes. They're in the extra bedroom here."

"Can I see?"

She stood slowly and nodded. "Sure. Come with me."

He followed her down the hall and she opened the door. The room where she kept her art supplies, her easel all set up, her pottery, her crafting implements, was a little bit of a mess. Her desk was cluttered, her case for her supplies overflowing. Canvases were stacked against the back wall. She had too many.

She pulled out her first one. A big splotch of red. Angry brushstrokes. Angry, angry, angry. Then she pulled the second one out. Black. Then the next one. Blue.

For all the sadness.

"Once I felt sad…" She held up the picture. "Well, once I let myself feel sad it was the beginning of moving forward. Once I got through the anger. The emptiness. And then I realized it was all I would have if I didn't change something. I had some hard things happen to me. My grief, my fear and my shame over the pregnancy and the miscarriage…no one could have stopped me from going through that. But I didn't need to keep putting myself through more hell. And once I realized that, once I sat with the part I'd played in my own destruction… I realized I didn't want to break myself anymore. I wanted to rebuild."

"What did you do after that?"

"I thought about getting certified in counseling,

specifically for addiction and recovery. Because the idea of immersing myself in sobriety seemed like a good one. But I kept painting, and the more I went back to painting for myself the more I realized it was such a great way to…to heal. All kinds of pain. To get to the emotional heart of that pain and figure out how to root it out. To put the feelings inside me that scared me so much, right out in front of me, for me and all the world to see. So I couldn't ignore it. Not anymore." A small smile tugged at the corners of her lips. "Somehow putting it out there like that made it into something I could handle."

She took a breath. "Anyway, I took some classes. Lots of classes. On different mediums of art, on color theory and line theory and then I did get training in counseling because that was part of what I wanted to do. I started programs at different community centers in LA."

"When you decide to do something you go all in, don't you?" he asked, the expression of awe on his face like a kick of adrenaline to her system.

"It was…freedom. I wanted to do as much as I could. I'd been crushed for years. Opiates were my boss, not me. And I suddenly found…me again. Motivation. Conviction. I was in charge, and I wanted to run with it. It's been five years, and I crave this, this control and clarity more than I ever craved any substance. And if I ever questioned myself, I looked at that picture in the kitchen."

"What does it mean?"

"She's looking ahead. She's looking to the light. And she has her back turned on the darkness. And I remember, that's what I did. I turned my back on all that ugliness so I could move on. And I have to keep moving."

He nodded slowly. "It's a good way to look at life. We've got to move forward."

"Yeah. How about we move forward to ice cream?"

"Sounds good to me."

He went back into the kitchen and helped himself to bowls from the cupboard, and found her silverware drawer, taking out a big spoon and digging it into the ice cream.

He was so big and broad, and he filled up the tiny kitchen in the little house.

A baby would look so tiny in his arms.

The realization made her stomach knot up.

She watched him dish two generous bowlfuls, and then gratefully accepted the offered portion.

She didn't have a dining table because she lived here by herself, and tended to curl up on the couch while she ate, or just stand at the island in the kitchen.

She took the bowl into the living room and sat on the end of the couch, drawing her knees up.

Jacob sat in the chair across from the couch. There was something absurdly human about him just then, sitting there eating ice cream. And it was a funny thing because the rest of him just wasn't…all that human. He was so muscular and broad, and quite frankly a savior in her memory half the time, and the act of eating ice cream on a small chair just seemed very mortal, all things considered.

"That was very nice of you," she said.

"I would love to take credit," he said. "But Aiden told me I needed to buy you ice cream."

"Aiden did?"

"Yes. He thought it might help me hook up with you."

Vanessa sputtered, "And he thought you might want to do that *why*?"

"I assume because I'm a man and you're a woman."

"Teenagers," she said. She took a bite of the ice cream to help cool the heat that was rising inside her.

"I have to tell you, that while the ice cream is a genuine gift, I did have a purpose other than ice cream behind my visit."

She blinked. "We did agree—"

"I know. And I'm not reneging on that. But I've been thinking a lot about my living situation, and yours."

"And?"

"I want to build us a house."

She dropped her spoon, the handle clattering against the edge of the bowl. "What?"

"I think it makes sense if we live together. At least for the first few years."

"I said that I didn't want to get married."

"And I didn't say anything about marriage. Or a relationship. But you have to admit, the idea of having two nurseries, two cribs, two of everything doesn't make a whole lot of sense. We live so close to each other anyway. It doesn't make any sense to have double the baby gear, does it? We could divide the labor so much easier if we shared a place."

"That feels…weird?"

"Are you telling me this entire arrangement doesn't feel a little bit weird?"

"I don't know. But I don't know how that would work." In fact, the very idea made her feel panicky.

Like she wanted to jump out the window. Or maybe jump out of her skin.

She had her space. Her little house. Her life.

Already, this pregnancy was completely outside her plan. But she could deal with it. The Jacob variable, though, that was something she was having difficulty wrapping her mind around.

"I don't like…sharing space," she said. "I have routines. I have a life. I don't like the idea of—"

"But this house would be ours," he said. "I mean, the design of it would be partly up to you. Decorating, I don't even care about that. It would have an art room. Bigger than what you have here. Way bigger."

This was the problem with sharing herself with someone. Then he knew how to use those things against her.

Was she so easy she was swayed by an offer of an art room?

Well. Yes.

But also it was an art room attached to a house made for her and the baby.

And he would be there. Close.

Which was both exhilarating and terrifying.

"But what about when it doesn't work anymore? What about when one of us ends up in a different relationship?"

"Look, I'm not a relationship guy. The fact of the matter is, Vanessa, if I was going to get married, it would be to the mother of my baby. I don't want to get married. I don't want to be in love."

"That doesn't mean you're not going to have relationships."

"Hookups."

The very idea made her skin crawl. She did not want to be in a house where Jacob was having hookups. She didn't want their child in a house where he was having *hookups*.

"Right, well, I don't want to be exposed to that, and I don't want our child exposed to it either. So it makes sense—"

"You're telling me that you're going to stay celibate for the next eighteen years?"

"I had been celibate for five. It went okay."

"Until it didn't," he pointed out.

"I don't know. But I just—"

"You can't actually predict the future, Vanessa. I guess neither of us can say for sure where things are going to be in five years. But I know for sure that the two of us are going to try to make this work for the baby, right?"

"Yes," she said.

"I think that it makes perfect sense for the two of us to try it this way. I need a house that's childproof anyway. We live close, we work at the same place…"

"Are you suggesting that we… That we be roommates?"

"I am," he said.

It was also weird and rational. As weird and rational as she had been attempting to be with him about the whole thing. And actually, this level of it threw the absurdity of the entire thing right in her face. They'd been very unsuccessful at being unsupervised together and not tearing each other's clothes off.

They were trying to act like the feelings between them were completely neutral, because it seemed safer for them to be, but once she imagined the two of them living in a space like that it was...

But as absurd as it was, they almost had to adopt that mind-set.

And he was right. It made more sense. It would provide more stability to the kid rather than migrating back and forth between places.

He was also right—and she hated to admit it— that they couldn't see enough years into the future to know for sure if it would work out. They would just have to try it.

"But if it doesn't work out, I'll need to find a different place?"

"We'll cross that bridge when we come to it."

"Well, if I pay for the house—"

"I don't want you to pay anything," he said. "I have the money to build the house. It's my property. I own it already."

"But how will that work? If something happens and I need to move out—"

"You will never be out on your ass," he said. "That I can promise you." His blue eyes burned into hers, and she couldn't breathe. "I'm not a perfect man," he said. "I'm not even overly convinced that I'm that good of one. What I can tell you is this—if I give you my word you can bet I'll keep it."

She believed it. That was the scary part. She believed it with a strange kind of effortlessness. It wasn't hard to believe it, not when he said it like that.

"So what do we...do?" she asked. "We're just going to start planning a house?"

"Yeah," he said. "I was thinking so."

"I..." She tried to breathe around the tightness in

her chest. "I just don't really understand what's happening to my life."

"It's becoming not just your life," he said slowly. "I mean, that's what I'm realizing. My life has to have something to do with yours. Because it's going to have something to do with our child. And if we want to be successful, I think from now on it's our lives. If you have a need, it's my need too."

She frowned. "Does that go both ways?"

"I don't know about that," he said.

"Why not?"

"It seems different. When you're the one carrying the baby."

"No," she said, shaking her head. "You're right, actually. It has to be… It has to be *our* lives. And that means…even if we aren't a couple, we have to consider each other's needs. Because otherwise we are going to find ourselves in a situation where we can't possibly cohabit for another minute, and everything is going to be toxic for the baby, and we don't want that."

He shook his head gravely. "No."

"So let's do it, then," she said.

"All right," he responded.

She took the last bite of her ice cream just as he did, and he stood up, reaching out toward her. She frowned, not quite sure what he wanted. He leaned in, taking hold of her bowl, and she realized he meant to take it to the kitchen for her.

"You don't have to…"

She scrambled to try to stand, but that brought her right up in front of him, their noses almost touching, a scant inch between their chests, between their bodies. Then she could feel his heat. Those blue eyes that had just shone with honesty now had heat in them, and they were burning into hers, and she found that she wanted to… She wanted to touch that heat again. Explore it.

No. This man was wound around her life in a thousand different ways, and right now she needed it all to work out for the sake of their child.

The last thing she needed was to hope for things to work out for herself.

This wasn't about her.

It couldn't be.

She shoved her ice cream bowl at him. "Thank you," she said.

"You're welcome," he said slowly, backing away from her and then walking into the kitchen, taking the bowls to the sink and rinsing them. She suddenly felt like this was all too much. Ice cream, a house and clean dishes.

The electricity every time they got near each other.

She didn't want to need him. Not like this. She couldn't afford to.

So yes, he was right. They needed to be an "us." But she also needed to remember to hold part of herself back.

To keep something of herself for her.

"So," he said, turning back toward her and crossing his arms over his broad chest. "When are we going to talk to your family?"

VANESSA HAD ASKED herself about a hundred times what she was thinking since putting together the dinner at her parents' house.

She didn't know why she was telling her entire family at once. What she should have done was get together with her mother on neutral territory, at Mustard Seed or Bellissima and tell her, and then see if maybe she would tell Olivia and her father on Vanessa's behalf.

All day at school, she hadn't been able to think of anything else. The dinner loomed large over her head. And Jacob was watching her, as if he knew something was happening, and was trying to figure out what.

She knew that he would want to be there. She did. But she was hiding the fact that it was happening from him because she just couldn't… She didn't want him charging in there and being a white knight for her again.

Like he'd done with ice cream and houses and any number of things.

Because it was just too strange. And she didn't think she could possibly handle it.

Plus, what was she going to do? Introduce him as the father of her baby, but not her boyfriend or fiancé?

The man she was going to move in with and make a joint family with?

Why not? Why are you still hiding yourself? Why are you still trying to make them okay with who you are?

Well, she didn't know. She didn't know the answer to any of it; all she knew were her panicked feelings, and the thousand ways she had run through the scenario in her mind.

Someone would probably ask if she had used drugs at all since the baby was conceived.

That was the really upsetting question that she was waiting for.

The one that she was going to have to call on all of her weaponized serenity to handle.

While no one might come out and call her irresponsible, they would certainly imply it. There would be a lot of concern, and that came back around to the fact that no one thought she was overly competent.

"Okay," Jacob said when they were alone in the classroom. "What's going on?"

"Nothing. Just…stuff."

"You are a really bad liar."

"That isn't true," she said. "I was a really good liar in high school. I used to get away with a ton of stuff."

"Well, you're bad at it now. Must be the sobriety."

"Probably," she said wearily. "I don't want to tell you what's going on."

"Then that's a sure bet that you should," he said, walking over to where she was standing and planting his hands on the countertop on either side of her.

He was so close, the scent of his skin teasing her.

She wondered how long it would take for her to forget that she was attracted to him. How long it would take for her to begin to see him as commonplace.

"Vanessa," he said. "It's us, remember?"

"I'm seeing my parents tonight," she blurted.

"And you don't want me to go with you?"

"No," she said.

"And why the hell not?"

"Because. Because they're going to ask questions. Uncomfortable questions. And I don't want to—"

"You're ashamed," he said.

"Yes," she confirmed. "And I hate that because shame is something that has created a whole lot of damage in my life, and I've done so much work to get rid of it. But my parents excel at making me feel that way."

"I want to go," he said.

"Are you going to...follow me there and come in without my permission?"

He looked at her long and hard. "Yeah," he said. "I am."

And in that moment, she realized she almost needed him to. Because asking for help felt beyond her. If she asked for help, it meant she needed it. If she needed his help, then she might need him.

But if he didn't give her a choice, then...there wasn't a whole lot she could do.

"I'm coming with you," he said like he'd read her mind.

She knew he couldn't read her mind, but even still, she wasn't offended by him pushing in that way. She wanted him to. She couldn't help herself.

"Fine. You can come with me. But it's going to be weird."

"Better weird on a team, right?"

"Who are you?" she said. "Because I have to tell you, my initial impression of you was not that you were a big team player. Or that you were just waiting to join your life to someone else's."

"I forgot what being alive was about," he said. "Up there on the mountain. Just feeling guilty over all the things that I've done that have been failures. But eventually, if I want to be better, I guess I have to make a choice to show up. That's what helping Gabe out here at the school is about. And it means I have to step up now too. I can't just not talk about this and make it go away. Facing it head-on… That seems the way to go to me."

That made her deflate a little bit. Because wasn't it so wrong to just hope that he wanted to be near her? That it was about her and not his desperate sense that he needed to make right things he had done wrong?

Well, it didn't really matter. That was the main thing. It didn't matter because the only thing that really mattered was the baby.

Do not need him.

"Okay," she said slowly. "Let's go to my parents' house."

CHAPTER SIXTEEN

VANESSA HADN'T BEEN back to her childhood home—by design—since she'd come back to town. It was full of so many memories—good and bad—and just looking at the beautiful two-story home now made her feel like she might be crushed by them.

By regret. For her own actions and the actions of her parents. The distance that felt impossible to bridge with a dinner.

But she supposed it had to start somewhere.

Yay. With a dinner where you tell them you're pregnant out of wedlock.

She realized Jacob had been here once before. When she'd miscarried in the downstairs bathroom while her parents had been out of town.

Pieces of her life were converging in such weird ways and she couldn't say she liked it much.

Vanessa took a breath and rang the bell. The soft chimes were very much in keeping with her mother's taste. Nothing too loud or startling.

Vanessa had always been loud and startling.

Oh, for heaven's sake, Vanessa. Stop feeling persecuted in advance.

The door opened, and Vanessa's eyes collided with her mother's.

A range of emotion moved through her face in a matter of moments. Happiness. Wariness. Irritation.

"Vanessa, it's good to see you."

"You too," Vanessa said.

She had her hands clasped in front of her. So did her mom.

Neither of them moved to hug the other.

Vanessa wanted to, but she didn't know if her mother did.

"I didn't know you were bringing a guest."

Her mother was smiling but Vanessa realized, too late now, that not telling her mom there would be another person would make Tamara Logan feel absolutely panicked about her hospitality.

She would be short food, short a place setting and wondering if the guest had dietary restrictions of any kind.

"I'm sorry," Vanessa said quickly. "It was a last-minute thing, I didn't think that Jacob could come, but he could, and I felt like it was important. This is Jacob Dalton. He isn't a vegetarian and he eats gluten."

Jacob shot Vanessa a strange look.

"Nice to meet you," Jacob said, sticking his hand out.

He looked every inch like the kind of man her parents would be thrilled for her to bring home. Salt of the earth, cowboy, a man who put on his Sunday-go-to-meetin' clothes for a dinner with a woman's parents.

Thankfully he didn't look like a dirty sex fiend who'd painted her like a canvas and screwed her till she screamed.

Because that would not impress her parents so much.

"Of course, I know your parents," her mother said to Jacob.

"I'm sure they know you," he returned. "But then, I think everyone in town does."

"Likely," she said, a small smile teasing her lips. It wasn't conceit. It was simply true. The Logans were a Gold Valley institution. "Come on in."

The house smelled wonderful. Like her childhood. Like her mother's Sunday dinners, like warmth and happiness and *together*.

It made her ache.

She saw her dad and her stomach twisted. It had been a few months since she'd seen him. They'd had lunch when she'd come to visit just before she'd decided to move back. But it was different to see him here. In this house that held so much of herself. So much of her history.

Her dad looked at Jacob, the crease between his brows deepening. "Jacob Dalton, right?" he said. "It's nice to see you again."

He stuck his hand out, and Jacob took it, his eyes never wavering from her father's. And her father had some scary eyes that often felt like they were looking through you, so as far as she was concerned it was an epic feat. "Good to see you too."

"Vanessa," her dad said, his greeting cautious.

"Hi, Dad," she responded, her voice small.

She hated that. That she shrank down the minute she saw him. Like he might scold her.

Olivia was already there. Early of course. She said that Luke and Emma had nasty colds and had stayed home.

"You might have called ahead about that too, Olivia," their mother said.

"Sorry," Olivia responded.

"Well, now we know we'll have plenty of food," Vanessa commented brightly.

"By accident," Tamara said. "Cole, will you help me with dinner?"

Her mother was obviously slightly stressed by the whole thing, but the exchange felt…normal. Normal family normal. Not Logan family normal. And that was a strange blessing.

Cole nodded and followed his wife from the room. That left the three of them in the dining room together alone.

And Vanessa hadn't spoken to Olivia since their fight at her house a month before.

"Hi," Vanessa said softly.

"Hi," Olivia returned, looking speculatively at Jacob. "I'm Olivia," she said to Jacob. "I'm not sure if we've met."

"Probably not formally," he responded.

"I guess some things have changed since we last spoke," Olivia said.

"Yeah," Vanessa responded. "Some things."

They would be getting into what things soon enough.

Her parents returned, her father with a roast chicken he'd no doubt carved for her mother in the kitchen, her mother with a bowl of salad. She retreated again and came back with rolls and green beans.

Vanessa's mouth watered, and along with hunger came a swell of emotion. She hadn't had her mom's cooking since she was eighteen years old.

She missed it.

And things might be hard with her and her parents, things might be hard with Olivia, but they'd both cooked for her. Meals they remembered were her favorites. And that counted for something. It counted for a lot in her world.

"Vanessa is working at your family ranch, right?" Cole asked.

"Yes," Jacob responded. "I'm sure she can tell you all about it."

She'd sort of rather he did. "I'm teaching art," she said.

She could see the confusion sweep her parents' faces. It occurred to her then they had no idea she painted and did sculpture. No idea of the role art played in her life, in her sobriety.

"It's made a big difference to the kids," Jacob said, bristling visibly at her parents' silence. "I'm not an art kind of guy, and I admit that I was kind of skeptical about some of the things she was talking about, but it has really changed the attitude of some of these boys."

"That's…very good, Vanessa." Her mom's smile was cautious and small, but it was there. And Vanessa clung to that.

They found a groove of light small talk. Her dad talked about retirement; her mom talked about her work planning charity luncheons and the holiday craft bazaar. They enquired politely about how she was adjusting to leaving LA and "all that sunshine" behind.

"Well, I might have lost some sun, but at least I don't have to pump my own gas," she said. "The thing I missed most of all about Oregon, not getting out of my car in the bad weather."

"Definitely an Oregon asset," Olivia said.

"Though in LA do you have bad weather?" her dad asked.

"Well, sometimes it's like the surface of the sun, so yes." She cleared her throat. "I do have…" She swallowed and looked over at Jacob. "I do have something to tell you all."

Three heads swiveled toward her, and the adrenaline made her start to shake. This was going to ruin it. She knew it right before the words came out of her mouth. And she still had to say it.

"I'm… Jacob and I…are having a baby."

Her father's expression shifted, and the friendly demeanor he'd treated Jacob to all evening vanished, replaced by pure ice.

"Are you getting married?" Cole asked.

The question was absolutely directed at Jacob. But Vanessa wasn't going to let him answer.

"No," Vanessa said. "We're not a couple."

"We're talking about some things," he said, right on the heels of her words.

"Are we?" she asked.

"We're in this together," he said, his voice soft.

Vanessa looked at her parents. Her mom was pale, her lips set in a flat line and Vanessa felt like she was living the moment she'd managed to avoid in high school.

And her mom was handling it just as well as she might have when Vanessa was seventeen.

Her mom looked at her dad, desperation in her eyes. And fear.

The fear Vanessa hated most of all. Because that actually was her fault.

She'd made them afraid for her for so many years.

"Vanessa," her mother said, her voice measured, "have you been…taking care of yourself?"

Heat rolled through Vanessa, her cheeks burning. She looked at Olivia, whose eyes had gone round and that meant that Vanessa was not imagining what her mom had just implied. And it was as shocking to Olivia as it felt to Vanessa.

She stared at her mom, waiting for her to revise her question. But Tamara Logan held her gaze, her eyes full of terror, full of steel. "Vanessa, it's important that we know the whole truth about the situation. Important for the health and safety of the baby."

Vanessa's stomach twisted.

"Is that your way of asking if I'm on drugs, Mother?" Vanessa asked.

"Well, can you blame me? Vanessa, I've done a lot of reading on the opioid crisis. Relapse is common. Ron Wyden is taking a whole thing to US Senate to try to address the growing epidemic."

"Well…great for Ron, Mom. I don't see what that has to do with me. I told you I was sober, and I am."

"You have a history of making irresponsible decisions," her mom said. "And you haven't got a long enough track record of doing the right thing for me to just assume—"

"Vanessa is one of the most responsible people I know," Jacob cut her off. "We wouldn't have hired her to work on the ranch if that weren't true. The way that she is with those kids… I've never seen anything like it. She doesn't deserve to have her sobriety called into question."

"You don't get to have an opinion," Cole said. "Not now that you've gotten my daughter in trouble and are refusing to marry her."

Rage prickled Vanessa's scalp. "*I* refused to marry

him," Vanessa said. "I'm not just going to get married to a man I'm not in love with and compound the issues we already have."

"You want us to believe that you make responsible choices, and then you go and admit that," her dad said, anger his default reaction to any high-stakes moment.

"I happen to think it's responsible to make sure you marry the right person," Vanessa said.

"Excuse me," Jacob said, cutting into the discussion. "This isn't my family. But what I know is that no one here is a teenager who's gotten in trouble. Vanessa and I are adults, and we are committed to doing whatever we have to do to make our child's life as good as possible. My parents might be unconventional, but they were happy to know they were having a grandchild. It's unfortunate that you don't feel the same."

The way he spoke, his tone even and cool, authoritative. And on her side.

It made her heart pound harder, made her hands shake.

"I didn't say that," Tamara said.

"It's apparent," he said. "Your low opinion of your own daughter keeps you from being happy for her."

Her mother looked like she'd been struck. "It's not a low opinion," she said. "But you tell me how you would react if you spent years not knowing where your child was. Sometimes not knowing if she was alive or dead. Tell me how I should trust her word when she lied every day she lived in this house as a teenager. When she hid bottles of pills and alcohol and sneaked out at night."

It was true. And that was the worst part. Sitting here, feeling angry—and in many ways rightly so—

didn't seem entirely fair when what her mother said was true.

"She isn't a teenager anymore," Jacob said. "And her entire track record, as far back as I can see, is a good one. And I trust that she'll keep being the woman that I've gotten to know. A woman that I am damn proud to have a baby with."

"Jacob," Vanessa said. "There's no point. I can only ever be one thing to them."

Because she'd been one thing for years. Because she'd withdrawn. Because she'd hidden from the judgment. Some of which she'd earned, and now she was in a tangle of pain she couldn't seem to get out of.

But someday it had to stop. Because she'd paid so much already, and she couldn't pay forever.

She swallowed hard. "This is why I've been avoiding you. And I did it until I couldn't anymore. Because you can't let me be different. You can't let me move on. It's too important to you that you hang on to all the pain that you feel over me disappointing you, to ever let me have a chance to do something other than upset you."

"It's not that simple," her father said. "We have to learn to trust you again."

Anger welled up inside her. Because her dad specifically…he had been so easy to disappoint. His trust an easy thing to lose, and once lost…apparently gone forever.

"Dad, I lost your trust the first time I ever did anything wrong. There was never any chance to come back from it with you."

"I don't need anything upsetting Vanessa," Jacob said, fury lacing every word. "She's been through enough. If you want to have any contact with her in the future, then I suggest you be prepared to treat her in the way she deserves. I won't allow you to come near her otherwise."

"I'm her father," Cole said. "You're not her husband, not her fiancé."

"I'm the man who aims to protect her with everything I am. If you need a label for that, that's too damn bad."

He took her by the arm and the two of them turned to leave the dining room. To walk out of the house.

A few moments later, she heard footsteps behind them, and when they got out onto the porch, Olivia followed them through the door.

"Vanessa…"

"Don't," Vanessa said, snapping immediately. "Don't start with your sanctimonious bullshit, Olivia. I can't stand it."

Olivia's eyes went round with pain, and Vanessa felt a kick of guilt.

Old patterns. Old habits.

The Logan family was lousy with both.

"They shouldn't have reacted that way," Olivia said. "It was wrong of them."

"Yeah, no kidding." Vanessa lifted her chin in defiance. "But you don't treat me any differently."

"I'm sorry," Olivia said. "Everyone is angry and they don't know what to do."

"*I'm* angry," Vanessa said.

"Let's go," Jacob said, putting his hand on her lower back.

"I doubt Mom and Dad expected you to come to dinner to announce your pregnancy," Olivia said.

"How did you tell Mom and Dad you were pregnant out of wedlock, Olivia? Because I know that's the one blight on your otherwise prudish record."

Olivia's face turned red. "I married Luke. And they knew that I was going to."

"Yeah," she said. "Just like they know that I'm a screwup. Forever. And there's nothing I can do or change or be to make it right for them. Or for you. Is there?"

"I'm sorry!" Olivia said, tearful. "I don't want things to be like this forever. I don't want to have you back and still not have you back."

"I'm not going to let my baby be around this," Vanessa said. "It's what made me lose it. The disapproval. Constantly. You don't know what it's like, Olivia, because everything you did was always perfect. Everything I did has been wrong. Even when I do basically the same thing as you, it's seen as wrong."

"It makes them more nervous," Olivia said. "Because of…"

"My past. But I wasn't born with a past. They never could deal with the way that I was. Neither could you."

"You didn't want me around, Vanessa," Olivia said, her voice thick with emotion. "You thought I was sanctimonious then too. Yeah, I did some of the wrong things. I know I did. When we were teenagers and I got you and your friends in trouble for skinny-dipping, you said you didn't want me to speak to you ever again. You told me you hated me. Don't act like I just walked out of your life on a whim. You didn't want me."

"*You* don't even know how much trouble I got in,"

Vanessa said. "Mom didn't speak to me for days. And then when Dad did, I wished he wouldn't."

"Yeah, well Mom got angry with me too," Olivia said. "She said she expected better from me. Like somehow it was my job to stop you. And that's how it always was, Vanessa. It was my job to be the things that you couldn't be."

"And you still think the problem is me? Did it ever occur to you it's messed up Mom and Dad can't just let us be…us. You chose their side. Not mine. A long time ago."

"What did you want me to do?" Olivia asked. "Did you want me to just let you hurt yourself? Because I know that I… I know I ruined your social life, and I know I made things difficult for you with Mom and Dad sometimes, but you were the one doing all those things. And I was afraid for you."

"But you never talked to me," Vanessa said. "You never asked me what was going on."

"What *was* going on?" Olivia asked.

Her breath caught, and she was tempted to say. But she couldn't add that to tonight. She didn't have the strength. "It doesn't matter now. What it amounts to is that they always assumed that I was doing wrong, and at a certain point I thought I might as well."

"I wasn't trying to hurt you," Olivia said. "I was trying to help you. And then after that…when I couldn't help anymore…I thought I had to be so perfect. To make up for the fact that you weren't. And the only time I wasn't was with Luke. My whole life I spent trying to make up for that. For you."

"I spent my whole life running from me," Vanessa

said. "Because Mom and Dad made me feel like I had to."

Silence settled between them, a thick blanket of tension.

"I'm sorry," Olivia said. "I'm just sorry."

"I'm done being sorry," Vanessa said. "I have to be done being sorry."

Jacob put his arm around her, and the two of them walked down the stairs.

"Wait!" Olivia said.

"We need to leave," Jacob said.

"Congratulations," Olivia said. "I don't know how to fix the past. I really don't. But I want to be in your life now. I don't want to fight with you. I don't care if you guys get married. It doesn't make any difference to me. Just be… Just be happy. Because that's what I learned I had to be. Not perfect. Happy. The life that Luke has given me is amazing. Happy. Messy. And with a lot of things that Mom would never have approved of. We took really different roads over the past ten years. But I feel like right now we're kind of meeting at a middle one. And maybe it's going to take us a long time to untangle why we're on those different roads. But in the meantime, can we just…meet here?"

She looked at her sister, at the pain on her face. Pain she'd caused. So much of this pain she'd caused. Including her own.

"I want to," Vanessa said. "I want to fix this. And I'm sorry. I'm sorry for the hurt I caused everyone. For the worry. For the pain. But at some point Mom and Dad have to quit asking me to pay for it."

"They're afraid," Olivia said. "They're afraid to hope."

"I need someone to hope with me," Vanessa said.

"I will."

Vanessa put her hand on her chest and tried to stanch the flow of pain radiating from there. "Thank you."

JACOB'S HEART WAS pounding from what had just happened. From the rage that was pouring through his veins. Yes, maybe Vanessa's family had a past history with her that meant they questioned her and her sobriety, but it wasn't up to him to feel sympathy.

Not when his job was to stand by her. No matter what.

Whatever she was to him, she was the mother of his child, and that mattered.

He opened the door for her and then got inside. Once the door was closed Vanessa put her hands on her face. "I'm sorry. That's what I was trying to spare you from."

"No, I wanted to be there. Because I wanted to make sure that you had someone there to protect you."

"Why do you want to protect me? We aren't…anything. Nothing but… We're having a baby."

"I could never say you were nothing to me, Vanessa," he said, his gut tightening.

Nothing. How could she be nothing to him when being near her like this made his skin feel electric?

The fact of the matter was, being near her was a particular kind of sensual torture. He missed touching her. He missed kissing her.

Both of the times they'd been together had been hot and frantic, and he wished more than anything that he could stretch her out in the bed and spend hours exploring her body.

He also understood why that wasn't the best idea.

"We should think about getting married," he said.

"I really can't do that," Vanessa said.

"Why not?" In his mind, marriage would solve a hell of a lot of things. At first, it had seemed like a bad idea. But…now…

"I don't want to get married to satisfy them."

"Is that the only reason you don't want to get married?"

"I don't want my children growing up in a weird, toxic home environment either."

"We are not them," he said, gesturing back toward the house. "And I'm not my parents either."

"I don't want to go home," she said abruptly. "Let's go to the saloon."

"The saloon that you've been avoiding?"

"I want a soda," she said. "And maybe chicken wings. That sounds good."

"All right," he said. "Bar food it is."

They drove in silence back into town, down the main street, past the quaint brick buildings that made up the small gold-rush town. They stopped in front of the Gold Valley Saloon, which miraculously had a parking space up against the curb right by the door. The neon sign outlined a gold miner, kneeling down and looking at sparkling pieces of the rock in his pan. Jacob came here all the time, but usually just to meet his brothers. Sometimes to hook up.

But never with a woman.

They would be making a statement, and it was only going to confirm what he was beginning to think was inevitable.

That they needed to make it official.

The inside of the bar was packed full of people. Some playing darts on boards against the scarred back wall, a couple playing pool. Some girls who looked like they might be packing fake IDs were at the jukebox and chose pop music that overrode the Tim McGraw that had been on a moment before.

That wasn't going to bode well with the locals.

He and Vanessa walked up to the bar, and Laz, the owner of the Gold Valley Saloon, came over, smiling broadly. "Beer?"

"I'll just take a Diet Coke."

"I'll have a Coke too," Jacob said.

"You don't have to do that," Vanessa said.

"I'm not doing it because you're sober," he said. "I'm doing it because you're pregnant."

"That doesn't make any sense," Vanessa said.

"Yes, it does. Men do that all the time. Because their partner is pregnant."

"Well, I'm not your partner, and I don't drink whether I'm pregnant or not," she pointed out.

"Still want a Coke?" Laz asked, looking between the two of them.

"Yes," Jacob returned.

"Congratulations," Laz added.

He didn't sound overly surprised, but then Jacob had a feeling that as a bartender, Laz was pretty difficult to surprise.

He got the rundown on everyone all the time. Whether he wanted it or not.

"Thanks," Jacob said.

And that was it from Laz, who didn't feel the need to interrogate them at all. Which was something of a relief.

The two of them looked over the menu on the bar top in front of them and decided to order french fries, chicken wings and potato skins.

They put in the order, and when Laz came back with their Cokes, they found a table to sit down at. No sooner had Vanessa taken a sip than a booming voice pronounced her name. "Vanessa Logan?" The man walked over to them, about their age, his hair thinning slightly, his stomach round with evidence from how much he enjoyed the beer here. "I haven't seen you in ages. Where the hell have you been?"

Vanessa froze, looking white-faced. "Jared," she said. "I…did not expect to see you."

"You should've let me know you were back in town."

She blinked. "Why…would I have ever wanted to see you?"

"Are you still mad about us having a fight when we were in high school?"

"I—I need to go."

She pushed back from the table and walked out of the bar, and Jacob went after her. "Vanessa," he said. But she was already halfway in the truck. "Vanessa!"

"Who the hell is that?"

"He—he's the man who got me pregnant. The first time."

"What happened?"

She looked over at him, her face white like a ghost, her eyes full of tears. "I don't know. Because I don't remember. I don't remember having sex with him."

"What?"

"We took, like, a grab bag of pills at a party plus alcohol. I passed out, I think. Or maybe I was in a blackout and I was conscious and talking. Maybe I told him I wanted to have sex. *He* said I wanted it. But I don't remember. And I wasn't totally sure what happened… But I was afraid. I was so afraid and then my period didn't come. And it just didn't come. And I knew… I knew that he… I can't even remember my first time."

"I will be right back," Jacob said. He stormed back toward the bar.

Vanessa stumbled out of the truck behind him. "What are you going to do?"

"What needs to be done."

He went back into the bar, and that Jared guy was standing there with his friends, talking and laughing, and Jacob saw red. He moved straight over to where the guy was standing and threw the hardest damn punch of his life, cracking him right in the jaw and sending him straight down to the ground.

"If you ever come near her again, I'll kill you. My dad owns a lot of land. They wouldn't find your body. And if they did, they'd find it one piece at a time. Do you fucking understand what I'm saying to you?"

"What?" the guy asked, sounding dazed.

Jacob bent down and grabbed Jared by the shirt, lifting him up off the ground. "If you come near Vanessa Logan again it'll be the last thing you do. She doesn't want to talk to you. You're disgusting. You're an animal, and you better pray that I don't see your face when I'm in a mean mood some night. This bar is not for you. This town is not for you."

"What the hell, Dalton?" one of Jared's friends asked.

"The hell is that your buddy here likes to take advantage of women when they're passed out. And then make it seem like they owe him an apology when they're not happy to see him. I don't take kindly to that. And I don't let anyone hurt what's mine. Vanessa Logan is mine. And you'll do well to remember it."

He straightened, leaving Jared flat on the floor.

Laz was standing at the bar, observing the whole thing. "Normally I would say don't get blood on my bar floor, but in this instance, I think I'll allow it," he said.

"Make sure that jackass isn't welcome in here again."

"He's not," Laz said, his mouth set into a grim line, his black eyes filled with anger. "Count on it. You want that order to go?"

"I sure do."

Jacob turned and saw Vanessa standing near the doorway, her expression unreadable. Then he turned back to the bar and collected their food, and they both went out toward the truck.

"I told you," she said. "I don't know how much of it was my fault."

"He should have known," Jacob replied after they were inside the cab of the truck. "He should have known you were too drunk. And he should have taken care of you, he should never have taken advantage of you."

She visibly shrank when he spoke that word. "I'm not sure if you understand a blackout, Jacob. I have a long history of them, and that was the first. But since that one, I know… I could say anything. Do anything. My body is still working, my mouth is still working… The Vanessa that makes good decisions and thinks of the future and cares about safety and…about anything at all, she's gone during that time. I've had a lot of evenings explained to me after the fact, nights I don't even have slivers of memory of. And the person my friends have described to me? I don't know her."

"He should have taken care of you, he should never have taken advantage of you." The idea made his stomach turn. He wanted to go hit him again. One hit wasn't enough. It never would be.

"Sometimes I feel like I was assaulted," she said. "Sometimes I feel like it was his fault. Sometimes I feel like it was mine. Sometimes I feel like his victim. Sometimes I feel like I'm a victim of myself."

"No," Jacob said. "No. He—"

"I'm glad you feel that way," she said, leaning in and sliding her hand over his shoulder. "It's you through and through. Black-and-white. Right and wrong. I don't worry so much anymore about what it makes him. Because I don't want to be around him either way." She swallowed hard. "I'm not ashamed anymore. I used to be. I was overwhelmed by shame. Like there was a stranger, a monster who lived inside me who came out when I took a pill or had too much to drink. And for a long time I worried it was the real me."

She took a breath and looked up at him, her dark eyes shimmering. "People say that so carelessly. That the real you comes out when you're drunk or high, and when you've done things like I've done, the idea that might be true is haunting."

"It wasn't your fault," he said. "It wasn't your fault. And he…he came over and talked to you and had the nerve to be in your face about how you're not over it?"

"Well, maybe I should be over it. The not getting

over it, where does that lead? To drugs, let me tell you. To a whole lot of questions that I can't answer. And… being over it would just be a lot better."

He grabbed her chin, holding her steady and looking her in the eyes. "There's been some shady people in your life. Who made you feel like you weren't worth what you should feel. Don't go trying to make it all your fault. Especially not this. It wasn't your fault. He deserves more than I gave him. I meant what I said. I'd kill him."

"I believe you," she said.

She took the order, stacked in white containers and put them on her lap, and Jacob started the truck. When he looked over at her again, he saw tears rolling down her cheeks.

"Hey," he said. "Don't cry…"

Then she pushed the food off her lap and lunged across the bench seat, wrapped her arms around his neck and kissed him on the mouth. It was over in a second, but when it was done, she was breathing hard and looking at him with glittery eyes. "Take me back to my place."

Jacob wasn't about to argue.

CHAPTER SEVENTEEN

VANESSA KNEW THAT some people might argue she wasn't thinking clearly. Not at the moment. Not with the upset of her family, and then the shock of seeing Jared in the bar. But somehow, deep down, she felt like she was thinking clearer than she had been for a long time.

Jacob was…everything. The way that he had stood up for her. The way that he had…

The way he looked at her and told her that it wasn't her fault.

Somehow, in that moment, she had been brought right back to the day that he had responded to her 911 call.

He'd been her only ally then, her advocate. And he was that now.

The one person in the world who seemed to look at her and see something else. Something more.

Excitement flooded her, her stomach getting tight. And there was something about this decision that blotted out all of the gross, awful things that had happened over the past few hours.

She had Jacob.

In this world full of darkness. Full of her mistakes that she couldn't seem to extricate herself from completely, that wrapped themselves like vines around her ankles and tried to hold her down, she had Jacob.

Who could stand up to her father, hold on to her tightly so she didn't collapse and destroy an enemy in a single blow.

Her desire to be with him, to be closer to him, was something primal and beyond anything she had ever experienced before.

It wasn't about loneliness or a lack of resistance brought on by an altered state.

She was fully and clearly in her own mind. She knew exactly who she was, exactly who *he* was.

This wonderful, heroic man who saw things so simply. Who was her champion, no questions asked, no qualifications.

Her need for him was sharp, cutting like a blade, that distinct, wonderful feeling that she hadn't even recognized as desire at first because it was so different to the fuzzy, half-realized sensations she'd had before.

Wanting him wasn't intoxicating. It was clarifying.

It burned everything else away and left this one thing shining brightly like a beacon. They took the drive in silence, the sound of the road filling the cab of the truck. And she looked out the window, watching the inky black trees blur against the midnight blue of the sky, the stars glittering there like jewels on velvet. It was all so real.

And she felt so connected to it. To her body. To what she wanted from him. When they turned onto the gravel drive that led up to the house, her hands began to shake. But it wasn't fear.

It was need. An intense shot of adrenaline that

signaled her readiness. She wanted him. She wanted this. There was no doubt.

But it was different. Different from the frantic, desperate times they had come together before.

There had been no thought then at all. No decision to get naked in front of him and be vulnerable.

This was something. Something else.

But like so many other things that she had shed over the past few years, she needed to let that past trauma go. To take it off along with her clothes. Because nothing that she wanted with Jacob made her feel ashamed.

And yes, it had come with a consequence yet again. But life did. That didn't make her past redemption. It didn't make her wrong. It made her human.

A woman who desperately wanted the man sitting next to her.

This wonderful, incredible man who had set himself up as a guardian for her.

When no one else ever had.

When they pulled up to her house, she tumbled out of the truck, leaving the food behind. She didn't actually care about the food, and judging by the fact that Jacob slammed his door quickly and didn't seem to give another thought to the foam cartons, neither did he.

They met around the front of the truck, the headlights shining on the two of them, and he grabbed her, pulling her into his hold, and kissed her on the mouth, deep and hard.

It took a moment for the lights to turn off, but when they did, the two of them were plunged into darkness, kissing there in front of her house.

"Let's go inside," she said softly, pressing her hands

on his chest and rubbing her palms over his muscles. Even covered in the thin cotton of the shirt, she could feel all his heat and hardness, and she wanted all of it.

She never had him completely naked before, and she wanted it.

She wanted *him*.

He took her hand, like they were walking through a park on a date, and not about to get into bed and ravage each other, but she liked that. Loved the way his large calloused fingers felt rubbing against the tender skin on the back of her hand. Loved everything about the comforting reassurance of his touch.

And she had been so bound and determined not to need. Not to need at all.

But tonight, she was going to let it all happen.

She was going to give him everything she had, because he had given her something no one else ever had.

He had made her feel like she might matter.

Are you really that sad?

Maybe. Maybe she was.

Maybe the bottom line was she still saw herself as something that didn't quite mean as much as any of the other people around her.

Someone who was damaged and lesser.

Someone who had atoning to do, someone who didn't exist outside the tightly controlled framework that she had built around her life.

Someone who only mattered as long as she was good.

But tonight a whole lot of ugly had been thrown in front of Jacob, and he had stayed the same.

He had been tested, and the bonds didn't break.

She unlocked the front door and they went inside, she threw her purse on the ground, along with her keys.

Jacob practically growled, pulling her up against his body and kissing her again, this time harder, deeper.

She wrapped her arms around his neck and melted into him, her tongue sliding against his, her whole body going liquid as the kiss went on and on.

She had never kissed like this before. Like it was a destination in and of itself. Like it was comfortable and new all at the same time.

Each pass of his tongue was a thrilling discovery, a new level of arousal that she hadn't known she could reach with just the pressure of a man's hand on her face, and arm curved around her lower back, and his lips fused to hers.

She could feel him against her body, hard and ready, and she wanted. So deep and real.

The present moment had never been so real. The rasp of his whisker-covered jaw against her hand, the heat of his mouth, the strength of his body. The sound of their breathing, mingling with the hum and click of the refrigerator and the gentle sound of the air conditioner coming on and off. Even the small things, the small details and sounds meant something. Grounded her in this moment. Where it felt like nothing had come before, and it didn't matter what came after. All that mattered was now. The heavy weight of those masculine hands on her body.

And if she closed her eyes and stilled for a moment, she swore she could hear the beating of his heart mingling with hers, fast and heavy like they'd been running a race.

He was the one who moved them from the spot,

who transitioned that kiss from the living room and down the hall.

He found her bedroom with ease, though in fairness it wasn't difficult, since it was the only door in the hall standing open, but part of her would like to think that he just had a sense for it, like he seemed to have a sense for everything else. How to touch her, how to hold her.

He flipped the lights on when they got into the room, and she was grateful.

He moved away from her, pushing his boots off with his feet, taking his socks with them, before gripping the edge of his T-shirt and jerking it up over his head.

She'd seen his chest the day they made love in the classroom, the day she'd used his body as a canvas, but it was even more spectacular than she remembered it.

His well-defined muscles shifting with each breath. His chest was broad and thick, his waist lean and narrow with perfectly defined abs and those hard-cut angular lines that seemed to create an arrow down to the part of him that was hard and ready for her, with only those low-slung jeans keeping him from being completely naked.

She had never been so happy to be fully engaged in a moment in her entire life.

Mindfulness, she knew, was a concept partly created to keep a person from drowning in anxiety, but she felt its primary use for her right now was to enjoy having a man with a perfect body standing in front of her, ready and waiting to be her personal playground.

She closed the distance between them and put her hands on his belt, undoing it and then the button and zipper on his jeans. She wanted… She wanted to show him how much she wanted it. How much she knew exactly what she was doing right now.

She wasn't distressed or impaired in any way.

She was ready.

She pushed his jeans and underwear down his lean hips and then stood back to admire his body, fully exposed for her pleasure.

He was a work of art.

She could happily paint him. Paint *on* him. All of the above.

He was a masterpiece of bold strokes and decisive lines, hard, masculine angles.

And she wanted every inch of him.

Beside her, over her, in her.

Her breasts ached, her core hollow and needy for him.

And then his lips lifted upward into a wicked smile, and he advanced on her, pulling her up against his naked body as he ripped her top up over her head, those knowing hands making even quicker work of her skirt and underwear.

Her bra was gone in a skillful second, on the floor with the rest of her clothes, and then she was blissfully naked, every glorious inch of his naked skin against every glorious inch of hers.

He was *everything*.

And so was this. Wonderful and powerful and unabashedly sexual.

He lifted her up off the ground, carried her toward the bed, but he didn't do what she expected. Instead, he gripped her ass tightly in both palms, bringing himself down onto the mattress on his back while he hauled her up toward his mouth, positioning her over him, his tongue finding her most sensitive spot unerringly as he pressed her to his face, his whiskers scraping against her inner thighs while he lapped at her like she was a dessert.

She gasped, holding on to the headboard as pleasure rolled over her like an uncontrollable wave.

In this position, with him gripping her so tightly and holding her in place, there was nothing she could do but submit to what he was doing.

If a man had ever given such focused attention to her pleasure in the past, she couldn't remember it, and she didn't think it had ever happened, because she would remember this. This feeling of sharp, intense pleasure, of blunt male fingertips digging into her hips as that slick, knowing tongue took her to places she thought only existed in fiction.

She tried to say his name, tried to protest, because in spite of the fact that he managed to give her multiple orgasms the last time they were together, she was always afraid that it wouldn't happen.

In general, orgasms had never been the goal of sex for her. Often there hadn't been a goal so much as just that sometimes it was easier to be with someone than to be without them.

Jacob didn't seem to see it that way. The man was goal oriented, and her pleasure seemed to be a huge part of that goal.

Not that she was complaining. It was just that…

She couldn't think anymore because suddenly he slid his hand from her ass, down between her legs, and teased the entrance to her body, sending a cascade of need raining down on her, crashing into a turbulent, jagged release that made her shake and shudder endlessly, until she was sure that it would never end.

He picked her up and lowered her down his body, so that his thick, heavy erection was pressed against her stomach, and their noses were touching, their lips nearly brushing.

"I've been dreaming about that," he said. "I can't get your taste out of my head."

"Oh," she said because she didn't have anything clever to say. She didn't have anything to say.

Her brain didn't work anymore.

He had transformed her entirely into a creature of sensual need, not one of thought or coherent phrasing.

He arched his hips upward, his hard length pushing insistently against her. "I want you," he said.

"I want you too," she said. But there was more in that declaration. More than she even wanted to admit to herself.

He reversed them so that she was pressed into the soft mattress, his large body over hers, his blue eyes staring down into hers. Then again, the moment felt sharp, just a little bit too sharp, with nothing to avail the connection between the two of them.

She was afraid he could see inside her. See things that not even she could see.

He claimed her mouth in a searing kiss, his mouth fitting perfectly over hers, his tongue sliding against hers, as he positioned himself at her entrance and slid inside her in one smooth stroke.

She gasped as he filled her, as their bodies joined together.

He slid one hand down her arm, gripped her wrist

and pushed it up over her head, before repeating the same motion with her other arm, capturing both wrists and his large hand, holding her in place as he thrust deep and hard.

The way he held her, the way he moved inside her, all of it brought them closer together, let her feel all of him.

And as he moved, the pleasure, the need, spiraled higher and tighter inside her.

She felt transported completely, and right there all at the same time. Their breath, his body, the bed, everything so real and clear. But nothing was more real than the orgasm that was building inside her, tightening every line in her body like a bowstring, so tight that she was afraid she was going to break.

And when it did, when it did, it was like a free fall, terrifying and exhilarating all at the same time. But at the end of it, when the shaking stopped, when the pleasure subsided, he was holding her in his arms because he had fallen right along with her.

Their skin was slick with sweat, their breathing harsh. But they were together.

And Vanessa realized she hadn't fully known just how alone she had felt, until she had experienced what it was to truly be with another person.

Their hearts beating together, their breath in the same time.

And whatever happened next, whatever happened tomorrow, or ten years from now…they would have this.

And maybe, just maybe, it would be enough of a foundation to build on.

She had wrecked him.

JACOB HAD NEVER in all his life had sex like that. Not the actions. Because he'd done all kinds of things before.

He'd been wild, and a life full of hookups, drunk nights and good times had helped him keep his demons at bay.

And handily, the thing that bonded all the careers he'd had in the past was that women tended to find them sexy. As little trouble as he had in his life with hooking up, it had only gotten easier as he'd gotten older, and he'd been able to lead with things like, *I'm a bull rider.*

So yeah, when it came to sex, he'd done most everything.

But it hadn't felt like this.

She took a breath and nuzzled against his chest, her cheek pressed against that place where his heart was raging hard.

And this all felt… It felt like something a man could build a life on.

Sometime, probably about the time he was ten years old, he decided that he didn't get to have a life the same as other people did. Because of what he buried down deep.

But now, that life, that normal, everyday life that most people aspired to, had come to him. He hadn't planned it, he hadn't chosen it. Really, he'd spent most of his life determined not to have it.

But here it was. Like a gift, and he could just reach out and take it.

"I have something I want to ask you," he said.

"What?"

He shifted, so that he could see her, so that he could

look down and see her pretty face. "I have to tell you something first."

"Okay," she said. "Tell away."

"It's just…it's not something that anyone knows," he said. "But I need to tell you, because you're not like anyone else in my life. You're not going to be. You're the mother of my baby. And that's real. That's forever. Permanent stuff. But I've got to tell you why I—I'm not put together like other people."

"Are you a tin man?" she asked. She slid her hand up to the center of his chest and felt his heart beating there. "Because I hate to tell you, but you've got a heart."

"Yeah, and about the only thing it does reliably is pump blood. I can decide things. For real, and I can stick to it. And that's something else you need to know about me. If I make a promise, it's for keeps."

"I believe it," she said.

"If you asked my parents about an October afternoon twenty-five years ago, they wouldn't know why you're asking. They might remember something happening, a local tragedy. Maybe. But they wouldn't have any idea what it had to do with me. You could ask my brothers, and they wouldn't either. Ask the police. No one would know."

"Okay, now you're scaring me a little bit."

"Good," he said. "I might need to scare you. So in October, twenty-five years ago, me and a friend of mine, Gavin Taylor, went on a hike. We were ten. We weren't really supposed to be out in the woods by ourselves, but the property that my parents owned was big, and it was easy enough to end up wandering off of it and get to God knows where. And that was the plan.

Neither of our parents knew where we were going. They both thought… I don't know. They didn't know we were together, though. So we ended up going into a part of the woods that I wasn't familiar with. There was a trail, and it was narrow. But we were small, and I think we figured we could make it across."

It was like being sick, telling this story. Like an illness you couldn't hold back anymore. His guts heaving it up, making his stomach cramp. This was different from having flashbacks. Dreams. Snatches of memory and thoughts of people falling. All sorts of people, not just Gavin.

His brothers. Ellie. Her daughter, Amelia.

But to actually remember what had happened.

"Gavin scrambled up ahead of me, and the trail was slick with mud. He lost his footing, and before I could react at all he went over the side." His chest went tight, the words now hard to force out of his throat. "It's the strangest damn thing," he said. "Something like that. I've responded to a lot of emergencies, but I can't tell you how awful it is when you have those kinds where it's all over in half a second. There is no calling for help. There's no stopping anything. You can't even buy time with CPR.

"Of course, I was a kid, and I couldn't believe that my friend would be dead. I looked over the edge and…I ran. I ran all the way until I was across the field at our neighbors' farmhouse. They weren't home, but the back door was unlocked, so I ran in and used the phone. I called 911 and called for help. And then I went back and hid and waited. Help came, but… They called for me. For someone. And I hid. I hid until they went down in the ravine, and then I ran. Because I didn't want to see them bring him back up. I didn't want to see anything. I ran home and went back into my bedroom and got into bed. And I covered up my head with the pillow, and I pretended that I had never gotten up that morning. And when my parents came to tell me… When they came to tell me that Gavin was dead…I didn't say anything."

He cleared his throat. "I couldn't fix it. I couldn't stop it. I couldn't bring him back by telling that I was there. I just kept it a secret. And I've never told another soul. I've never told the story to anyone. I don't talk about him. I don't talk about that day. I pretended that it happened to someone else," he said. "Like that could protect me. And it worked. For a long time. If no one knows about a bad thing, they can't feel sorry for you. They can't bring it up, you can't be connected to it for the rest of your life. And I just… I forgot. I jumped headlong into being the guy who didn't care about anything. The guy who just wandered through life having a good time."

"But you didn't," she said. "You didn't. You became a paramedic. And when I needed you, you were there for me."

The words hit him strangely at the center of his chest.

"I reckon," he said. "But it didn't protect me. It didn't stop what happened with Clint. In fact, the way that I treated life is what caused it."

"The two aren't connected," Vanessa said. "You're building a case against yourself like there's a crime and you're law enforcement, but you didn't… You didn't do any of those things. They happened. Clint died twenty something years after your friend. I'm so sorry. I'm so sorry you saw that. That it…stays with you like it does. No little boy should have to see that. No one should have to. You were ten years old. If you weren't… If you weren't completely messed up by it, you wouldn't be a good person."

He laughed. Hollow and bitter. "It doesn't matter. It wasn't lesson enough to teach me so that I could… keep a bad thing from happening later. And it doesn't change that… You can't see something like that and not be changed, you're right. And I've never much felt like I was put together like other people. Not after that."

"That must be lonely," she said. "Feeling that way, and never being able to tell anyone why."

"It's not fun to talk about," he said. "I don't feel sad that I never told anyone before. It's too hard. It's too hard to tell that story, to have someone else carry it too. But like I said…you and me. This is something. It has to be. For a long time. And if I don't always give you what you need, I need you to understand where I'm coming from."

"It's not a burden to understand you," she said. "I'm sorry you had to go through that, but this isn't a burden for me. Not any more than you knowing about the miscarriage. About what happened before that, about what happened after. It's just part of knowing each other."

"I want to get married."

"What?"

He could see how for her maybe there was no direct line between the conversation they were having and marriage, but for him, it made total sense.

"I want to get married," he reiterated. "Because we can't be with each other and just be friends. God knows

I can't. All I thought about for weeks is being with you again, and I know—I damn well know—that I cannot be in the same house as you and not want you. I spent my life avoiding domesticity, and here it is. Well, I'm avoiding it, and contorting myself into weird shapes to just not do the obvious thing. You didn't want to get married because you don't just want to do something you think might please your parents. I don't want to get married because…well, I never wanted to. I don't feel like I'm a man that's built for love in a traditional sense. But I can do commitment. And no, I can't promise you there won't be times when we're miserable, and there won't be times we want to leave each other. But I can promise you that I'm not Hank Dalton. I won't sleep with other women. I won't hurt you that way. You'll be the only woman in my life, and I'll be the man in yours. We can be a team. If you can accept what I can give. If you can accept me like this."

"What does that mean? 'Like this.' You mean someone who isn't going to fall in love with me?"

"I don't know that I really believe in love in that way that a lot of people do. People fall in love, I expect, partly because they want to. Or expect to. My brother gave… He's in love. And he means it. I know he does. I do know that I believe in that. But I might believe in fate. Because I looked at you…and it was the damnedest thing, Vanessa Logan. I swear I saw the future when I looked into your eyes, and I think we can make that future something good. As long as we make that choice."

"Yes," she said breathlessly. "Yes."

And he'd done it. A naked-in-bed proposal that had

ended in a yes. Committed to spending his life with someone else, rather than alone.

And he told her about Gavin.

She'd still said yes.

In just a few moments, Jacob Dalton's whole life had changed.

But unlike a free fall, it hadn't ended in destruction.

For the first time, an instantaneous change felt good.

And he was just going to sit with that for a little while.

CHAPTER EIGHTEEN

THE NEXT MORNING, Vanessa was buzzing, and still trying to process everything that she and Jacob had talked about the night before. The story about his friend. The proposal.

She felt like she hadn't even fully gotten to take on the heartbreak of the story he'd told her before the proposal had come, and that made it all a little bit muddy.

She'd said yes.

And she really hoped that it had been the right thing to say.

But tangled up in bed with him, completely naked, she couldn't imagine a scenario wherein she would want to live with that man and go to a separate bed at night.

She didn't even think it was possible.

And anything less permanent than marriage…

It really had to be friendship or husband and wife. There could be no middle ground. Not when it came to trying to give their child a stable home life.

And yeah, she knew it was coming down to admitting that she just didn't have the self-control required to not sleep with him.

Sex.

Sex was the dividing factor between marriage, and not.

It was a strange thing. And some people would say, sex could be a small thing. A casual thing.

She would have said that in the past.

But that was because she'd never had sex the way she did with Jacob.

Sex with him went down beneath her skin. It touched places inside her that she hadn't known existed.

She would never be able to share him, not when he was hers. Not when he had been in her bed at night, naked and pressed up against her, skin to skin. She would never be able to keep her feelings neutral.

And it made her wonder how much ground was between not neutral and…love. And what that even meant, considering Jacob felt able to offer commitment but not love.

She didn't know how she felt about it. Or why it mattered.

It was forcing her to be philosophical about things that she tried not to be philosophical about.

But one thing she did know, was that often commitment was much more important than feelings.

As someone who had—in the beginning—had to be committed to sobriety, rather than in love with the entire experience, she felt uniquely qualified to look at it from that angle.

And she had never really imagined that a big head-over-heels kind of love existed in her future anyway.

Truly, she had more than she'd ever imagined, and Jacob was right.

Not getting married just because she was trying to prove that she didn't need to get married to please her parents was…stupid.

For a moment, she imagined a real wedding, with her in a white dress and Jacob in a tux.

No, it wouldn't be that.

They were going to have to get married at the courthouse, and quickly.

But theirs wasn't a marriage like Luke and Olivia's, so she wouldn't be having the big elaborate wedding her sister had had.

But she was a pregnant bride too. She wasn't better than you.

No, but her groom had been wildly in love with her.

She thought back to attending her sister's wedding. The first time she'd seen her family in years. It had been like a painting she'd seen once in church, of people meeting each other in heaven. Hugging. Laughing. An ecstatic reunion where everything bad had been beautiful and brilliant. In her memories it was wreathed in gold. It had been simpler. Because it had just been a relief to be together again. And none of the darker feelings had had a chance to creep in yet.

It had been pure emotion.

Pure. In a way so few things in life ever were.

"You look very serious," Ellie said, walking into the classroom carrying a small basket. "A bundle of sandwiches was left for me today, and I assumed that some of them were for you," she said.

Vanessa smiled. "Why do you think that?"

"Because Jacob brought the basket today."

In spite of herself, Vanessa blushed.

"Oh," Ellie said, sitting at Vanessa's desk across from her. "That doesn't look like a we-are-friends-and-only-friends-raising-a-baby-together face."

"He asked me to marry him," she said.

"Now, that's what I expect from a Dalton," she said. Then she pulled a face. "Well, I guess Hank maybe not so much. But Caleb, Gabe and Jacob, I would expect a marriage proposal if they got a woman pregnant."

"I didn't want one," Vanessa said.

"Indeed."

"I said yes obviously."

"Obviously," Ellie said, smirking slightly.

"Oh, there's ice cream in here." She pulled out a tiny tub of marionberry pie ice cream and Vanessa's heart practically glowed.

"Is that a craving of yours?" Ellie asked.

"I guess so," Vanessa said. She sighed heavily. "I wasn't going to marry him," she said. "I wasn't going to marry him just because we were having a baby because that's just… It's old-fashioned and it's silly."

"It's kind of logistically sound, though," Ellie said.

"But we might be miserable."

"Every marriage might be miserable," Ellie said. "You take a risk when you get married. You vow to stay together forever, but things happen. Sometimes death happens sooner than you think. Not that I'm trying to put that in your head. I just mean… We don't have guarantees in life, Vanessa, and you can't plan and expect that nothing bad will happen. Maybe you guys will be miserable. But maybe you won't be. You have just as much chance as anyone."

"Why? We're not…in love or anything."

"Mmm," she agreed. "Right. So that's something. Believe me. I think there's all kinds of different relationships. I had that…childhood-sweethearts thing. I mean, not childhood, I guess. But I met him when I was eighteen. Going to college, and I came to Gold

Valley to visit with friends on a break. And I met him. I just… He was the sweetest thing. We had a sweet relationship. He was lovely. It wasn't like wildfire or anything. But it was…" Her smile went dreamy. "Wonderful. I can still imagine growing old with him, even though he's not here." Ellie blinked, her eyes full of tears. "I loved him with my whole heart. And I still don't know what would have happened if he would've lived. If we would have had to figure out what it was like to be in a relationship while raising a kid. People change. The years change them. We would have been different just because of years, and I'm different now because of what it's been like to go through losing him. My point is…you can't project. And yeah, you have just as much a chance as anyone."

"I'm so sorry that you lost him," Vanessa said, her heart feeling fragile.

The world was so big and scary, and full of so much loss. Clint's death had profoundly affected Ellie, and it had wounded Jacob too. Jacob, who was already so badly damaged from the death of his friend.

Jacob, who had seen things that would destroy a grown man, let alone a little boy.

"Me too," Ellie said. "But I'm trying to get to the point where I'm just happy that I had him."

Vanessa could only wonder what it would be like to be in love like that. Because *wildfire* was the right word for her and Jacob. But it wasn't that soft kind of sweetness that Ellie spoke of when it came to Clint.

There was nothing soft or sweet about them.

They had chemistry. Chemistry she hadn't ever imagined could be real.

"Marry him," Ellie said. "I think you'll be happy."

"I want to marry him," Vanessa said. "That's the part that scares me, though. When I first thought about it, I thought of it as a grim march that I would be doing just to fulfill an obligation. But that's not how I see it now. I want to…be with him. And that scares me."

"Are you falling in love with him?"

The word made Vanessa's stomach feel hollowed out.

"I really hope not."

"There are worse things than being in love with your husband," Ellie pointed out.

"Not if your husband doesn't love you back."

"Jacob is a good guy. He probably will—"

"He won't."

It was the easiest thing for her to believe.

She wasn't the kind of woman who inspired those sorts of feelings.

She didn't even inspire unfailing loyalty from her family.

But you got it from him.

She cleared her throat. "It doesn't matter. I'm marrying him. Whatever the feelings end up being. We are… We're doing this."

And she ignored the little bubble of hope that appeared in her heart as she confirmed her decision.

Right now, her life wasn't anything like the plan she had formed before she had moved to Gold Valley.

And right now, she was actually feeling pretty happy about it.

"So I HEARD that you started a fight at the saloon last night." Gabe leaned against a fence post and stared Jacob down.

Jacob looked up from his work on the fence line. "I did," he said. "Though, in fairness, it wasn't a fight. Because I hit the gutless bastard once, he went down and not another punch was thrown."

"Well, that's how it's done," Gabe said, sounding approving. "Can I get some backstory on the punch?"

"It's a long story. He was hassling Vanessa." He frowned. "I guess it's not a long story."

"No," Gabe said. "Makes perfect sense to me. If some bastard walked up to Jamie and tried to give her a problem, he'd go down and not get back up too."

But Vanessa and Jamie weren't the same. Not really. Oh, Jacob believed that Jamie had changed his brother. He'd seen it in action. Had watched her take all his scattered pieces and turn them into laser focus. She was like his muse, if Jacob believed in that stuff. Mostly, he believed in good sex. And he had a feeling that his brother and Jamie had plenty of that.

But Gabe had it all wrapped up in a pretty package and tied with a bow that he called *love*.

This wasn't love. It was primal, possessive rage wrapped in something kind of terrifying.

And there was no bow.

"Anyway, Laz is on my side," he said. "He said the bastard's not allowed back in the bar."

"Well, good for you. You gotta protect your woman, there's no question about that."

Well, there was no point denying that Vanessa was his woman. In fact, he might as well deliver the good news to Gabe. "I'm getting married."

"You what?"

Caleb chose that exact moment to walk into Gabe's office.

"I'm getting married," Jacob returned.

Caleb looked somewhat thunderstruck. "You. You're getting married."

"I am. It seemed like the thing to do."

"Yeah," Caleb said slowly. "Suddenly? Because you were pretty fixed on not marrying her."

"And things change."

"Well, congratulations," Gabe said. "It's for the best anyway," he said, his tone confident.

"Why do you think that?"

"Because that's what makes a family."

"A marriage license?" Jacob asked.

"No. But being in the same household as your own child is probably a pretty good idea, don't you think?"

"Well, clearly I do," Jacob said. And he was going to pretend that it was all about that, and had nothing to do with the fact that mostly, he couldn't keep his hands off Vanessa and didn't want to. Not now, not for the foreseeable future.

"Obviously, Dad didn't," Gabe said.

"Hey," Caleb said. "Dad didn't know about the kids."

"No, I know. It's just…the deeper I get into all of this… I don't know. I don't know how two parents who, I think, honestly do love their children as much as anything can cause so much trouble," Gabe said.

"It always suited me," Jacob said. "I was able to more or less sit back and not be hassled."

"You were always doing crazy stuff," Gabe said. "Like you were begging them to notice you."

Jacob frowned. "Maybe begging them to notice something. But not me."

That was about as authentic as anything he'd ever

said to his brothers. And it was the truth. He wanted everyone to see a happy, wild, undamaged guy when really, there was a traumatized kid beneath all of that. And he hadn't wanted anyone to know that. Hadn't wanted anyone to see it.

His brother Caleb looked at him, and Jacob felt his heart twist up with guilt. He and Caleb had always been as thick as thieves, and even Caleb didn't really know the truth. Now that he'd told Vanessa, part of him thought maybe it would be better to tell his brothers. But he didn't quite want to. Not yet.

"Well, I meant it. Congratulations. Both on the punch and on the engagement." Gabe clapped his brother on the back. "But I have to go check on some things. See you both later."

He walked out past Caleb and Jacob, and Jacob had a feeling that Gabe—however insensitive he was—knew that the two of them probably needed to have a few words.

"Engaged?"

"Yep."

"I have to say," Caleb said slowly, "I did not think you'd get married before me."

"Oh yeah?"

"Yeah. I figured we'd do it maybe when we were in our sixties."

Caleb was smiling, but Jacob sensed that there wasn't any real happiness underneath that.

"Really?"

"No," Caleb said. "I'm not the marrying kind."

"Yeah? Since when?"

He shrugged. "I always figured I wouldn't. Mom

and Dad. You know. Around the time I was twenty or so I gave up on it altogether."

And without putting too much thought into it, Jacob realized that it was around the time Caleb had met Ellie. Around the time Ellie had come to town already engaged to Clint.

"That could change," Jacob said.

"Now," he said, "I don't really want it to."

"Neither did I. And look where that got me."

"Well, you were doing things that I have not been doing."

His brother's admission of celibacy wasn't all that surprising. Because frankly, Jacob couldn't imagine him taking care of Ellie the way that he was and carrying on with other women.

It wasn't Caleb's way.

"Well, sometimes things happen that surprise you," Jacob said. "Vanessa was a pretty big surprise to me."

"You don't have to feel responsible for Clint," Caleb said. "Ellie doesn't hold you responsible, you know that."

"Yeah," Jacob said, his voice rusty. "I know that. Or she wouldn't be here. She wouldn't talk to me."

"In our line of work, I don't really think you can overthink the concept of faith to quite that degree."

"Maybe not."

"But you are."

"I don't know. I just… I feel responsible."

And for some reason, the idea of letting go of it felt terrifying, and Jacob couldn't even quite figure out why. Like holding on to it was protecting him from something, somehow.

"He wouldn't have wanted you to."

"Bullshit," Jacob said. "You don't know that. If we were on a ship and it was going down, he would've been the one that you'd sacrifice your life for. He had Ellie. And Amelia. He would have wanted to live."

Caleb's face went carefully blank.

"That is true. He did have them. But now you have Vanessa. And you're going to have a baby. Though I'm not sure that you should need those things to give your life more value."

"The irony is not lost on me," he said. "That I have all those things now. And that he's gone."

"You can't change it," Caleb said. "No amount of wishing changes it. Things just are, sometimes. Because life is a cruel and fickle bitch. Sometimes people who should be here are gone, and sometimes people who should never have survived the dumbass stuff they did do. And sometimes… Your heart is just made to beat for a certain thing, and there's nothing you can do about it, not in all the world. No matter how much you wish you could."

Jacob had the sudden feeling they weren't talking about him anymore.

"Well, one thing's for sure," Jacob said. "No amount of regret is going to change the way things are now. I've got what I've got."

It was strange, because he hadn't known how he felt about the baby when Vanessa had first told him. And now it felt like something real. Like purpose.

Something that connected him to the earth when he'd felt disconnected from it for a long damn time.

"Hold on to what you got," Caleb said. "Because if there's one thing both of us know, it's that there aren't any guarantees."

Yeah, well, that Jacob was well acquainted with and certain of. He didn't need a hell of a lot of reminders to know that. And that made his heart feel cold.

Because whatever he had now, it was no guarantee he would keep it.

"Well," Jacob said. "You think you might want to be my best man?"

"Do I have to wear a tux?"

"No. Ellie can be a bridesmaid. You can walk down the aisle with her."

His brother's face went granite. "You don't have time to have an aisle anyway," he said. "You gotta get hitched too quickly."

"Fair enough."

And he considered it some kind of truce that Caleb wasn't going to get in his face for that crack shot he'd made about Ellie.

He didn't know why he'd done it. Except that Caleb's words, that he'd meant to be comforting in some way, had only gotten beneath his skin.

CHAPTER NINETEEN

VANESSA DIDN'T REALLY think she needed Jacob to come to every art class, not anymore. She'd developed a rapport with the boys, even though Aiden was still being stubborn. She wasn't afraid of them. Not remotely. They weren't all good kids, not really. They were complicated. A little bit messed up. Sometimes they painted dark and disturbing things. But none of them were beyond redemption. They might not be good, but they weren't bad either.

That was the trouble with people. They were often complicated. Prickly and difficult like her sister could be. Self-destructive and inaccessible like she had been.

Unbending like her father. Too interested in the opinions of others, like her mother.

And Jacob…

She didn't even know.

But it was easier to pretend that someone was wholly good. Easier to pretend that another person might be worthy of nothing because so many of the pieces of them were difficult. There was no comfort in complicated.

None at all.

But there was a richness to it, depth that made life more interesting.

Complicated was the fact that she really didn't need

Jacob in this classroom anymore, but she loved him being there.

Complicated was the fact that the man didn't seem to think he was a hero, while he was utterly and completely heroic in the eyes of every boy who stepped into the class.

He was patient with them. He didn't take any crap. He gave as good as he got when the kids mouthed off. And he forgave them day after day when they said terrible things. When they tried to get everyone around them to hate them, to hurry up and fast-forward to the part where they had destroyed the goodwill of others and could never earn it back, because that was the world as they knew it.

But they were given complicated. And that was something new. The complication of humanity, forgiveness. Mistakes. Imperfection, not met with wholesale anger or acceptance.

Complicated was the fact that her feelings toward Jacob were shifting, evolving, and she couldn't stop them.

Even watching him now…

He was talking to Calvin, looking at the boy's most recent painting. And she knew that Jacob didn't actually understand art specifically, she knew he didn't care about it in a deep way, but he cared about the kid holding the paintbrush.

So he talked to him. Asked him what things meant.

"You're all improving a lot," Jacob said. "Today's *fuck this* is really coming along nicely," he said to Aiden, who shot him a side-eye.

"I've never been good at anything before," Calvin said, staring at the canvas.

"What do you mean?" Vanessa asked.

"I mean…I'm not very good at school. I don't have any friends. I'm not good at being a son. I don't have any siblings. I've never been good at anything. Except maybe this."

Vanessa's heart twisted, and she thought it might break altogether.

"You're very good at it," she said truthfully.

"It makes me feel better," he said. "I don't know if it's the painting or feeling like I'm good at something."

"Might be both," Jacob said. "Things can be both."

Oh, Jacob. Her heart broke for him. Because he was absolutely a hero. The way he was talking to Calvin now… He would be such a wonderful father.

And he was going to be her *husband*.

The very idea made her heart feel full; it made her feel like she might float up off the ground.

She felt happy. To have him in her future. The possibility of having him in her life. He was… He was everything. And she was pretty sure she might be falling in love with him. She hadn't wanted that. Because she just couldn't… She couldn't imagine ever deserving it. Ever deserving him. And that was the strange and funny, yeah, complicated thing. He didn't think he was a hero, and she thought he was the best man she'd ever known. And that made him too good for her, while he…probably thought he wasn't enough.

Life was absurd.

But he said that he wouldn't love her. Another thing he seemed determined to not let himself have, but that was okay.

She had him. And the feelings in her heart that were starting to grow. She didn't need to have everything.

That was one of life's complications, after all. But she could have him. As her husband, as the father of her child. And there was little to her that was more important than that.

"You know," she said to the class. "Even if art isn't what you love," she said, primarily addressing Marco and Aiden. "I hope that you see that when you try different things, sometimes you find an unexpected thing you like. Sometimes you find out that you have talent you didn't know you had, or you're interested in things you didn't even know were out there. Art doesn't have to be your thing for you to learn a lesson from this class."

"You don't think my art is great?" Aiden asked.

"It might be," Vanessa said. "But you haven't really shown me anything deeper. You haven't shown me anything more than your anger. And that's fine. It's something. But I just haven't seen anything more."

"Maybe there's nothing else there," he said.

Jacob looked at Vanessa, and his eyes held hers. There was something deep and determined there. Something raw and real, and Vanessa's stomach clenched in anticipation of what he was going to say.

It was so strange, to look at his face and feel what was happening inside him.

"There's only nothing else there if you choose that," Jacob said. "A man gets to choose who he wants to be," Jacob said. "You hear me? You're all men. Life didn't let you be boys. That sucks. But it's how it is. Let me tell you something, if you're men, you get to make choices about what your life is going to be. You like art? Do art. Don't tell yourself you can't. I've been irresponsible in my life. And now I'm choosing to make different choices. At a certain point—" his eyes met Vanessa's "—life can't be about what happened to you. It might've been a bad thing. A lot of bad things. Really terrible stuff. I get that. But you can't let it make you who you are, not forever."

"What do you know about terrible stuff?" Marco asked. "Didn't you grow up on this ranch? Where they send kids like us to see that there are better things in life? You grew up in the better thing. Don't talk to me about letting go."

Jacob turned, his jaw granite, and he looked at all three boys square in the face. "When I was ten years old I saw my best friend fall off a cliff."

Vanessa's heart squeezed tight. He was sharing it now, this thing he'd been hoarding inside like a dragon hoards a cursed object. He'd been trying to protect people, but it had poisoned him instead. The bravery she knew it took for him to share it now humbled her. Made her want to go to him and put her arms around him.

But instead, she just listened.

"I saw what it looked like when someone died," he said, his voice rough. "And I learned really quick that life is fragile. You ever walk around feeling bulletproof? I always knew I wasn't. Because I saw what life can do to your body. Throw you around, mess you up. Steal the soul right outta you. I've seen it. Don't tell me what I haven't seen. And I let it decide who I was," he said. "For a long time. With consequences. So trust me. I know plenty. I'm telling you this because I'm a hell of a lot of years older than you. And you can get yourself straightened out now, instead of waiting until you're my age."

When the boys cleared out later, Vanessa was still reeling from Jacob telling the kids about himself when she knew that until the other night he had never told anyone.

"You didn't have to do that," she said. "You didn't have to—"

"I could never figure out what purpose it served," Jacob said. "But you know what? It's never going to serve any purpose at all if it's just sitting inside me. It won't make a bit of difference in anyone's life. And maybe it won't now. But it's not doing anything—not getting better, not helping at all—just being there inside me. If it will help the kids…"

She reached across the space between them and cupped his face, kissed his lips slowly. "I'm gonna marry you," she said.

"You say that now," he said. "But you haven't actually tried being married to me yet."

"No one has," she said. "Unless there's something I don't know about you."

"No," he said. "You're right on that score."

"So there you have it."

"But that means not even I know what kind of husband I'm going to be."

"Choose what kind," she said, echoing his words back to him, a small smile curving her lips. "You're a man, after all. Choose what you want to be."

"That's dangerous," he said.

"I'm open for a little bit of danger where you're concerned."

She was. He was worth it. Every sharp edge. Every complication.

She was resolved in that.

She looked right into his eyes, the blue in them glistening like diamonds, and she was positive they could cut into her soul like glass. But she didn't want to run from it. Not from the intensity. Not from the potential hard road that might lie in front of them.

Because it wouldn't *only* be hard. There would be good to it also. There would be easy and fun along with any potential pain. She couldn't see the future. There was no way. And what she knew for sure was that she was committed to a complicated road, whatever twists and turns it might take.

She smiled. Because growth, at least in her life, wasn't about being perfect. It was accepting this. That she couldn't guarantee what lay ahead, but she could accept it. That sometimes this all felt too close and too real, but she still wanted it.

She didn't want to dull it, didn't want to hide from it. Didn't need to use "therapist-speak," as Jacob called it, to get any distance between him and her.

"I'm pretty open to whatever comes our way," she said.

There was a sadness in his eyes suddenly, and she didn't know what she'd said to put it there. But just like that it was gone, and the intensity had returned. "Well, that's good to know," he said. "Because I can't guarantee you much, but I do guarantee you life will continue to happen."

"I'm pretty sure that I can deal with it. As long as it's with you."

He said nothing to that, but she kissed him anyway, because that was the choice she was making. Regardless of what was going on inside him.

"Why don't you come up tonight and look at the property? We need to find a site for the home."

"Okay," she said, looking up at him, her brown eyes looking slightly startled.

"I guess you haven't been in my place, have you?"

It seemed strange. Given the intimacy they'd shared. But she had not actually been inside his cabin. And she certainly hadn't wandered all over the property.

"Should I bring some pajamas?" she asked, smiling coyly.

"Hell no."

"Because we're going back to my place?"

"Hell no," he said. "It's just that you never need pajamas when you wear nothing but your skin."

She blushed, and he liked that.

She made him feel grounded. Connected in a way that he wasn't used to. She was so damn resilient. So hardy, and in many ways, he felt like she put him to shame. Everything she'd been through… She made him want to stand taller. Stand stronger.

She made him…

Well, she had always made him want to be a hero.

For that brave girl going through that loss the first time he'd seen her. That fear. That pain.

He'd needed to be a hero for her then. And he damn well wanted to be one now.

But you know you can't do anything to keep her safe.

He pushed that to the back of his mind. They dropped her car off at her property and then piled into his truck and drove up the dirt road together, all the way to the top of the mountain, where his cabin sat.

It was a beautiful spot. And he loved it, but he still didn't want his child anywhere near the edge.

"Why did you pick this spot?" she asked when she got out of the truck and looked around. "Knowing what I do about you now…I guess it doesn't make sense that you would pick it."

"Well," he said slowly. "You're back in Gold Valley, aren't you? And in some ways, that doesn't make any sense. Because it was a place where a whole lot of bad stuff happened. But you came back."

She frowned. "I guess…sometimes you have to face it, don't you?"

"Maybe," he said, wandering past the cabin over to the rock face that overlooked the valley below. "I haven't found an answer standing up here, though."

"Do you think if you keep looking you might?"

"I always have. At least, I did when I bought the place. It was damn beautiful." The sunlight taking all the green and dipping it in gold, and the ends of Vanessa's hair too, all lit up in the sunlight.

"That's the frustrating thing," he said. "You stand there, and you look for answers, and after time there isn't a damn thing out there. Just nothing but…silence."

"It was the silence that always used to scare me," she said. "I thought if I sat in the silence for too long I was going to hear things I didn't want to. Or just have to start feeling my own feelings."

"Yeah, I'm not a big fan of the silence."

"I found a lot of truth in it, though," she said. "I think that's the real problem. Getting down to that silence is one of the hardest things any of us can do. But that's when you hear it."

"Hear what?"

"Call it what you want. The voice of God. Your conscience. But it was in the silence that I heard some real answers for the first time in a long time."

"How did you get to the silence?"

She laughed. "Court-ordered rehab? I mean, I didn't go quietly, and I didn't particularly go willingly. It seemed preferable to going to prison for possession, and that was about it. But once I did go...when I was quiet, I was able to hear my own self for the first time in years. That's when I painted. It's when I fell. All these things that I'd been avoiding. I think it makes sense in a way that you go back. To the thing that hurt you. Try to find the answers there once you look for them everywhere else."

"I'm sorry that your family hurt you," he said. And he meant it. From the bottom of his soul he meant it. Because if her family hadn't... Maybe if her parents had been different she never would have gotten on the path she had. Maybe if they'd been there when she'd been in pain...

He clenched his teeth. "I'm sorry I didn't know you. I'm sorry I wasn't there for you more than I was."

Her eyes glossed over. "You were there for me more than anyone else. It was real. It was real for me."

"I wish I could've punched him back then."

"It's okay."

"It's not okay," he said. "What happened to you wasn't okay."

She took in a sharp breath. "I know. And I wasn't okay for a long time after. I wasn't. But I am now." She put her arm around his waist. "Here with you, I feel pretty all right."

"Come on," he said. "Let me walk you down the

trail, and I'll show you where we might build our house." They tripped up into the trees, beneath the thick, shaded canopy cover.

"We have to cut some of these down, wouldn't we?" she asked.

"Just some. It'll be pretty easy to widen this into an access road. But you don't want to just walk in every day. Not when you have baby stuff."

"We're going to have to get a babysitter," she said.

"Well, we do work on my parents' property. I'm sure that we'll have help there."

"Your relationship with your parents seems complicated," she said.

He thought about it. "I think it's more complicated for Gabe. My issues come from somewhere else."

"Well, in large part, so do mine. But that base-level stuff tends to come from your parents. The stuff that gets you into the other—"

"Yeah," he said. "Fair enough."

"I think my dad taught me to run. When things got hard he just…went back on the road." He looked down at her. "My dad is a nice man. But he's hurt a lot of people. He loves my mother, but he's spent a good portion of their marriage betraying their vows. That is… Well, either he's not actually a nice man, or he's great at running."

"Yeah. Sounds like it." She sighed heavily. "I know too much about doing things that make you hate yourself to say that your dad isn't a nice person. But he's probably a damaged one."

"Definitely." They stopped in front of a space that was mostly clear. "Can you imagine it?" he asked. "Isolated, quiet. Just trees for company."

"You know, most people would consider that lonely."

"Woman, I consider it a gift."

"I said *most* people," she said. "But…I think I'm okay being lonely here with you."

Her words made his heart ache, made him long for things that he didn't have a name for.

But that feeling in his chest, bittersweet and perfect, described by her words perfectly.

Being lonely with someone else. He couldn't think of anything better. At least, he couldn't think of something that would work better for himself.

He wished he knew a way to get rid of the lonely. But the very idea… The very idea made him feel threatened in the same way the suggestion that he let go of his guilt over Clint's death did. Like it was something he needed, though he couldn't for the life of him figure out why. "I think this is perfect," she said, touching him softly. He felt it like the impact of a bullet. She slid her fingertips down his arm, took his hand and led him back toward the cabin.

The sun had sunk behind the mountains, and the gray sky was beginning to pop with the appearance of silver stars.

He looked down at her, and she smiled up at him, and something about it suddenly felt so easily broken.

So temporary.

She was the most beautiful thing he'd ever seen in his life. Almost beautiful enough to block out the ugly things he'd seen.

The body of his friend. His other friend in a coffin, his widow weeping over the casket.

There was new life in this period with her. But it

was also so fragile and tentative that he wasn't sure he could bear it. He wasn't sure he could breathe past. And for a man who had learned to read through anything, smile through anything. Drink through anything, it was world stopping. World ending.

"Do you think that you could be happy here?" he asked.

He was happy to change the subject away from any and all internal musings. And get back to more practical things like plots of dirt where he could put a house. A way that he could take care of his woman and his child.

"Yes," she said softly. She walked up to him and put her hand on his chest, moved her hand up to his shoulders and back down.

He groaned, but not just with desire. It was something deeper than that. Something that touched him in a way that seems to go beyond the surface. That went beyond the physical.

Her touch did something to him, and it always had.

He didn't believe in fate or any other kind of mystical crap. If he believed in fate, maybe it would be easier. Easier to excuse himself because everything that had happened in his life would have simply been about a force beyond himself.

Sadly, he believed that what he did affected things around him.

And that was a much harder reality to bear.

But there was something about Vanessa that felt a lot closer to fate than anything else he ever experienced.

And it terrified him. Down to his core.

"Why don't we go check out my cabin?" he asked.

"I wouldn't mind," she said, looking at him from beneath her lashes.

They both knew what he meant by that. That his intentions weren't really to give her a tour of his one-room Lincoln Logs setup.

When they came out of the trees, it was dark, the stars really blanketed overhead. He opened the door to his house and let her inside.

It was rustic. To say the least.

He hadn't come up here to be comfortable. He had come up here to be alone.

To cut himself off.

To make sure that he didn't care. That he wouldn't hurt so bad anymore.

Those thoughts, like bullets, tore through the skin.

Guilt.

Guilt was a much easier way to interpret his actions.

Fear was something else entirely.

He gritted his teeth, pushed it away.

"This is it," he said, gesturing around the large great room. The only other room was the bathroom, through a door just next to the kitchen. Everything else was all there in one space. There was a skylight at the center of the room, filtering pale moonlight inside. There was a table shoved up against the wall with one chair added, a fridge, a microwave that he never used.

And a bed in the corner. It worked for him. It was all he needed all this time.

"This is where you live?"

"It was never my intention to keep the house. I was going to build something new."

"And then you didn't."

"It didn't seem necessary."

She reached for him again, her fingertips rising up the side of his neck, moving to touch his face. She brushed her fingertips along his stubbled jaw, her eyes never leaving his. "Sweetheart, you have to stop punishing yourself someday."

"A cabin in the woods isn't my idea of punishment," he said, but his voice had gone rough because she had called him *sweetheart*, and looked at him like she meant that word, and he didn't even know quite what to do with it.

He swallowed hard, not certain why it was such a difficult thing to do.

"If you say so," she said softly. She lifted her other hand, pressed her fingertips to his face and stroked him gently. "You're a beautiful man," she whispered.

"I'm glad you think so," he said. "Since you're going to be looking at my face for the next eighteen years at least."

A small smile tugged at her lips. "You know I don't even mean your face."

"Oh yeah?" He was about to say something crass, something about his body, but the look in her eyes stopped him.

Made him feel like there was a rock lodged in his chest.

He didn't think he could speak. Wasn't entirely sure if he could breathe.

She stepped back away from him, moving beneath the silver light coming down through the ceiling, and she slowly pulled her shirt over her head. She took her bra off, wiggled out of the rest of her clothes, and the breath rushed out of his lungs. She was the most beautiful thing he had ever seen. Ever.

And he just stood there and stared, let her silhouette burn into his brain. Because something felt so strange and tenuous about this moment. This moment where they were planning their future, planning their forever.

And somehow, he just didn't feel it. Didn't feel like it was possible.

Like it could happen.

His brain rejected the thought, and he pushed it away, moving to where she stood. He didn't want to touch her. It was like there was some kind of spell cast over them in this moment, like she was a vapor, a silver wisp that he might frighten off if he approached.

There he was, thinking magic things because of Vanessa Logan.

The woman was a phoenix. Reborn from ashes while he just lay there burning. Reduced and unable to figure out the way forward. And here she was, in all her glory, magic and new and better for all the things she had overcome, not damaged irreparably, but glorious and glowing and everything a man could need.

That thought terrified him.

Another stone thrown down into the pit of his stomach, where all that heaviness he'd been ignoring his whole life lay.

He approached her, and he leaned in, kissing her lips, not touching any other part of her as he did. Slowly, achingly so. He took it deeper, sliding his tongue across the seam of her lips and requesting entry.

And when she gave it… Oh, when she gave it, he took it.

He kissed her like that, his hands down at his sides, until neither of them could breathe. And then he fell to his knees. He touched her calves, running his hands up the sides of her smooth legs, until he came to grip her hips, eye level to that gorgeous V between her thighs, that he craved more than just about anything else.

He leaned in and tasted for himself. He lost himself in her. In the sounds she made as he pleasured her, and the way she coated his tongue, and the feel of her.

He wanted to remember it forever. This moment. The way that she consumed him as he consumed her. There was nothing else like it.

There had been other women. But he couldn't remember them. And he didn't want to. Because right now, his past felt burned clean, magic done by Vanessa and her strengths, a gift that he didn't deserve, not even for this moment.

And it was a beautiful moment.

He ached with the need for her. And he didn't know that he would ever be able to get his fill. Not if they had tonight, not if they had forever.

She threaded her fingers through his hair, holding him tight, and he pushed and pushed until she went over the edge, until the sounds of her pleasure filled his cabin. A space that had never heard the cries of a woman's pleasure—at least, not while he was here.

And now he would hear an echo across these walls for the rest of his life.

He didn't know why he had that thought, because in theory, he wouldn't be living here.

But it all felt temporary, and he couldn't shake that sense. Couldn't shake the bittersweet edge that burned across every breath he took.

But she cried out her pleasure, and he stood, lifted her up off the ground and wrapped her legs around his waist, carrying her over to the bed.

He brought her down onto the mattress, loomed above her. She smiled, her hand back on his face.

She liked to touch his face, and he didn't know why. But he liked it too.

"You have too many clothes on," she said softly, moving her hand over his chest.

"You going to do something about it?"

"I suppose I could," she said, treating him to a coquettish grin. She pushed her hand underneath his T-shirt, pushed it up higher, those clever fingertips teasing his stomach, and everything in him went hard.

He helped her get his shirt up over his head and then marched forward, and she gasped as his denim-clad body brushed up against hers. She arched into him, pleasuring herself on his body, her eyes going glassy. He could feel her heat, could feel her intensity, and her desire. And it mirrored his own.

He wanted to extend the moment, to make it last, but he didn't know if he had the strength. Didn't know if he had the willpower. At this moment, he didn't know he had anything in the whole world except for Vanessa, soft and naked in his arms, and he didn't care if he did.

Because she would be enough. This would be enough. As long as the moment didn't have to move on.

But time was a bitch. It made sad lonely boys into lonelier men who were hard around the heart. Made wives into widows. Friends into cold stone grave markers.

And he didn't know how to stop that. He didn't know but he wished he could. He wished he could stop right here, because this made sense.

This made him feel good.

And very little in his life had. Not at his own hand. But her hands were good.

Soft and sweet as they skimmed over his shoulders and down his back, as she pushed her fingers beneath his jeans and belt and scanned his ass. As she grabbed him and dug her fingernails into his skin. He moved his hands down her hips, lifted up her thigh and draped it over his lower back, moving forward slowly, back and forth until she cried out against his mouth, until she came again.

It still wasn't enough. But he needed to be inside her, and he didn't know how to fight that.

Wasn't that the thing? The fact that he just didn't know how to fight himself. Not at the end of the day. He didn't know how to do anything but get in, and that was part of why time slipped through his hands. He couldn't stop it. Even with that realization. Even as he shucked his jeans and underwear and came back to her body, every inch of his naked flesh against every inch of hers.

She reached between them, wrapped her hand around his cock and explored him thoroughly, moving her hand up and down, over the head, down underneath, and he saw stars. He growled, his mouth crashing down over hers, as he thrust inside her, into her warm, welcoming heat.

She arched up against him, and he went deeper, silver light flashing behind his eyelids and giving the impressions of stars as he gave up all his control and surrendered. To the moment, to the passing time, the end of tonight, which came closer with each thrust. As if each increment of pleasure cost him precious moments.

But he didn't know how to fight it.

And ultimately, he didn't want to. She shuddered against him, her internal muscles pulsing around his cock as she found her release again, her fingernails making half-moons on his skin to mirror the one in the sky.

And that was when it slipped from his hands completely, time unraveling all around him as the world splintered and the world shattered like a glass pane, raining down pleasure on him in a thousand glittering pieces.

When it was over, he lay there with her, not alone, in this cabin for the first time.

With someone who knew all of his secrets.

Who knew what had happened to him when he was a boy. Who knew the guilt he carried as a man.

Who knew his body, and every fractured piece of his heart. The enormity of it was so big he couldn't breathe.

So he turned away from her and closed his eyes, like he might sleep, because he didn't know what else to do.

Because if there was one thing he'd proved to be consistently, it was a man who avoided things he couldn't handle.

But she didn't leave him there.

Her hand stretched across the space between them, and soft fingertips came to rest on his arm.

She stayed like that. All night. Just touching him gently, never breaking contact. And he stayed awake. And when the sky began to turn gray, and the morning light began to show through, he felt a sense of dread growing in his chest.

The night was over, and damned if he knew why, but it felt significant. Damn Vanessa Logan and that sense of faith she seemed to carry around with her. Damn Vanessa and the fact she made him believe in things he would have said he didn't. Made him want things he would've said he never could.

And that hand. Damn that hand that rested on his shoulder. It belonged to a woman who knew all that he was, and was still there in his bed.

He didn't know what to do with it. If time was still moving forward.

They couldn't stop it. Couldn't control it. Couldn't slow it, not with any amount of pleasure, pain or alcohol, because he had tried.

This woman had reached into his chest and wrapped her hand around his heart, and he had no idea what he was supposed to do with that. It choked him. Terrified him. Made it so he couldn't breathe.

He needed to breathe.

He needed distance.

He couldn't stop time.

But one thing he thought he might be able to do was speed it up.

So Jacob sat up and swung his legs over the side of the mattress. Then he got out of bed.

CHAPTER TWENTY

"JACOB?" VANESSA WAS GROGGY. She could hardly think. Even this long after her third orgasm she was fuzzy.

There had been an intensity to Jacob that she couldn't quite untangle. But she couldn't complain either.

Because he had been amazing. A leader and a partner all at the same time. The man was magic in ways she hadn't realized a person could be. He was so dear and precious, and she didn't know how he had become all of that.

She thought that with him she'd made a mistake of some kind. But she hadn't. Not really. She had come home to Gold Valley, but she hadn't really come home until she had been in Jacob's arms. This man, who had been a constant to her for so long. This man, who had been an anchor and hope on the worst night of her life.

The man who had become, not just her past, but her future.

But something had happened in the past few moments. Something had shifted. She could feel it in his body language.

In everything.

Really, she'd felt it when he had turned over after they'd finished last night.

He had put deliberate distance between them, and she wasn't sure if she knew why that was.

"GO BACK TO BED," he said.

He was hunting for his clothes, and he pulled his jeans on, then pulled his T-shirt over his head.

"Where are you going? I rode up here with you."

"Nowhere," he said, his expression blank.

And she could tell that he had just realized that. That he was her ride, and he couldn't just wander off somewhere.

"Thank you for showing me your house," she said.

Maybe if she backtracked the conversation, if she moved it to a place where they had both been comfortable, to a topic that had been acceptable, he would come back to bed. It would go back to how it had been. But she didn't really think so. She just wished it could be true. So much. But when he looked at her, there was something blank and terrible in his expression, and she knew that she wasn't going to be able to win this. Not by going backward.

But then, that was the story of her life. Going backward didn't work. She had to go forward. Even here.

Of course, she hadn't been doing that, not totally, not with her family. She had gone back. Back to old patterns.

Not into addiction and drugs, but into being assured of her victimhood and of the fact that no one could understand her. While not being forthright about the fact that she wanted to be understood. About how she needed to be understood. About how she needed them to simply love her as she was or walk away. Everything just moved forward. And she had to find a way to move forward with it.

"Jacob," she said.

"What?"

"I love you."

She did. She loved him in ways she didn't think she could have ever loved another human being.

Because he made her feel…precious. She hadn't had to ask him to give that to her.

He had listened and understood. He had defended her at every turn. The only person who had—even when he was angry—been on her team from the beginning. Without being asked.

She had talked so much about valuing herself, about never taking less, not anymore.

And he had showed her, in a thousand different ways, that he did.

Right now, she realized she needed to value herself enough to ask for this. To ask for love.

Because otherwise it would always be a series of moments where she wondered. Wondered if what they had could last, and she didn't want to wonder. She wanted to know.

"I don't know what love has to do with anything," he said.

"It has to do with everything," she said.

"Since when? You were perfectly happy to marry me without any talk of feelings, and now suddenly you're talking about love?"

"Are you going to tell me that you don't feel anything? After that?" She gestured to the bed as if he might be confused about what she meant. "I mean, the connection that we have… There's no way that is just physical. We've both had sex with other people. We know that this is more than that."

"It's very good sex," he agreed.

He agreed easily, casually, and there was something unspeakably painful about that.

Because she was dredging up feelings from deep inside her heart, and he seemed to be letting it all glance off like blows against heavy, thick armor.

"I want this to be more than just convenient," she said. "That's the point. I just… I love you. I love you, and I have come into a deeper and deeper understanding of that recently. I want… I want more. I want everything. I was willing to take convenience, because I thought it was all I could have. Because I've never… I've never been able to trust in anyone's feelings for me. And I can't sign on for that with you. I don't want to. I want all of it. Everything. The whole deal. Love and vows and promises. Because we can have that. I know we can. I can have it. You can. We don't deserve to be defined by mistakes or pain. We deserve better. We can have better. We just have to ask for it."

"No," he said, his voice flat. "I don't… That's not what I want."

"You don't want everything?"

"No. Some people can't have everything, Vanessa. They can't."

"Why not?"

"Because some people are broken," he said.

"Am I?" she asked, her voice getting immeasurably small. "Am I broken? Is that why I can't have everything?"

"It's me," he ground out. "*I* can't have everything."

"Well, if you can't, then neither can I." His face was blank as she said that because he still didn't understand. That if he hobbled himself he did the same to her.

"We can have… We can have good things. We can have a life. It doesn't need to be…this. It doesn't need to be dramatic and over-the-top. It doesn't need to be anything more than a logical decision, because let me tell you, every decision I've ever made that didn't lead with my head ended badly."

"That's not… That's not even reasonable," she said. "Life is full of decisions. You can't walk it back and rethink every one of them. Your brain edits the details out. You think of defining things, traumatic things, and I'm sorry that you've been through them, but you can't allow them to be your entire life."

"Yes, I can."

"Should *I*? Should I let my—my assault and my miscarriage and my drug use be all that I am?" She shook her head. "I don't want that. I want to be loved. I want to be more than Vanessa Logan, druggie and disappointment. I want to be Vanessa Dalton, Jacob Dalton's wife. I want to be a mother. I want to be loved. And most important, I want to be me, and you made me feel like I could be all those things at once, and before, I never thought that was possible."

"I already explained to you the way things were going to be with me. I can't stop you from…feeling how you feel. But it will fade. After years of living with me, if you want something I can't give, then you're not going to be happy."

"Don't tell me how I'm going to be happy," she said.

But inside she knew that he was right. That if she took a fraction she would be selling them both short. Because they could do better. They could. They could do so much better than this half life. Where they pretended at marriage and danced around feelings. Where they loved a child between them but wouldn't allow themselves to love each other.

If she accepted it, she would be selling them both short. She would be agreeing with him that he was broken. That they were broken and that they couldn't or shouldn't be whole. Everyone had left him alone up here. His family, in spite of how much they loved him. Everyone had accepted—to a degree—the level of brokenness that he chose to show the world.

Like a boy painting *fuck this* all over a canvas, that was how Jacob went through life. And he didn't let anyone close, and he didn't let anyone see deeper. But he had given her an insight into what he was, into who he was. And if she did the same thing everyone else did, if she left him alone on the mountaintop, if she didn't demand that he come down, if she didn't demand that he meet her there, then she was not really loving him.

She would be a crutch. She would be a hindrance to them both. Devaluing herself yet again, and what she deserved. Afraid to demand love because she had always been afraid to demand that.

And letting him stay closed off.

Letting him stay the way he'd been. That boy who'd seen something so devastating he couldn't speak of it.

She didn't want to allow him to stay locked inside himself, because they could have better. They could, and they should. And if he wouldn't demand it for them, then she would have to.

She felt like she was standing on the edge of an abyss, because her only experience with this had been failure.

Any other time she had ever thought to test the

limits of love, she had found the edge of it. But she believed that she and Jacob had the potential for love that stretched endlessly, that went on forever. That could cover an entire life. A life of happiness, sadness, mistakes and triumphs.

But it would have to be tested now. It would have to be demanded now. Otherwise they were doomed.

Because love—*commitment*—was a choice. And this was the crossroads. Either they took it or they didn't, but it had to be decided.

"I love you," she said again. "And I want you to love me. I think you can. Jacob, I think you *do*. I have lived in places for years at a time and never grown an attachment to someone the way I have to you. It's not time that we need, it's something else. We needed something that was in each other, and I think we found it. I am so damn glad that we did. I think we've been dancing around something real and deep since we saw each other again for the first time. I think we covered it up with fighting and sex. Because there was something on the other side of it, and we can step into it, but we have to be brave. We have to think we're worth it. We can't believe we're broken. I refuse to believe it," she said. "Because if I'm broken forever, then there was never a point in trying to put myself back together."

"You're not broken," he said, his voice rough. "You're not broken, and you deserve better than someone who is. I wanted to make it work. I wanted to make this something, because I like my life to be easy. And God knows that being married to you would've been easier than trying to sort out a separate life. You deserve better than that. You deserve better than someone looking for easy."

"Is that what you think of yourself? Still? You think that you're easy? That you don't take chances on life? That you don't put yourself out there to save people, to protect them? Because you have a whole history of that. You were there for me when no one else was."

"It was my job," he said flatly. "You were one of any number of women who I helped, one of any number of people. It wasn't special. And it wasn't personal. And it is not any evidence that I am a damn hero."

The words lanced her heart like an arrow. "Don't say that. Please. I needed you and you were there, and it mattered. And you've been there for me—"

"I was there for you and I got paid, and I was there for you when you were naked. It's not anything. It's not anything that anyone else wouldn't do. I'm not your hero. I can't save anyone. I never have. Not when it counted. Not off the clock. Don't make me into something that I'm not. Make yourself and what you can be, go right ahead and do that, but don't confuse all the strength you have inside yourself with something you're going to find in me. This is what I am," he said, gesturing around the room. "I am Hank Dalton's son through and through. I've never done a thing but let people down when it counted. I chose my own pleasure over responsibility, my own comfort over anything else. No matter which road I take, it seems to be the path I end up on. Thoughtless, careless. Down to having sex with you without a condom. No, I'm not a hero."

"For somebody so married to that narrative, you've sure taken a lot of work where you could be one."

"Because I tried," he said. "I tried to be someone who could save another person. If you get paid to do it, you figure that you get put into those situations and you can, and then… When there's a call on the radio, and it's all coming down, I guess I can be. But in my life? I've never once managed. I don't feel it. I don't feel anything."

"I don't believe that either. Look at you. Look at the way you are with those boys, the way that you have helped your brothers with this ranch. The way you've been there for me. You do feel things. You feel everything."

And she could see all at once the terror in his eyes, and she knew that she was right. She knew that he felt things. That he felt them deep and heavy, and that the mere idea of it scared him to death. "I can be your husband," he said. "I can protect you, support you, sleep with you. But I can't do…everything else. And if that's what you need to be happy—"

"Yes," she said, her voice almost failing her. "It's what I need. It's what I need. Why should I be the only person who doesn't…doesn't get to be loved? You get to be loved. I love you. Your brothers love you. Your parents love you. Even Ellie loves you while you sit around mired in guilt that isn't yours."

He flinched at that, and she wondered if she'd finally made it through the armor.

She went on, hoping she had. Hoping she'd reach him. "Guilt you seem to need to protect yourself. All those people love you, Jacob, you asshole. Is loving me so damn difficult? My parents can't do it, my sister can't do it without a heaping dose of effort on her part. And you can't. The father of my child. The man that I let into my body. The first man that I've ever been with sober. I gave myself to you in a way that I've never given myself to anyone else. I gave my heart to you in a way that I've never… In a way that I never even knew I could. You can't give me this. Because you—you need to protect yourself. Because you're a coward," she said. The words were flying faster now. She was spitting them out like acid, and she couldn't stop herself because if she let them inside her chest she knew they would burn a hole straight through her heart. It wasn't fair. It wasn't there at all, and he was just standing there. Standing there looking like granite. Like the mountain that this cabin was built on. He was immovable.

And she was falling off a cliff.

"It's not about you," he said. "It's about me."

"Then you really haven't learned anything. All this stuff you've been through and you haven't learned a damn thing."

"You don't have any therapy talk for me?"

Rage burned right through the pain in her heart. "No. I'm sorry. I can't detach and make us both more comfortable. I don't have therapy talk, I just have a broken heart. What do you have to say to that?"

Nothing. He said nothing. He simply stood there and stared at her. She launched herself forward and hit him on the chest with her closed fist. "I love you. I was never going to love anyone like this."

"We can still get married," he said.

The world's worst consolation prize. The lamest and most ineffectual offering after she'd cut herself open and bled for him.

"I don't want to marry you," she said. "I want to move as far away from you as I can and forget that I ever met you. But I can't. Because we're having a baby.

Now I'm stuck with you. I'm stuck with this. Stuck with this feeling... Right now I think I hate you as much as I ever loved you."

She slipped her clothes on. Not talking. Not saying a damn thing. No amount of bile that she spit out seemed to change anything. He didn't relent. Didn't say never mind that he loved her, he was sorry that he hurt her.

He just didn't say anything at all, while she collected everything and made her way toward the door. And she hoped, even still, that he would stop her. That he would tell her to wait. That he would realize he was making a mistake. Because surely, he would. What they had was so real, and raw, and it felt deeper than any feeling she had ever experienced before in her entire life. How could he not feel the same?

She just didn't believe what he said. She just didn't believe that he couldn't feel. Not when she felt so much.

But he remained unmoved. He was just watching her go.

And then she realized she couldn't go. Because she didn't have a car.

And she wasn't going to give him the satisfaction of stopping now. Not at all.

"You don't have a car," he said, his words feeling maddeningly redundant given she had already realized that.

"I'll call for a ride."

"You don't have to do that. You live two miles down the road, I'll drive you."

"I do," she said. "I can't stand to be with you for another second."

And she wasn't sure she could stand not being

with him either, but something had to give. Something had to.

She stormed out the cabin door and into the still, cold morning. She took out her phone and looked at it.

She could call Ellie, and really, she wanted to, but Ellie was probably at home by herself with Amelia, and she wouldn't be able to leave her little girl to come and get Vanessa.

Olivia.

She would have to call Olivia, who had a husband at home with her, so she would be able to leave.

And why not? She was bleeding all of her feelings all over everything. She might as well show Olivia what a mess she was. That she hadn't changed.

She wrapped her arms around her waist for a moment like it might hold her together, keep her from flying into pieces. Then she pulled out her phone and dialed her sister's number as she began to walk down the driveway.

She would just hope she didn't get eaten by a cougar.

If she did, maybe Jacob would be sorry.

She let out a heavy breath and lifted the phone to her ear. On the fourth ring, Olivia answered. "Are you okay?" she asked.

She stopped in the middle of the gravel driveway and looked around, at the sad gray sky fading into lightness with very little morning glory to be had, at the grim, gray trees that lined either side of the road. "No," she said. "I need a ride."

"From where?" She could hear her sister springing into action already.

"Just from Jacob's house down to mine. But I don't

really want to walk on the road because it's, like, two miles and I might get eaten by a large predator."

"Well, don't get eaten."

It took Olivia about ten minutes to arrive. When her car pulled up, Vanessa was bathed in a glow from the headlights.

She trudged sadly to the passenger side and got in.

"You want to just go get some coffee?" Olivia asked.

"Yes," Vanessa said.

She buckled, grabbed hold of the shoulder strap and leaned her head against it as Olivia turned around and they began to head down the driveway and toward town.

"What happened?" Olivia asked finally.

"I think he broke up with me," Vanessa said, misery washing over her in a wave.

"That dickhead," Olivia snarled, hitting the steering wheel. "Did he really?"

"Wow," Vanessa said. "I don't think I've ever heard you use that sort of language."

"Luke is a bad influence," Olivia said. "And I'm kind of okay with it at this point."

"I think I am too."

"Plus, he hurt you." They pulled up in front of Sugar Cup. It was just now six o'clock, and it was starting to open. They sat for a moment at the curb in front of the little coffee shop.

The old white brick building was a staple of Vanessa's past, and for some reason it made her feel unaccountably sad now.

Maybe because she'd gone there before her life had gotten cruddy and complicated.

Because it reminded her of nice times in Gold Valley, and she couldn't access any feelings about nice times right now.

"I know I've hurt you," Olivia said. "So maybe I don't have the right to get angry at him for doing it too. But I'm angry at him all the same."

"You came to pick me up," Vanessa pointed out.

"I'm sorry," Olivia said. "I'm so sorry that I was so...useless when you needed me."

"You weren't useless, Olivia. I pushed you away, and you didn't know what to do. We were young, and we were stupid. I think every time we interact now we carry a little bit of that with us."

"Yeah," Olivia said. "I've changed, though. I think I still default back to prickly prude, though. I try not to."

"I think you're going to have to tell me about how you ended up with Luke."

"Maybe after you tell me what happened with Jacob?"

"I'd rather hear a nice story first."

They got out of the truck and pushed on the black door, walking into the coffeehouse, bathed in a cozy, welcoming aura, a welcome change from the cold light outside.

It was empty, all the tables vacant, and Vanessa knew that would change within a half hour.

The place was as adorable as ever, the redbrick wall at the back decorated with a large photograph of the main street of town, the floor all made of scarred barn wood and a giant rustic chandelier hanging at the center of the place.

Home.

A piece of home, and a happy piece of it, at that.

"Do they still make sugar bars?"

"They do," Olivia said. "Though, I'm partial to cinnamon rolls."

The two of them ordered coffee and their preferred treats, and went and sat down at the table.

Olivia told Vanessa about how she had been dating Bennett Dodge. And how she had broken up with Bennett when he'd failed to propose when she had expected him to, and then had landed upon the bright idea of using Luke Hollister to make Bennett jealous.

It hadn't worked.

And Olivia had found herself falling in love with unsuitable Luke, even while trying to win back the man who she had decided was suitable.

"I was obsessed with being perfect," Olivia said. "At the expense of other people, I might add. I'm sorry... I think I did the same to you."

"Mom and Dad are hard," Vanessa said slowly. "I felt like they needed us to be perfect too. But my response to that was not to...try. Because I didn't think I could ever be good enough. So I tested the limits, and I found them."

"They never quit loving you," Olivia said. "But that doesn't make it okay that they couldn't show it."

"I don't know," Vanessa said, sighing heavily. "We all could've made some different choices, probably."

"That's probably the truest thing," Olivia said. "We all could have done a little bit better."

"I wish I knew how to do better now. I'm ready to ask for better," she said. "I'm ready to...have better. And Jacob doesn't... He doesn't love me."

Olivia looked down blankly at her cinnamon roll, then looked up at Vanessa. "Does he really not?"

"I thought he did, and he was just being afraid. I yelled at him. And I figured he was bound to come to his senses and stop me from leaving."

"If there's one thing I've learned about big, bad cowboys," Olivia said slowly, "it's that they are big and strong, and often their fear is bigger and stronger. Luke was like that. Do you think he went quietly into falling in love with me? Hell no. He really didn't want to."

"But here you are, together," Vanessa said.

"Yes," Olivia said. "Here we are. Don't give up on him just yet."

"It's different. He feels stuck with me because we're having a baby."

"Clearly he doesn't, since he found it easy to break up with you."

"Well, how will I know? How will I know if he loves me, or if he just regrets breaking off the marriage."

"You'll know. Because when a man loves you it's pretty damn obvious. Even if he says he doesn't."

Vanessa closed her eyes and took a bite of the coconut-and-white-chocolate confection in front of her. She chewed for a moment, hoping that the sugar would pour a little sweetness on her soul.

But not even that did it.

"I don't know what to do."

"Well, I'm not going to walk away from you," Olivia said. She reached across the table and took Vanessa's hands in hers. "Whatever you need, I'm on your side. I'm so sorry that it took me this many years to say that. I am so sorry it took me this many years to reach out. But I will never, ever watch you drown.

Never again. You were right, Vanessa. I turned away from you when you needed me."

"You can't take all the fault," Vanessa said. "It's too easy for me to give it to you, and that's not fair."

"None of it's fair," Olivia said. "But I could use a lot less self-righteousness, and a lot more humility. Because it was self-righteousness that kept us apart in the first place."

"Well, it's easy to see now at twenty-seven, isn't it? But we were sixteen."

"I know," Olivia said. "But we're not now."

"No," Vanessa said. "We're not." She sighed heavily. "I need to call Ellie and tell her I'm not coming into work for the next few days. I can't face him."

"Fair enough."

"When Luke said he didn't love you...did you feel like your life was over?"

"Yes," Olivia said. "It turned me into the dramatic emo teenager that I never was before. It was funny, because I thought that I was in love with Bennett, but being without Bennett just felt inconvenient. Being without Luke made it hard to breathe." She blinked. "But I did keep breathing. Because in the end, whatever had happened between the two of us, what he couldn't take back was what I got from being with him."

Those words struck a chord inside Vanessa. And Olivia kept on talking.

"He made me a stronger, better version of myself. He made me the girl who could stand in front of him and say that she loved him even while he rejected me. And I was miserable. Absolutely miserable. But I was stronger. Stronger because of him. I think that's how

you know it's real. Whatever happens in the future...
You take a piece of the love forward, and it adds to
you. Makes you better."

"I know he did that for me," Vanessa said softly.
"And it was all that better he made me that ruined us.
Because I can't take less than love. Not now."

"And you shouldn't," Olivia said. "None of us
should ever take less than love."

"I think...I have some thinking to do," she said.

She might not be able to change the way things were
going with Jacob. She might never be able to fix it.

But there were other things in her life she might be
able to repair with the strength that he had given her.

Whatever happened with him, she wasn't going to
waste these changes.

"Can you take me home?" she asked when the coffee was drunk and the sweets were gone.

"Sure."

They drove home in silence, and when Olivia
dropped her off, she frowned. "Do you want me to
stay with you?"

"Thank you. But I need to be alone."

Alone with her feelings. Her very bad feelings. The
sharp, awful feelings.

And as she stood there alone in her living room with
those feelings bearing down on her, she knew that she
could withstand them.

And that was the biggest gift she'd been given, one
that had been building across all these years, and so-
lidified with him.

The giver of the heartbreak, the provider of the
strength to withstand it.

Because she was worth more, and that meant she would have to walk through this pain to get there.

Because she was worth too much to dull her feelings and turn them into a muddy river that might sweep her away.

So she stood strong in her pain, and she felt it. Felt it slice through her like a knife. Until she thought she might bleed out there all over the floor of her little house.

And in the midst of all that pain, she gave thanks. Because she didn't want drugs, and she didn't want to drink. She wanted him, that was true. But more than anything, she wanted to be her, even now, even when it was hard.

Because she had work that she loved. She had a strength cultivated from pain. She had a future.

Her child. This relationship that she was growing slowly and steadily with Olivia. Her friendship with Ellie.

Even now, even in all this pain, she wasn't a black hole. Not anymore.

She was Vanessa Logan, and she would endure.

And she was damn proud of that.

CHAPTER TWENTY-ONE

VANESSA DIDN'T SHOW up to work the next day, or the day after that. And the only person who knew why—Ellie—wasn't speaking to him at all.

You asshole, you know why.

Because of him. He was worried, worried sick because of course he was afraid that there was something going on with her physically. Something to do with the baby.

Yeah, that's all you're worried about.

He knew enough to know that she was alive and well, and had made it home safely after she'd stormed out early that morning. But beyond that…he didn't know a damn thing. Art class was canceled for the remainder of the week, and Jacob felt like the boys—boys who had acted like they didn't care at all—weren't very happy about it.

They built in more time for outdoor stuff, did extra writing, and he knew the kids all enjoyed that, but they did miss Vanessa.

But it was Aiden who rounded on Jacob with dark, angry eyes one afternoon when they were doing chores. "So what happened to her?"

"She's just taking some time off," he said.

"Liar. Something happened. I can tell."

"You're just a kid. You can't tell anything," he said,

immediately regretting the words, but not rushing to take them back either.

"You did something wrong," Aiden said. "And I don't know why I'm surprised. You're just an asshole like everyone else."

"I didn't even think you liked art."

"I like *her*," Aiden said. "She—she cares about people." He shifted uncomfortably. "I think she knows… I think she knows how hard stuff is."

"She does," Jacob said. "And she'll be back."

"No, she won't," Aiden said. "I bet you she won't."

He turned and stormed away from Jacob, leaving him stunned.

"What the hell?" Caleb asked, moving over from where he'd been by the barn, helping one of the kids tack up a horse.

"He's just pitching a tantrum. He'll be fine."

"About Vanessa not being here?"

"The kids really love her class."

"And they love her," Caleb said. "What's going on? Because you've been a snarling asshole for the past few days."

"We broke up," Jacob said. "So sorry, I guess you don't get to be my best man anymore."

Caleb shook his head. "You dumb asshole. What did you do?"

"Why the hell do you think I did anything?"

"Because we're related. And we're related to Hank. So I assume that it all runs in the family."

"I'm not… I can't love her. And I told her that."

"Why the hell not?" Caleb asked.

"I don't…want to talk about this with you."

"Why not?"

"Because you're the sad sack wandering around after a woman he can't have, and I am not in the space to get a lecture from you."

And just like that, Jacob found himself getting knocked backward, his back crashed up against a tree, and his head hit pretty hard. He almost saw stars, and his brother didn't look at all apologetic. "Watch it," Caleb said.

"Get out of my face, then. You know what, Caleb? If it wasn't the truth, you wouldn't feel the need to hit me."

"You're a coward," Caleb said.

Jacob turned away from him. "And if it wasn't the truth," Caleb continued. "You wouldn't have to walk away."

Jacob turned around. "What can I give her? What am I going to offer her? I can't… I haven't done anything right. Not ever. What makes you think it's gonna be different with her?"

"I don't know," Caleb said. "What I do know is you could have her. You literally got her pregnant. It is the clearest path to having the woman that you want. And the only thing in the way is you. From where I'm standing I think that makes you a dumbass."

And then it was Caleb's turn to leave him there, and Jacob spent the rest of the day feeling pissed off. And at the end of the school day, when the kids were getting rounded up to go back to their homes, there was one person missing.

"Has anyone seen Aiden?" Jacob asked.

"No," Gabe said, shaking his head. "I haven't seen him anywhere."

"When was the last time you saw him?"

"Around lunchtime," Gabe said. "When we went out to do chores."

"He walked away from me then," Jacob said. "I haven't seen him since."

"Dammit," Gabe said. "Well, let's see if he turns up at his foster home, and I guess until then we'll keep an eye out here. We don't know that he left intentionally."

But as night began to fall, and they heard from Aiden's foster parents that they still hadn't seen him or heard from him, it became apparent that he'd left.

The police department didn't have the manpower to mobilize a search party. SAR could get involved in the morning, but as far as they were all concerned that wasn't soon enough.

Jacob went into the art studio. It was dark, and it made his chest feel tight. Because memories of Vanessa were all over, and it smelled like paint, which made him think of her. Of the way they'd made love in here. The way her hands, her body, often smelled after a long day at school.

He wandered through the room and looked at the canvases. And he saw one he knew he hadn't seen being worked on in class.

It was of a boy with dark skin and black hair, his head bent down over his forearms. Alone. On a blank black background.

Aiden.

Aiden had finally painted his heart.

And Jacob had never felt more like a coward.

He felt like a rock had settled in his gut. He tore out of the studio, to where his brothers had assembled in Gabe's office.

"This is my fault," Jacob said.

"Why?" Gabe asked.

"Because we exchanged words, and he walked away. And I didn't try to stop him."

"This isn't time for your guilt complex," Caleb snapped. "It doesn't help anyone."

"Fine," Jacob said through gritted teeth and didn't argue as much as he would've liked to, because Caleb was right, there was no point sitting around casting blame when action needed to be taken. "We need to form a search party. We gotta go into the woods. Make sure he's not in there. For all we know, he's somewhere hale and hearty on the property, but if he went back in there…there's all kinds of places he could've gotten hurt. There's places he could fall." Specifically, he was thinking about the cliff that Gavin had fallen off all those years ago. The very idea of Aiden finding himself in that situation made Jacob sick. "Let's get the horses. I'll call Dad and see if he wants to come out."

In half an hour, Caleb, Jacob, Luke Hollister, Gabe, Jamie, Hank Dalton and the Dodge brothers were all on horseback, lined up at the entrance to the woods.

"We'll ride in and comb the place," Jacob said, turning the headlamp on his cowboy hat on. "Canvas the area as best we can."

"Let's go."

They rode into the dark woods, forming a grim line, their headlights casting a glow across the bush as they searched.

Periodically, someone would yell Aiden's name. Taking the chance that he wouldn't run away from rescue and was likely ready to come back to civilization by now.

Jacob looked to his left and saw Gabe there, and then to his right, at Caleb.

There was something comforting about having them there. His brothers at his sides.

And it made him realize how difficult it had been all this time, to be isolated the way that he had been.

Not just in the past couple of years since Clint's death, but in all the years before that. When Gavin had died and he had shut everything out, because he didn't want to face the feelings that existed inside him.

But they had always been there. Always. It was Jacob who hadn't always been able to reach out.

He turned his focus back to the task at hand, urging his horse forward.

When they were about an hour into the woods, they had all put some distance between each other, brush and ridges spreading out the search party.

Jacob felt compelled to head to that place where Gavin had fallen. A combination of dread, terror and what he hoped was paranoia spurring him on.

He kicked the horse's flanks and urged him up the side of the steep mountain. "Aiden!" he called over and over again, his voice echoing across the space. Rebounding back off the side of the mountain across from them.

"Jacob?"

The voice he heard was faint, but it was there all the same.

"Aiden?"

"I'm down here!"

"Dammit," Jacob said, dismounting and moving over to the edge of the narrow trail.

He looked down and saw Aiden, wedged into a small outcropping on the side of the cliff.

He was hanging on, but just barely, and he looked terrified.

"Are you all right?"

"I think I broke my ankle," Aiden said. "I fell off the side of the trail and I can't move. If I do I'm gonna fall."

"I won't let you fall," Jacob said, terror like granite in his chest. But if he was certain of anything in his life, it was this: he would not let Aiden fall. Not now.

He grabbed the radio that was strapped to his belt and called to the channel his brothers were on. "I've got him. I'm sending you coordinates on the GPS. We might need the fire department."

Jacob had a rope stashed at his side, and he unhooked it. He tied one end of it to a rock, and the other to his waist. "I'm going to come down toward you."

"Shouldn't you wait for help?"

"I don't want the ground to give way. If you fall... I'm not waiting."

"Okay," Aiden said, clearly not about to argue about a rescue.

Jacob made sure the rope was secure, and he slid down partway, toward Aiden. "I have done this before," Jacob said, talking to the kid as he made his way toward him. "I was an EMT. And a firefighter."

"My hero," Aiden said drily.

"I might just be," Jacob said.

When he got down to him, he grabbed hold of his arm, and then the rest of him. "Now the hard part. I just have to drag us both up."

He heard brush crashing above him. "Jacob?"

"Down here," Jacob called up.

"Do you have him?"

"Yes," Jacob said. "Help me out. Grab hold of the rope and pull us up."

Jacob climbed, and with support from Caleb and Gabe, he managed to get both of them back up onto the narrow trail. A burst of adrenaline went through his chest, and suddenly all of the strength drained from his body. He lay on his back, right next to Aiden, who was panting.

And then he hit him. "What the hell were you thinking?"

"I was mad," Aiden said. "I just wanted to go for a walk."

"You don't know the area, you didn't tell anyone where you were. You are in big trouble. You are grounded for the rest your life."

"You're not my dad," Aiden croaked.

"Maybe not. But I'm going to be somebody's dad. I might as well start practicing on you."

They got away from the ravine, and Caleb helped Aiden up onto the back of Jacob's horse, and they all rode into the edge of the woods. By the time they got there, the fire department was waiting to take a look at his ankle.

"You're gonna want to go to the hospital," one of the guys said. "You need to get that set."

"Will do," he said.

Aiden's foster parents weren't far behind the fire department, and they bundled him into the car and took him off toward the hospital.

Jacob knew they didn't need him, but he struggled with wanting to follow them all the same. "You're a damn hero," Caleb said. "Whenever something like that goes down…you show up. It's what you do."

"I'm not a hero," he said.

"Yeah, except that everything you do proves that you are," Caleb responded. "And I don't know why you're so married to the idea that you can't be. But you are, aren't you?"

"I haven't done anything that anyone else wouldn't do," Jacob said.

"Um," Caleb said. "I'm pretty sure you have. Most people wouldn't tie a rope to their waist and go down the side of a cliff to save someone else's life. That, in my book, is a hero. Look what you do, look what you've always done for work. You are a hero, Jacob, and I don't know why the hell you can't seem to handle that."

"Because I've never been able to do it when it counts."

"What's tonight? Aiden. He counts. He matters."

"He sure as hell does," Jacob said. "But he could have died. He could have died, and ultimately, there would have been nothing I could do to stop it. Great. I showed up, and I was able to act. But it might not have ended that way. It might not have ended that way, and we can't know when something is going to go bad."

Caleb looked at him, his expression blank. "No," he agreed. "We can't. We can't know that, and that's why we have to do everything that we can to make sure we're there when it counts. That's what you did tonight, that's all anyone can do."

"Not enough," Jacob said, desperation clawing at his chest. "It's not enough, and it's never going to be. I can't… I can't be a hero."

"Why not?"

"Because I—"

"Don't say it's because you feel guilty about Clint."

"I need to feel guilty about it," he said, the words bursting out of his mouth. "I need to feel guilty about it because if I don't…then I just have to feel it. Then I just have to feel it like everything else. And I don't know if I can do that. How are you supposed to do that? Walk around with all that shrapnel in your chest. That loss. That knowledge that…any given day one of us could wake up and not come back home."

Caleb nodded slowly. "I mean, I get it. I know what it's like to walk around feeling bulletproof for a long damn time and then realize we aren't. What we do… It's not without risk. But of course we've done it so many times, been right in the thick of it and come out of it okay. Losing Clint like that, it drives the whole reality of it home."

"I've always known," Jacob said. "I've always known that it could end. That you could be here one minute, and the next be gone. When Gavin died… When Gavin died, I knew then. I was ten years old and I knew it."

His brother knew Jacob had lost a friend as a child, but he didn't know the details, and Jacob wasn't about to get into them now. Caleb clearly wasn't going to press.

"It's not the not-being-bulletproof that gets me," Jacob continued. "It's that the people around me aren't. It's that I can't predict it or control it. That I can't stop it. That no matter how hard I tried… Dammit, Caleb, I went into being an EMT, went into the fire department to try to make some kind of difference, but it doesn't help protect the people around me. It's still not enough. Me being a damn hero isn't enough. I will never be enough of one to stop time from moving on, to stop…fate, or whatever the hell it is that I don't even want to believe in. Because I want to believe we have choices, but I can't seem to… I can't seem to be able to make the right ones."

"That's just life," Caleb said. "We can't know what's going to happen day to day, and we can't control or stop everything. That's just…the way it is."

"And that's just fine with you?"

"No," Caleb said. "Hell no. It's not fine with me at all. But what else can we do?"

"How am I supposed to live with Vanessa? How am I supposed to love her, knowing that… I mean, what if I deserve her? What if I'm not broken? What if I could have her? What if she could be my wife? The mother of my child, and she could live with me, for the rest of our lives. What if all that's true? But what if I lost her? What if I couldn't protect her? Then what? Then what would I do?"

His brother's ice-blue gaze collided with his. "A man can't live on what-ifs, Jacob. Believe me, I know. What-ifs don't make reality. No matter how much you might want them to or might want them not to."

And Jacob had a feeling that his brother was talking about Ellie, but it was one of those things he wouldn't mention, even now, because it was one of those un-spoken things that Gabe and Jacob didn't even really talk about with each other. Out of respect. Not just for Clint, but for Ellie and Caleb themselves.

"But it's the what-if that kills me," Jacob said. "It's the what-if that makes me…" He shook his head. "Maybe I'm a damn coward," he said. "But I don't know how to live in a world where I might lose something I care about so much."

"Do you know why death is a tragedy?" Caleb asked slowly. "I mean, do you know all the reasons it makes us so sad?"

"What the hell is that supposed to mean?"

"You know. Death is sad because of love. Because it leaves people who love that person behind. And it leaves a hole inside them that can't be filled. It's love that makes it matter. And it's the possibility of everything those who went before us will miss that makes it even more tragic. Why is it tragic that Clint is gone? Because of love. Because look at everything that he left here. Because of Ellie, because of Amelia. Why is it tragic that your friend Gavin is gone? Because of all the life that he didn't get to live. You have that life right in front of you. You have that choice. You're not in the grave, Jacob. And there isn't a damn thing stopping you from being with Vanessa other than you. Other than fear. And that's a real damn tragedy. But you could have this woman, this woman who loves you. She loves you, and there isn't an earthly power standing in your way except for your own self, and you won't take it."

The words hit Jacob like a bomb, pain exploding inside his chest.

Because Caleb was right. The tragedy of death was in the hearts that were left behind, and in the possibilities of life missed by those who were taken too soon.

"You're here," Caleb said. "You're here, and Vanessa loves you. That's a gift. That is a gift that...so many men would give a whole hell of a lot to have."

"You make it sound easy. You make it sound like there's nothing to it at all."

Caleb laughed, hollow and bitter. "Well, I'm not the one who's in love," he said, the word sounding dry. "But you are. You are, and that means you have a choice to make. Are you going to live like you went over the cliff with Gavin? Are you going to live like you went down in that helicopter, which isn't living at all? Or you can live like these years are a gift. A gift that some people don't get. No, you don't have a guarantee about tomorrow. None of us do. Whether you're with Vanessa or not, something could happen to her, and you wouldn't be any happier about it if you weren't married to her, because the fact of the matter is…you love her. You love her already. And you damn well know it. Being apart from her is just punishing yourself more. Protecting yourself, really. But from what? Maybe from the full spectrum of pain, but the full spectrum of happiness too."

"You think a lot about this?" Jacob asked heavily.

"Yeah," Caleb said. "I do. I spend a lot of time looking around at the life that Clint left behind. It's a beautiful life. And if you could have something like it…"

"I love her," Jacob said, the words bursting from him, filled with truth that he'd been avoiding for the past few weeks.

"I know you do," Caleb said. "Love is the strongest thing on this earth. I think it makes everything hurt a lot more."

Jacob laughed, but it was hollow and humorless. "Is that supposed to be an endorsement?"

"I don't know," Caleb said. "I can't really endorse it one way or the other. Anything that matters is heavy. That's all I know. But what's the alternative? The alternative is going through life caring about nothing. Not letting it touch you."

"And I suppose that's when you become Hank Dalton," Jacob said. "Happy-go-lucky and hurting people without meaning to, because you don't let yourself feel."

"I expect that's true," Caleb said. "We have our very own cautionary tale available to us in the form of our father."

"I want her," Jacob said. "I want her so much it hurts to breathe."

Caleb was silent for a long moment. "If you want someone that much, and you could have them, but you don't…life isn't worth living anyway."

And he knew then that Caleb was talking about Ellie. He didn't know the whole situation with their relationship. They were connected, that was for sure, but one thing he never asked, and never wanted to ask, was if Caleb had ever had any kind of romantic involvement with her. It was clear to him now, based on the anguish in his brother's voice, that those feelings were only on one side.

And nothing drew a line under the absurdity of the situation Jacob found himself in quite like that.

"I don't know why she loves me," he said. "She's… she's the strongest woman I've ever known. Strong and brave. I've gone through a couple of hard things, but Vanessa has been walking on a hard road for half her life. But she does it. And she's just…everything."

"Maybe that's why she loves you," Caleb said. "Because when you look at her, that's what you see. And maybe…maybe it's worth asking her what she sees when she looks at you."

Fear and hope burst inside Jacob's chest in equal measure. And his heartbeat, loud and strong and insistent.

His heartbeat, because he was alive.

And where there was life, there was hope.

Where there was love… Well, where there was love was a life worth living. Really living.

"I think I've got some work to do."

"I still want to be your best man."

"Oh, you can count on it."

If Vanessa would still have him.

He just had to pray that Vanessa would still have him.

CHAPTER TWENTY-TWO

VANESSA STOOD OUTSIDE her childhood home and took a deep breath. She had spent the past couple of days thinking a lot about what Olivia had said. About how she needed to take the strength that she had gotten from being with Jacob and use it. How she needed to make those changes count, rather than sinking into despair and losing everything that had been remade inside her.

She took a breath and looked over at her sister.

At least they were here together. Olivia squeezed her arm. "Are you okay?"

"Yeah. I will be."

"Do you want to go it alone?"

"I probably should."

"Okay. But I'm right here. If you need anything."

Vanessa nodded and looked back toward the house. And there was one thing that she had to get off her chest. One thing that maybe mattered, and maybe didn't. "I don't remember the dollhouse," she said.

"What?"

"The dollhouse. When I went to your home, you told me it reminded you of the dollhouse. And I don't remember the dollhouse."

"Oh," Olivia said. "I played with it all the time. By myself. It was downstairs in the rec room. I played with the dollhouse, and then I graduated to playing darts. I'm very good at darts."

"I didn't know that," Vanessa said.

Olivia shrugged. "I didn't really have a lot of friends. And…I just spent a lot of time being quiet by myself."

The wealth of loneliness that she heard in Olivia's voice stunned her. It hadn't really occurred to her before that Olivia might have been lonely. But then, she supposed that made sense. She felt that loneliness reflected inside her. Olivia had been surrounded by no one and had felt isolated, while Vanessa had often been surrounded by whole roomfuls of people and had still felt completely alone.

"I'm sorry," she said. "I'm sorry that you were lonely."

"I'm sorry that you were," Olivia said. "I just didn't know how to talk to you anymore. You know, after I told on you, and I got you in so much trouble."

"The skinny-dipping?" Vanessa asked.

It was such a silly thing. In her long list of transgressions, such a small one. But it had been the beginning of the change in her relationship, not just with Olivia, but with her parents.

"I shouldn't have gotten so mad at you," Vanessa said. "But it wasn't about you, not really. It was about Mom and Dad. They were… They were so disappointed in me. And Dad… He made it very clear that there was something…flawed in me that I needed to watch out for. That I was wild, and I needed to get it under control or something bad would happen. And all I knew was that disappointment in his voice. And the shame that came with it. I wasn't angry at you so much as I was embarrassed. Because I thought maybe you could see the same thing in me."

"He said that to you?"

"Yes," Vanessa said. "And so after that I just… I just wanted to test him. To test and see if I could go too far. And I could. Eventually they just quit talking to me. They acted like I wasn't there. And…it seems ridiculous to be angry about it because I pushed for that. I pushed for that breaking point."

"There shouldn't have been one," she said.

"Maybe not," Vanessa said. "But there was. And something in me always knew that. And I still…"

"I'm so sorry," Olivia said. "For all the misunderstandings. For all of the hurt. And mostly for the fact that we were both so lonely, and we didn't need to be. Because we were right there."

"Well," Vanessa said, "we're here now, and we are here together."

"Yes," Olivia agreed. "And I promise that I'm here. From now on."

"Okay. Well, stay here, just in case this goes very badly."

"I will," Olivia said.

Vanessa took a deep breath and walked up the front steps to the door of the house and knocked.

The door opened, and her dad was standing there, looking at her. "You wanted to see me?" he asked.

"Yes," she said. "I did."

She followed him into the house, into the living room, where he took a seat in his favorite easy chair. She was pretty sure it was the same chair that had been there when she'd left nine years ago.

And suddenly, she felt very small, the way that she

always had when she'd been called in to speak to her father.

But then she looked at him, really looked at him. At the shock of white hair that used to be dark, at the deep lines around his eyes.

He wasn't the same, and neither was she.

She took a breath and sat in the chair across from him. "Jacob and I broke up," she said. "So I am now single and pregnant, and basically everything you were afraid I would be."

"Vanessa…"

"I needed to come and tell you that, because in the past I was afraid to tell you when something bad happened to me. But I'm not afraid now. And whatever that means for us, whatever it means for our relationship… Whether you can deal with the fact that I am someone who doesn't do things the way that you would, that I'm someone who makes mistakes, then I need to know. Because I can't exist in this middle ground anymore. I would like to have a relationship with you. I would love for you and Mom to have a relationship with your grandchild. But I am who I am, and I've done the things I've done. I'm not proud of some of it, but I'm proud of where I am now. So if me being a single mother is going to make it so you can't treat me the way you treat Olivia, if it's going to make it so you can't treat my child the way you treat hers, then I need to know now."

He just sat there for a long moment, a strange expression on his face. And finally, he spoke. "Of course it won't," he said. "Vanessa, I—I'm a man who's made a lot of mistakes. I got sick a couple of years ago. I don't know if you know that."

Vanessa's heart twisted. "I didn't."

"I don't tell you that to make you feel bad. But just to say that when I was there staring down my mortality, I started thinking a lot about the things I've done. And then I doubled down on them. Because I'm a fool. I tried to control your sister's life. I asked Bennett Dodge to marry her, to take care of her. And that would've been a disaster. It wasn't until she ended up with Luke Hollister that I realized what I was doing. That I was controlling my children with such a tight hold that I was breaking things. That's what I did with you. I thought that if I made you afraid of my disapproval that it would set you straight."

A tear rolled down Vanessa's cheek and she didn't do anything to stop it. "It just made me think that I… That I could never be good enough for you and there was no point in trying. Because I wasn't Olivia, and I never could be."

"I know," he said. "I know."

"That's where I'm at now," she said. "I need you to know… I need you to understand what happened. Before I left. I just need you to know."

She poured out her heart. She told him everything. Everything she had held from him for so many years. About that party, about the fact that she couldn't remember what had happened. About the miscarriage. The terror she had felt, both when she had lost the pregnancy, and when she had begun to suspect it. And all the while, her father sat there in stony silence. She couldn't read his expression, and mostly, she didn't want to. Because she couldn't take scorn on top of everything else. She simply couldn't. When he finally spoke, he sighed heavily. Leaned back in his chair and dragged his hands down his face.

"Why didn't you tell me?" It wasn't the question she had expected. In fact, she hadn't really expected a question at all.

"Because," she said, her voice scratchy, "you had already warned me about my behavior. You had already made it clear that you were angry with the way I was acting. And you had told me that it was leading to a bad place. And I—I figured that you would tell me I deserved it. Because I felt like I did. Because I made a mistake. And I was foolish. I was stupid. So I was sure that I brought it on myself. And that I had deserved it. And after everything... I couldn't face that I might have to stand there and have you look at me and confirm what I already thought. I was just too weak. I couldn't do it then. But I can do it now, if we have to."

Her father leaned forward in his chair and covered his face with both of his hands. His large shoulders lifted and shook. She had never, not once in her life, seen her father overcome by any kind of emotion unless it was anger. She had never seen him cry, but she was sure that was what was happening. Right in front of her, and she didn't know what to do about it. So she just sat there, feeling numb, because she had spent so many years figuring out how to not cry when she thought of this moment that right now, all she could do was watch like she was an observer. Like she was an alien and this was happening to someone else.

He gathered his composure slowly and looked up at her. His eyes, the same color as her own, filled with regret. Plain and simple.

"What hurts the most," he said, "is that I don't know what I would have said to you."

He paused, the only sound in the room the ticking clock on the wall. "And I'm worried," he said finally. "I'm very worried that I would have told you it was your fault. That I would have yelled at you. That I would have blamed you. I've had years. So many years to imagine this moment. And all this time I dreaded it. Because I knew that you were going to look me in the face and tell me how I had failed you."

He cleared his throat. "Because over the years I have come to that conclusion. That I must have. And now I know I did. Because you were afraid that you wouldn't get unconditional love from me, and I can't even assure you that you would have because I didn't know how to be wrong then. I didn't know how to express fear in any other way than anger. I didn't know how to support you without just trying to make you afraid of consequences. So I was hard. Because I didn't want you to be hurt, but also because I didn't want me to be hurt. Because I didn't want to look like a failure as a parent. I didn't realize... I didn't know how profoundly I could lose you. I didn't know how badly the lack of support would hurt. I thought that if I... If I froze you out it would be incentive enough for you to want to do right. What I thought was right."

His throat worked, emotion overcoming him. "But how could I... I took support away from you when you needed it most. I see it now. I've been coming to that realization slowly over the past few years and now I know. I know for sure. What I did is the reason you couldn't come to us. The way I handled you. And I have nothing but regret for that."

Vanessa was shell-shocked. By the pure emotion in her father's voice. By the conviction there. By this re-action, which she hadn't expected. Not even remotely. "I made the choices that I made," she said. "There's no pretending that I didn't. I chose to handle my pain the way that I did. And that isn't your fault."

"Don't absolve me," he said. "That's not what we're here for. I think absolution to make things smoother doesn't do either of us any favors, does it? You made the choices you did. I made the choices I did. But what-ever you did, my job was to be here when you came back, and I didn't give you any sense that I might be. That was wrong. It was my fault. I regret it with ev-erything I have. You deserve better from me, Vanessa. This town, appearances, none of it has ever done any-thing for me. Not really. You're my daughter. And if none of that benefited you, then it didn't matter."

"You had Olivia—"

Her father moved from behind the desk, leaned over and grabbed her arm. "You're not Olivia. And you never were. You're not interchangeable. It wasn't just as good having her here. It was in a trade. There is no trade. You might look like her, but you're not her. And there wasn't a day that went by that I didn't feel the lack of you, but I wasn't strong enough. After a cer-tain amount of time, I just wasn't strong enough. To sit here, to have you tell me why it had all gone the way it had. I'm strong enough now. Now that it's too late. My biggest regret is that you had to get stronger first."

Fear. Fear was the theme. Fear was what was keep-ing Jacob from her. Fear was what had made her father push her away, fear was what had kept her from con-fiding in her parents when she had needed them most.

If there was a bigger barrier to love, to life, than fear, Vanessa didn't know it.

Change required unaccountable bravery, and she knew that, because she'd done it.

The strength to decide to change patterns of behavior that were ingrained in you.

It was hard. It was hard as hell.

And it wasn't over. Even now.

Because she had to change her feelings about her father if she wanted to have a relationship with him.

And that meant exposing herself potentially to pain.

Pain she didn't want. But there was no other way. There was never any other way. Except walking around with your armor stripped off, with a willingness to take the blows as they came.

Because if you didn't, you ended up like Jacob. Unable to accept love. Like her father, full of regret because he had been paralyzed by fear when he had needed most to be open. When he had needed most to be brave.

"I was afraid. I was afraid to come home and deal with the mess I made, with the pain I caused you, the fear I created in you. I was afraid of my feelings when I was a teenager, and so I hid them with drugs. I am so sorry that I had a hand in making your fear worse. Because fear is the cause of all of this. Fear has a lot to answer for."

"I have a lot to answer for," he said. "I have been considered powerful and important in this community, and that has been insulation for me. It gave me a place that I was certain of, secure in. And it also provided me with a sacred cow that I didn't want to tip over. I protected that too fiercely because it was my security in the world. When my security should've been in you. In your sister. Your mother. The love that we had for each other. Because that's the only thing that's real. But instead I failed you. I failed you when you needed me most."

Vanessa didn't give platitudes to absolve him, because she needed these words. Needed to hear that, so very desperately.

"I'm sorry," her father said. "I can't go back and change what was. I can't be a better dad, then. But I can be a better one now. Whatever you need, Vanessa, I'm here for you."

Her heart felt swollen, like it might burst.

"Thank you," she said.

"I'm awfully proud of you," he said.

And those words meant more than any apology ever could.

Her throat tightened. "Thank you."

"I can't imagine the kind of strength it takes to change the way you did. Because I'm sixty-five years old, and it just about killed me to come to these realizations, and it was only just a couple of years ago. To fix what you did when you did… You're a stronger person than I'll ever be."

Vanessa stood up, and so did her dad. And then very cautiously, Vanessa wrapped her arms around her father and rested her head on his chest. And he hugged her and said the words that she had needed to hear her entire life.

"It doesn't matter what you do, I'll always love you. No matter what."

She nodded, unable to speak. But in her heart she thought, *Me too. No matter what.*

She was still hurting. She was still broken from Jacob, but there was a place inside her now that was healed. And it was less to do with all the things her father had said and done, and even more to do with the fact that it was because she had chosen it.

Because it would be easy to not allow her father to be absolved with words, to stand firmly in all the pain that she'd experienced as a result of the way things had been done when she was in high school.

But she didn't want it. What she wanted was love.

What she wanted was this. It was a choice, and it was hers to make.

And she would do it.

It was her gift from Jacob. Because watching him fail to make the choice had driven that point home.

She smiled a little bit sadly.

It was a gift she was sure he hadn't meant to give her, but he had all the same.

And that was power in and of itself. To decide what to do with her heartbreak.

Though it still didn't give her Jacob. After what she'd been through, only a fool would go after him again.

A fool, or someone who was brave.

And she had decided that she was brave now.

Because what was fear? Self-protection.

Something to cover up the truth of what you were feeling.

A safety net, like drugs.

And Vanessa didn't do safety nets, not anymore.

It was so funny to think that most people would imagine she'd lived recklessly back when she had been using.

She hadn't. She had looked cautiously. She had lived small. Had lived for one thing, which existed to dull the pain of what she was and had made her life feel simple in so many ways.

And now life was big and bright, loud and dangerous, and she was making the choice to step into it all.

And so she would.

"Thank you," she said, finally stepping away from her dad. "Thank you for this."

"Thank you," he said. "For giving me forgiveness that I don't deserve."

"I think the best kind of life is one where we get what we don't deserve, isn't it? If we all got exactly what we should…it would be a lot sadder."

"That is true."

"I need to go try to fix some things with Jacob now," she said. "Because I love him. And…and I'm greedy and I want everything. I want things fixed with you, and I want things fixed with him."

"You're worth it, baby girl," he said. "Go get what you want."

CHAPTER TWENTY-THREE

JACOB HADN'T SLEPT for days, and when he'd gotten back home after the search for Aiden, he'd crashed out.

When he woke up, he knew right where he had to go.

He threw his shoes on and went outside, disoriented. The sun was setting, light shining down from the mountain, spectacular gold and glimmering rays lighting up the valley below.

He stood there and looked at it, and he didn't feel like he was falling.

He felt like he was broken. But he didn't feel like he was falling.

And that, he supposed, was something.

He was going to go to Vanessa's next. Because he had to talk to her. He had to find her, had to tell her that he was choosing her. Because there was nothing else that he wanted. Nothing else at all, not in the whole world.

And then he saw her car headed up the road, headed to him.

And he just stood there, watching, because he couldn't breathe. Couldn't think.

She parked and got out, moving toward him quickly, her expression full of fierceness. "I need to talk to you," she said.

"I was on my way to go talk to you," he said.

She stepped up toward him, so they were both standing on the rock that looked out over the view below.

She was so damn pretty. Glowing in that yellow dress she wore, her hair loose and curling around her.

And he wanted her. Wanted her with everything.

"Vanessa," he said.

But his words failed him, so instead, he closed the distance between them and kissed her on the lips. Kissed her as the sun and its last remaining rays shone on them, lit him up from the inside out.

But the warmth wasn't coming from the sun, it was coming from her.

"I'm so damn sorry," he said roughly as he looked down at her face. "I am so, so sorry that I wasn't ready to be as brave as you."

"Jacob," she whispered.

"I love you," he said. "I love you so damn much. Vanessa, I…I can't even explain the way I feel when I look at you. Like I'm looking at a promise for the rest of my life that I thought was too beautiful, too dangerous for me to have. But that's just it, sweetheart. It was never about guilt or what I didn't deserve. It was about me being afraid. Afraid of losing you. Of wanting something so much, something that I might not be able to hold on to forever. Time scares the hell out of me, and it doesn't care. It moves on forward, and there's nothing I can do to stop it. Even when I want to freeze a moment… Well, none of us can."

"No," she said. "None of us can. But sometimes time marching on is the best thing ever. Because if it had stopped, I wouldn't have been able to become the person that I am now. We wouldn't be together. We wouldn't be having this baby. We wouldn't... We wouldn't be in love."

"That's true," he said, his voice rough. "And I want all those things."

"Time can be a thief, Jacob, and you know that better than most. But time can give gifts too. The gift of us. Of the future that we'll have together."

That word. The *future*.

That was the thing he'd been avoiding thinking about. That when he saw her, he saw a future, stretched out in front of him, beautiful and bright, and it didn't even terrify him. It was something he wanted, something he craved.

"I never believed in fate," he said. "I never wanted to. But you... I can't deny that there's something with you and me."

"I feel it," she said. "But I don't think it is fate. I think it's choices that brought us here. To this moment. Mistakes, but some good ones too. And they made us both who we are. They made us this. And I can't regret any of that, because the woman I am now loves the man that you are. Oh, she loves him so much."

"I don't know why," he said, his voice scraped raw.

"Don't you know," she said. "You're my hero. And it's not just because you were there the night of the miscarriage. It's not just because you punched Jared in the face, although that will always be a treasured memory for me. It's not because you're perfect, or because you always come through. A hero doesn't stop every bad thing from happening, Jacob. But a hero shows up all the same, even knowing that he can't win every time. And you're a hero to me. My hero."

"I hurt you," he said.

"Yes," she replied. "You did. But I'm still standing. And now we are standing here together. And that's what matters. Not being perfect. Knowing that we aren't and trying anyway. That's what matters."

And he looked down at her, at this woman who knew all that he was, all of his failings, and all of his fears, and he saw more than just the future reflected back at him in her eyes. He saw himself. In a way that he never had before.

He had been alone, from the time he was a boy, because he had decided that alone, isolated, was better than pain.

But not now. Not when he could have her. Not when they could have everything.

"I want to marry you," he said. "Not because you're having a baby, not just because I like sleeping with you an awful lot, but because I want to do whatever I can to come close to showing what I feel in my heart. That this is permanent. That this is part of me. That you're part of me."

"I want to marry you too," she said. "I was scared at first, to let you into my life. To let anyone into my life, because so much of what I've built is about control. But I'm not afraid now. I'm not afraid of my feelings. Good or bad. Because I know what is broken can be healed. I know we can be healed. As long as we choose it."

"I do," he said. "And I choose you."

"I choose you too."

Jacob pulled her in for another kiss, just as the sun sank behind the mountain, and a sense of peace washed over him, a sense of peace he hadn't felt since he was a little boy. Since he'd learned that the world could be ugly.

But in all that time, he'd let himself forget just how beautiful the world could be.

And with Vanessa by his side, he knew that he would never forget that again.

Because when he looked at her, he realized it wasn't fate that he saw. It was love. And the chance to choose it every day, to embrace the hope, the beauty and the joy in life, instead of fear.

And he knew that he would spend the rest of his life choosing that. Choosing her.

Loving her.

VANESSA THOUGHT HER heart might burst as she melted into his arms. She had come up here to fight for this, to fight for them, and had found his arms open. Had found a man stripped of his armor, for her.

And she'd never felt more loved.

Vanessa Logan had spent years avoiding coming home. And all this time, she hadn't realized that home could be with another person.

Home was with Jacob Dalton.

EPILOGUE

"DON'T GET TOO EXCITED."

At the sound of Jacob's voice, Vanessa couldn't help but get excited. They were in the new house. Well, not officially, but in the shell of it. And they would be all moved in before the baby was born. The house was very nearly finished, an impressive feat of both design and construction.

"I'm trying to contain myself," Vanessa called from her position in what would be the living room.

"I'm going to paint for you."

She turned just as her husband walked into the room, two cans of paint and a roller in his hands.

"Oh really?" she asked.

"Yes. Okay, not an art piece. But…the nursery. I thought about painting you a picture, I really did. But I couldn't think of what to paint. What I wanted to show you was my heart. This life, this house, our child, who I want so much… That's my heart, Vanessa."

Vanessa launched herself across the empty space and into his arms.

"I told you not to get excited," he murmured into her hair.

Oh, this man. This man, who had held her at her most broken, who held her now at her most whole…

She loved this man. Now and forever.

"Then don't be so exciting, Dalton."

"It's the way we Daltons are," he said. "Starting with Hank."

"Hmm...you know, I kind of like that. Hank. Henry. Henry Dalton."

"Oh, honey, my dad's ego can't possibly handle getting any bigger. We can't go naming babies after him. And anyway...he's...a disaster. A mess."

"We all are sometimes," Vanessa said. "We all are. And shouldn't our child be free to be his own kind of mess?"

Henry Dalton stuck, and that was exactly who he became.

But no matter what messes and scrapes he got himself in, his parents loved him all the same.

Because they weren't alone anymore. They had each other.

When Vanessa finally did paint a piece for the nursery, it was of three people holding hands, looking straight ahead.

Walking forward into their future.

A future full of love.

* * * * *

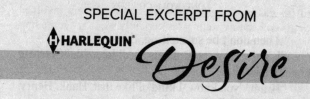
She smiled at him sweetly. "Thank you, Roarke."

There was something so enticing about hearing her
utter his given name in that soft, sweet voice. It made him
imagine what it would be like to hear her say it again as he
hovered over her.

Roarke shut his eyes briefly and tried to scrub the sound
and image from his mind.

He was only in Houston for one more day, and then he'd
be off to Dallas again. Besides, the object of his infatuation
was Ryder Currin's daughter.

Could he possibly make his life any more complicated?

He'd lived his life in a comfortable realm that existed on
the corner of sarcastic and serious. He didn't have room for
gorgeous women who looked like Greek goddesses, tossed
around smart-ass nicknames and randomly kissed strangers.

Besides, Sterling seemed to honestly respect his accomplishment in getting him released on house arrest. And how

hard he was working to clear his name. Getting involved with his archenemy's daughter certainly wouldn't score him any brownie points with the old man.

"Well, it was nice to officially meet you, Annabel." He set his half-finished drink on the bar and wiped a hand on his tuxedo pant leg. "But I'd better check in with Angela and make sure everything is good."

"Of course." Annabel's tongue glided over her full lower lip. She raked her manicured fingernails through the loosened, wavy ends of her hair, tugging it over one shoulder. "Save me a dance later?"

"I look forward to it." Roarke turned and made his way back to the main ballroom and the table where they were seated.

He'd done the right thing walking away. Though what he'd really wanted to do was lean in and steal an unexpected kiss from her this time.

She was young. At least five years his junior. Fresh faced and idealistic. She'd just broken up with her fiancé. His father hated hers. And he lived in Dallas while she lived in Houston.

He'd made the right decision to turn tail and run.

So why did every step he took away from Annabel Currin feel like he was walking away from the sunshine and into the cold dead of night?

What will happen when Roarke and Annabel meet again—and this time she needs his help?

Find out in
Off Limits Lovers
by Reese Ryan.

Available August 2019 wherever Harlequin® Desire books and ebooks are sold.

www.Harlequin.com

HDEXPRR0819

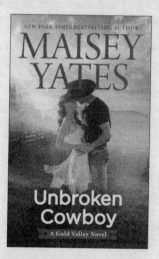

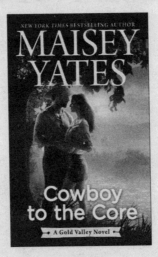

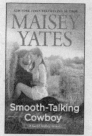

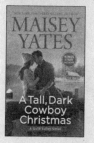

The countdown to Christmas begins now!
Keep track of all your Christmas reads.

September 24

- ☐ *A Coldwater Christmas* by Delores Fossen
- ☐ *A Country Christmas* by Debbie Macomber
- ☐ *A Haven Point Christmas* by RaeAnne Thayne
- ☐ *A MacGregor Christmas* by Nora Roberts
- ☐ *A Wedding in December* by Sarah Morgan
- ☐ *An Alaskan Christmas* by Jennifer Snow
- ☐ *Christmas at White Pines* by Sherryl Woods
- ☐ *Christmas from the Heart* by Sheila Roberts
- ☐ *Christmas in Winter Valley* by Jodi Thomas
- ☐ *Cowboy Christmas Redemption* by Maisey Yates
- ☐ *Kisses in the Snow* by Debbie Macomber
- ☐ *Low Country Christmas* by Lee Tobin McClain
- ☐ *Season of Wonder* by RaeAnne Thayne
- ☐ *The Christmas Sisters* by Sarah Morgan
- ☐ *Wyoming Heart* by Diana Palmer

October 22

- ☐ *Season of Love* by Debbie Macomber

October 29

- ☐ *Christmas in Silver Springs* by Brenda Novak
- ☐ *Christmas with You* by Nora Roberts
- ☐ *Stealing Kisses in the Snow* by Jo McNally

November 26

- ☐ *North to Alaska* by Debbie Macomber
- ☐ *Winter's Proposal* by Sherryl Woods

Harlequin.com

XMAS0319BPA

Get 4 FREE REWARDS!

We'll send you 2 FREE Books plus 2 FREE Mystery Gifts.

FREE
Value Over
$20

Both the **Romance** and **Suspense** collections feature compelling novels written by many of today's best-selling authors.
